The Summerhouse

Alison Prince

WALKER BOOKS
AND SUBSIDIARIES
LONDON • BOSTON • SYDNEY • AUCKLAND

This is a work of fiction. Names, characters, places and
incidents are either the product of the author's imagination
or, if real, are used fictitiously.

First published 2004 by Walker Books Ltd
87 Vauxhall Walk, London SE11 5HJ

2 4 6 8 10 9 7 5 3 1

Text © 2004 Alison Prince
Cover illustration © 2004 Phil Schramm

This book has been typeset in Galliard and Myriad

Printed in Great Britain by Cox & Wyman Ltd, Reading, Berkshire

British Library Cataloguing in Publication Data:
a catalogue record for this book
is available from the British Library

ISBN 0-7445-9098-1

www.walkerbooks.co.uk

*To the children and staff of
Brown's C of E Primary School, Horbling,
who were in from the start.
With love, and thanks for all your help.*

One

Abby had overslept. She'd heard the alarm and switched it off, then heard her mother call up the stairs, but she'd drifted back into sleep. Now she was running down the steep path from her house to the road, feeling faintly queasy because of the gulped glass of orange juice lumping about in her stomach – and because of having to take the short cut. The path was a lot quicker than the curving drive that led down from her house, but it ran through the kennel-people's place. And that was scary.

Abby ducked under the branches of the big walnut tree that overhung the Kennels' summer-house built into the side of the hill, and kept going. Weird noises came from the summerhouse some-times, and its blinds were drawn so you couldn't see in, but that wasn't the worst. What she really hated were the dog pens behind the bungalow down there by the road. Sometimes the dogs all started barking, and their claws rattled on the wire mesh as they jumped and scrabbled at it. What if they got out?

The pens were quiet today, thank goodness. Perhaps it was too cold for the dogs to come out of their wooden houses. A sharp wind was blowing, and the grey sea was ruffled with white horses. The salty air made Abby's eyes run, but she didn't mind. She wasn't scared of the sea, although it could toss stones and seaweed all over the road when it was rough. It had storms, but it was reliable. She liked the way the straight line of its horizon was always there.

Most days Sue waited on the road so they could walk to school together, but she wasn't there today. She'd have gone on; she hated being late. Abby ran past the small shops that backed onto the beach, then slowed to a walk, so out of breath that her lungs were aching. She must have made up most of the time by now – and anyway, she wasn't alone. A boy was dodging between the boats that were pulled up on the beach, trying not to be seen. He wore a khaki camouflage jacket patterned with black blotches.

Chokker Bailey, Abby thought. He was in her class at school. A lot of people thought Chokker was nuts, but Abby rather liked his fierceness and his sudden, unexpected grin. She wished she knew him better, but nobody knew Chokker, not really. She paused, waiting for him to come out from behind the boat that leaned sideways on the stones, but he didn't appear.

He's waiting for me to go on along the road before he moves again, she thought. *One of his weird games.* After a few moments she shrugged and carried on. There wasn't time to hang around.

Out of the corner of her eye she saw the boy make a dash from behind the boat to the shelter of the hut at the edge of the putting green. She waved and called, "Hi, Chokker!"

He didn't answer, of course. Abby heard the crashing of pebbles as he ran down the shingle to the sea's edge, pretending he hadn't heard her. The thicket of tall knotweed growing by the chain-link fence hid him from her sight, then she saw him walking along the sandy part of the beach with his hands thrust into his pockets, head bent to look down as if he was seriously interested in the shells and stones at his feet.

Abby gave up watching him. Mrs Currie was still outside the school with her STOP notice, ushering children across the road. That was all right, then – Abby wasn't going to be late. She joined the next group and waited with them on the pavement. As she crossed over, she glanced back. Chokker was following at a distance, but he still gave no sign that he had seen her.

I failed, Chokker thought. *She saw me.* The Grand Master would not be pleased. He'd stare from under the dark hood and frown. *Luma, you have been careless*. And he'd be right, of course; he was always right. A moment of inattention could cost you your life. *A good fighter must be ready to defend himself at all times.* Or to defend someone like Abby, who didn't even know there was any danger.

Here's the school. Duck across the road behind the yellow van; don't go up there to the lollipop woman at the crossing: that's exactly what they'd expect. Never know who's watching – could be a man at a high window, a crack shot with a telescopic rifle. Not a good technique, though – too noisy, too public. More likely to send in a quiet expert, someone who can kill and leave no mark. He could be waiting round any corner, looking ordinary. Smiling. Wearing a sports jacket, a flashy watch on his wrist. Can't trust anyone.

In the open now. Go through the gate with the other kids. Luma has to look ordinary. Be like them, even though they're idiots. It's not their fault they think there's no danger; that's the way they are. Untrained.

It was still cold and windy when Abby came out of school with Sue. They weren't in the same class, so they hadn't seen much of each other during the day.

"Sorry I didn't wait this morning," Sue said. "I did for a bit, then I thought perhaps you weren't coming, so I went on."

"That's all right," said Abby.

Sue had neatly cut brown hair, much tidier than Abby's long, fair strands, but she wasn't as well behaved as she looked. She was always getting told off for talking too much.

Fraser and his younger brother Neil charged past.

"See you up there!" Fraser shouted over his shoulder, and Neil waved, still running.

"OK!" Sue shouted back, and Abby waved.

They were going to the summerhouse. Touching the windows had started as a dare, because there had been weird shrieks and yells inside the glass, and now it had turned into a sort of fascination. Everyone in the village thought the kennel people were strange. They hadn't been here that long, and Mrs Kennel or whatever her name was didn't speak proper English. Her husband never seemed to speak at all, just went into his summerhouse and spent hours there behind his closed blinds. Neither of them joined in village life at all; nobody knew what they were up to. And all those dogs. Some people boarded their dogs there – mostly newer people – and they said the foreigners were all right, but there was a farmer in Kildownie who'd always looked after dogs if their owners were away. He was cheaper than the Kennels too. The older village people used him.

Abby wasn't bothered about all that, but she liked it when the others went to the summerhouse, because she could go up the short cut without having to pass the dog pens on her own.

"Hey, I meant to tell you," said Sue. "My mum says the kennel man writes books."

"Go on?" Abby was surprised. "How did she find that out?"

"Someone told her in the paper shop. But I don't think it's right," Sue went on. "I mean, what about the noises? All those screeches and yells. I think he could have wild animals in there. If they keep all those dogs, they could have a zoo as well."

Abby shook her head. "Zoos are enormous."

"Just a *small* zoo," said Sue. "Hamsters and gerbils, things like that. Maybe monkeys. Marmosets, the little sort. A zoo would be great. I wanted to have one of Mrs Kennel's puppies for my birthday, but Dad said we've got enough animals. And anyway, her puppies are really expensive."

Abby didn't say anything, and Sue glanced at her as they walked on. "You don't like dogs, do you?"

"They're all right."

Abby didn't want to talk about it, even to Sue. Nobody talked about it at home, either. They never had.

"Your house would be perfect for a dog, up there in the Castle grounds," Sue said.

Abby shook her head. "They make messes on the lawns, and dig things up, and Dad's supposed to keep the gardens nice for the visitors."

"But your mum could—"

"Mum's busy showing people round the Castle all day; she hasn't time to look after a dog."

"I suppose not," said Sue. "Pity, though."

They came to the bungalow at the road's edge, with the dog pens behind it. There was a wooden sign at the gate that said: PROSCHYNSKI KENNELS: BOARDING AND BREEDING, and Abby wondered again how to say Proschynski. Nobody in the village knew. Halfway up the hill, the summerhouse stood out in the darkening afternoon like a huge paper lantern, lit from within. Its pale-coloured blinds were drawn as usual, and the dark shapes of Fraser and Neil moved around outside it like black bats, trying to peer through any crack they could find.

Fraser turned as they approached and put a finger to his lips. "Music," he whispered. "Listen."

There was no need for him to tell them. The music coming from the summerhouse was quite loud. A lot of people were singing together, but it didn't sound like a proper choir. The voices were fierce and foreign, with a hard, jerky rhythm.

"Weird or what?" said Fraser.

The music stopped just as he spoke, and his words sounded very clear. A screech rang out from inside the screened windows, followed by a string of garbled words and a wild, shrieking laugh.

Sue screamed and ran away down the hill, followed by the boys. Abby went the other way, up the path towards her house in the Castle grounds. When she had climbed high enough to be level with the top of the big walnut tree, she turned and stared back. The summerhouse was quiet again now, glowing peacefully in the gathering darkness – then her heart almost stopped.

Something large and heavy was moving in the branches of the tree, making walnuts in their leathery cases crash through the leaves and hit the ground with a sharp thud. Abby gasped, too scared to move. The thing in the tree rustled as it turned a pale face towards Abby, and she caught a glimpse of black and brown patterning.

"Chokker!" she said.

Chokker jumped out of the tree. He landed in a shower of leaves and broken twigs and rolled over, then got to his feet and came towards her, brushing at his camouflage jacket.

"You want to be careful," he warned. "You don't know what you're dealing with. The bloke in there could be up to anything."

Abby didn't answer. Chokker must have been out of school like a shot, to have got here before the others. Perhaps he'd gone at the end of PE. She stared at him, frowning. He stood with one hand on a branch that leaned down above his head. His close-cropped hair and combat clothes made him look more like some wild kind of outlaw than an ordinary boy. But he wasn't an outlaw. He stayed in the village with Mr and Mrs Finbow, who ran a foster home.

"You think I'm kidding?" he went on. "I tell you, bad things can happen. Things you'd never believe."

Abby felt a sudden surge of anger. "Yes, I would," she said.

"No, you wouldn't. You think everything's safe. But it isn't." He gestured at the pointed wooden roof of the summerhouse. "The guy in there could be doing evil experiments or running a spy network or dreaming up new ways to kill people. Look at that doctor who killed hundreds of people before anyone found out. Everyone thought he was OK. You probably did too."

"You can't say what I think," said Abby. "The summerhouse man could be all right." She didn't feel sure about it, but she had to be fair. "Sue's mum says he writes books."

Chokker snorted in contempt. "People who write books can do other things as well. I've got a book by a man who was in the SAS. He knows every way there is to kill people. When he was training, he had to eat rats."

"That's horrible," said Abby.

"There you are, you see. Like I said, things can be bad."

"I know."

He laughed. "Go on, then – tell me something bad."

Abby shook her head. She had never told anyone about the dreadful thing, and she certainly wasn't going to tell Chokker Bailey.

He gave her a last, withering glance, then ran off down the hill.

Abby turned and went on up the path towards her house. The thing she would not talk about began to replay itself in her mind, as it did so often when she was going to sleep at night, a dream that wasn't a dream. Rain on the road, light reflecting from the vehicles that had stopped, Mum screaming, Sylvie's feet sticking out from under the car. They were in her blue wellies; they looked perfectly all right. And the dog that had rushed and scared her was shrieking because its owner was thrashing it.

Later that night, Chokker sat in his bedroom, watching his Total Fight video. It was the one decent thing the Finbows had given him in the two years since he'd been living with them, and he'd only got it because he'd kept asking. It had been in a dump bin at the post office, among the ex-hire videos that were on special offer.

Punch, turn, chop, swivel, left kick, crouch, turn, right kick. He knew the patterns by heart, but it was important to keep studying. The Grand Master was firm about that. *Never relax,* he said. *The attacker won't send you a warning. Surprise is his advantage.*

16

You have to be ready at all times.

The Master only appeared in the video as a dark silhouette in a hooded cloak that hid his face. *It could be dangerous for you to know who I am,* his deep voice said. *I care about my students. Each one of you is important to me, and I want you to be safe. I know you are there, and I know what you are going through. The work is hard and your muscles ache, but it is worth it. Follow what I tell you, and you will become strong, and bring strength to those about you. One day, you will earn their gratitude.*

The video moved into its final fight sequence, where the student in his barred mask and his black sweater with the Total Fight logo took on five attackers at once. They came at him from all sides, but he whirled and kicked and punched so fast that the eye could hardly follow his movements. At the end, Chokker rewound the film and watched it again.

He heard the bathroom door open. The three younger children came chattering along the landing with Mrs Finbow, who liked to be called Dorothy. Chokker groaned inwardly.

Dorothy tapped on his door. "Charlie!" She sounded cheerful and coaxing, as always. "Time to think about bed. Have you done your homework?"

"Haven't got any," said Chokker. He had, but it was easier than promising to do it in a minute.

"That's all right, then."

He shot her a contemptuous glance through the closed door. Dorothy belonged to the Charlie people. It was only his friends who called him Chokker – the kids he watched out for in case they were attacked. Some of the teachers had tried to use that name, but Chokker didn't answer and they soon gave up. There hadn't been any choice about the children. The way they'd said his official name made him sound a total prat. "Oi, *Char*lie!" So he'd told them about Chokker. But nobody knew about Luma. Nobody at all.

"Now come on, you little ones," he heard Dorothy say. "Story time."

She tried hard, he had to admit. Full marks for effort. Better than most of them. He couldn't stand her husband, though, awful Gerald with his brown beard and his brown-rimmed glasses and that horrible sports jacket. He had the social-worker look, saintly and miserable at the same time, as if he was counting up the brownie points for being so patient.

Chokker clicked the *off* button on the remote.

If the man in the summerhouse knew he was being watched, he might already have called up some defenders. They could be anywhere up the hillside, hidden under the bushes, prepared to strike. Like the Master said, you had to be ready at all times.

Dorothy's voice droned gently from the next room, reading the younger ones to sleep. Chokker felt a sudden pity for her and the children. They were so helpless. Apart from the unknown others who watched the video and listened to the voice of the Master, he was alone in his skill and his knowledge.

He swung his feet to the floor, and in the small space between his bed and the TV set went silently through the patterns again. *Punch, turn, crouch, kick, swivel, back kick, turn.* It wasn't just for fun. It was his duty.

The next day, Chokker found himself thinking about the man in the summerhouse. He thought about him through the noise of the little ones banging spoons at breakfast time, and while he was walking to school, and all through the boredom of the morning's lessons.

Evil can be anywhere. That was what the Master said. And he was right, of course; he was always right. *I am Luma; I am his student. One day I too will be a master.*

"Charlie, could you possibly do some work?" Mrs Long enquired. "You haven't even picked your pen up."

Sarcastic old bat. Chokker gave her a withering glance. He picked his pen up and leaned his head on his hand, then went on thinking about the man in the summerhouse. Yes, he knew what he would do.

❧

As they climbed up past the dog pens after school, Abby stared at the walnut tree, wondering if Chokker was there. He was. The others saw him too.

"What's he doing?" wondered Neil.

"He's off his head," said Sue.

Chokker was leaning down from an overhanging branch, with a long stick in his hand, and he was tapping on the roof of the summerhouse. Tap – tap – tap, quite steadily and slowly.

Abby gasped. It seemed like poking at a sleeping dog – terribly dangerous. "Chokker, don't!" she called, but he went on tapping. She and the others scrambled up the hill towards him, and as they arrived at the summerhouse, its door was flung open and the kennel man came out. He was wearing old corduroy trousers and carpet slippers and a checked shirt, and his grey hair stood up wildly because he was clutching his head with both hands.

"For Pete's sake," he said. "What do you *want*? You creep about outside, trying to look in like I'm a peep-show, and now you're knocking on the roof." Abby had expected him to sound foreign, but he didn't, except for a faint trace of American. "It's tough trying to work at the best of times," he went on, "but you're making it totally impossible. You trying to drive me crazy or something?"

Nobody answered. Abby glanced at the others. They seemed as stunned as she was. Neil's mouth was open, but as she looked at him he shut it and swallowed hard. Up in the walnut tree Chokker was watching silently, narrow-eyed and motionless.

"Sorry," Abby said. "We didn't mean..." Her voice tailed off. What *had* they meant?

The man stopped tearing at his hair and waved a hand at the summerhouse instead. "If you want to come in and see the place, then you'd better do it now," he said. "Get it over with." And he stood aside from the door to let them enter.

Something hit Abby lightly on the shoulder. A walnut. She looked up and saw Chokker frowning down at her from his perch on the branch.

He was shaking his head fiercely. *"Don't go!"* He mouthed the words with hardly a sound, but the urgency of them was clear.

They all hesitated. "I don't know if we should," Sue said quietly to Fraser.

The kennel man wasn't supposed to hear her, but he did. "Quite right," he agreed. "Never go any-where with strange men. Please yourselves. But if you're not coming in, then leave me in peace, OK?"

"Come on," said Fraser to Neil, and the pair of them started towards the summerhouse.

"It wouldn't hurt just to *look*," Abby said, almost to herself.

Sue nodded. "I mean, we've always wanted to see what's in there," she said.

Another walnut hit Abby, on her head this time – Chokker was a good shot – but she didn't look round. She followed Sue towards the open doorway.

When they had all gone in, Chokker climbed quietly down from the tree and skirted round behind the summerhouse, careful to avoid the open door. *See, but don't be seen.* He crouched behind the dark leaves of a rhododendron, watching.

With its clutter of books and shabby furniture, the summerhouse looked like a cross between an office and an untidy sitting room, Abby thought – but the thing that caught her attention at once was the parrot. It was bright green, clambering around inside the big cage by using its claws and curved beak. It looked at the children and let out a loud scream.

"Shut up, you ill-mannered old bag," said the man.

Sue giggled, and Neil asked, "What's the parrot's name?"

"Agatha. Bossy old thing she is too."

The linen blinds drawn down over the windows gave the summerhouse a strange, shut-in feeling. *If this was mine,* Abby thought, *I'd want to see out.*

Fraser had wandered over to the big desk. A computer stood on it, complete with a scanner and two printers, but everything was switched off, and the screen was blank and silent. Piles of paper littered the desk, all of them covered with scrawled handwriting. A lot of the pages had slid off onto the floor, and the waste-paper basket was overflowing with crumpled sheets. Fraser thought that was quite funny. "You're using up a rainforest," he said.

"I *know*," the man said irritably. "Don't nag."

"Sorry," said Fraser.

Abby wondered if it was all right to think of the man as Mr Kennel. She didn't like to ask.

"Why do you have the blinds shut?" asked Neil.

Mr Kennel sat down on a collapsed-looking sofa that had a fringed shawl over the back of it and sighed. "If I open them, I just sit here looking at the sea," he explained. "And the more I look at it, the more I wish I was going somewhere. And that's no way to get any work done."

"My mum says you're a writer," said Sue.

"Don't know how she found that out. But yes. Supposed to be."

"Do you mean you're not really?" Fraser asked.

The man made a face and said, "I'm beginning to wonder. It was all right when I was on the move. I guess it suited me, travelling around."

"Where did you go?" asked Neil.

"Pretty well all over. My parents came from Poland. They ended up in the States. I was born there." He shrugged. "They got fed up with it, though. We came back to Europe when I was still a kid. It was meant to be just a visit, looking up various relatives, but we stayed on." He ran a hand through his hair. "Why am I telling you all this stuff?"

"It's interesting," said Sue.

Fraser was frowning, trying to get the picture. "Do you write books about travel, then?"

"I write thrillers. At least, I used to. Each one set in a different place."

"Are you writing one about being here?" Neil asked.

"I'm trying to. But it's not happening."

Abby looked at the scattered papers on the desk and the floor. "Are those the book?"

"Yes. But they're rubbish."

"Why are they?" asked Fraser.

"It's just not working, that's all."

"I don't see what you mean," Fraser said, and Abby groaned inwardly. Once started, Fraser could never be stopped. It was the same at school. He'd go on and on asking questions until the teacher lost patience and told him to shut up.

Mr Kennel sighed. "I don't suppose you'll understand this, but before you can write a book, you've got to know what it's going to be about. It's the same for you, I guess, when you write some-thing at school."

"The teachers mostly tell you what to put," said Sue.

"Lucky you. That makes it easy. Writers have to sort it out for themselves. And it can be really dif-ficult."

"You could write about the dogs," suggested Sue.

"No, I couldn't. My wife does the dogs. I like animals – I don't mind giving her a hand sometimes – but they're not my thing. And don't ask what is my thing," he added, "because right now I don't know."

"Do you mean you've run out of ideas?" asked Fraser.

The man stared at him for a long moment, and Abby wondered if he was annoyed. After all, the question was rather a rude one. Then he said, "Well, yes, if you must know. I haven't had an idea for weeks. Nothing there. Zilch. Just a load of muddle."

"That's awful!" said Sue.

"You can say that again," agreed Mr Kennel.

The parrot let out a squawk and shouted, "BLAST! BLAST! BLAST!"

The man glared at her. "Shut up, Agatha."

"SHUT UP, AGATHA!" the bird repeated. "SHUT UP! SHUT UP!"

Abby knew the parrot didn't understand what she was saying, but the words she spoke were charged with such furious frustration that Abby felt quite worried. Perhaps she and the others were intruding. "I think we ought to go," she whispered to Sue, but neither of them moved. Abby liked the way Mr Kennel didn't mind telling them about his difficulties. It made her wish she could help.

Sue seemed to feel the same, because she said,

"We could think of some ideas, if you like."

Mr Kennel gave her a tired smile. "You do that."

"No, but we could," Fraser said, taking it with his usual seriousness.

"That would be very nice," said Mr Kennel.

Abby knew he was just being polite. She made herself move towards the open door. "Thank you for letting us in," she said.

"Didn't have much choice, did I? And by the way," he added, "you can tell your friend out there, if he keeps knocking on my roof I'm going to turn him into dog meat."

"We will," Fraser promised.

"Can we come again?" Neil asked.

"What for? You've seen the place now." Then he looked at Sue's disappointed face and relented. "Well, all right," he said. "I might let you in if you bring some real humdingers of ideas. Written down."

"Yes, we will!" Sue said happily. "Lots of them. See you tomorrow!"

"Perhaps," said Mr Kennel.

They all trooped out, and he shut the door behind them.

Nobody said anything until they'd gone down the hill a little way, then Sue said, "Let's all go to my house and write ideas down!"

"Can't," said Fraser. "I've got a saxophone lesson straight after tea."

"Neither can I," said Abby. "But tomorrow's Saturday."

Sue brightened up. "So it is! Come round to mine in the morning?"

"All right," said Abby, and the boys nodded.

"About eleven," said Fraser.

"You can't get him out of bed," Neil said, then ducked as his brother pretended to hit him.

"Eleven's fine," said Sue. She and the others went on down the hill.

Abby turned and retraced her steps upwards. A figure stepped out from the bushes to bar her way, but this time she wasn't startled.

"Hi, Chokker."

"What did he say?" Chokker demanded. "The guy in the summerhouse. What's he up to?"

"Nothing much," said Abby. "He's trying to write a book, only he can't think of anything. He's quite nice, really."

"You can't be sure," said Chokker. "Bad people are good at seeming nice. That's how they work."

Abby didn't argue. "Mr Kennel's got a parrot. That's what makes the screams and things. She's called Agatha. Oh, and he said if you went on tapping on his roof, he's going to turn you into dog meat."

She saw Chokker's face tighten. "Only a joke," she added quickly, but it was too late. His eyes were staring into hers with fierce excitement, and in some mad way, he seemed pleased.

"Told you, didn't I!" he said. "OK, so he wants to kill me. But he'll have to catch me first."

"Don't be *silly*," she said. "Of course he doesn't want to kill you; he's all right."

But Chokker just laughed. The next moment he had slipped away between the bushes and disappeared, like Robin Hood in his forest.

Abby listened, but the fading rustle of leaves gave her no idea which way he had gone.

 # TWO

"Now," Sue said, "who's got an idea?" She wanted to be a teacher when she grew up, and Abby thought she would be quite good at it. They were sitting around the table in Sue's kitchen, and her mother had left them to it.

"Neil and I thought the parrot could escape," Fraser said. "In the book, I mean. And Mr Kennel would have to find it in some foreign place."

"He could call it *The Mystery of the Missing Parrot*," Neil added.

"Brilliant," said Sue, writing it down.

Abby wasn't so sure. "But he's not going to foreign places," she said. "That's the whole thing. He's stuck here."

"So what do *you* think?" Fraser asked.

"I don't know." She'd woken in the night from a bad dream, and it was still lurking about in her mind. The dogs had broken out of their pens and turned into huge black lizards that breathed fire at the windows because they wanted to eat the children. She didn't want to talk about it, but it was driving everything else out.

"Come on," Fraser urged. "You must have thought of something."

"Maybe he could write about dragons," Abby said reluctantly. "Dogs turning into dragons."

"Ooh, scary," said Sue, writing it down.

Neil didn't look scared at all. "What if Mrs Kennel bred dragons instead of dogs?"

"Perhaps she does," Neil said. "You wouldn't know. She never talks to anyone, does she? Just goes for walks with all those dogs on leads."

"She's all right," said Sue. "Dad asked her about the price of her puppies, and he said she's quite nice, really. She sounds a bit funny, being foreign, but she's mad about her dogs, loves them to bits. I thought the summerhouse could be a castle," she added. "With a princess shut up in it, waiting to be rescued."

"Yuck," said Fraser.

"Oh, *be* like that." Sue sat back in a huff and folded her arms.

"Well, it's boring. We thought there could be a haunted chocolate shop," Fraser went on, and his brother chimed in.

"If you eat a particular chocolate you get turned into a ghost."

"Mm, that's good." Sue picked up her paper again. She never stayed in a bad temper for long – it was one of the things Abby liked about her. "You mean, it would be in the box with all the others, looking just the same, but—"

"The minute you ate it, you'd be dead," said Fraser.

"Doing haunting and stuff," Neil agreed. "And we could have a fairground ride that changed you into something else. Like when it turns you upside down and your hair stands on end, there's a sort of magic that gets into your head in between the hairs."

"Great!" said Sue, scribbling hard. "We could call it *The Bad Hair Day Ride*. You'd go on as an ordinary human, but when you came off, you'd be something else."

"Like an apeman or something." Neil swung his arms about and made gibbering noises.

"But everyone would notice," Abby pointed out.

"Yeah, but it's only a story," said Neil.

Abby groped for words that would say what she vaguely felt. "He'll want something kind of – bigger," she said.

They all looked at her, and Fraser said, "Go on, then."

"Perhaps he'll need a sort of hero." It sounded feeble. "Or heroine. Someone who goes through a whole lot of adventures and things."

"Only it's all right in the end." Sue was trying to be helpful.

"But then you've got to think up the adventures," said Fraser. "And that's what we're doing, aren't we?"

"Yes, I suppose so," said Abby. It was beginning to seem very difficult.

Sue consulted her piece of paper. "We've got five ideas. The vanishing parrot, dragon-dogs, a chocolate shop, the bad hair day ride, and my princess."

Fraser rolled his eyes at the princess, but Abby said, "Five is quite a lot."

"He'll have to let us in, won't he?" said Neil. "He said he would if we brought some ideas. I want to see the parrot again."

"So do I," agreed Abby. But there was more to it than the parrot.

Abby walked the long way home from Sue's house to avoid going past the dog pens, and went on thinking about Mr Kennel. She'd never met a grown-up person who'd admitted he was in a mess. Her mum and dad got in a muddle sometimes and lost things like the car keys, but they tried hard to behave as if everything was fine. And at school the teachers were always in charge. They looked a bit desperate sometimes, and you could hear them saying things like "All this paperwork – it's impossible", but they went on running things. They didn't let you in on the job they were trying to do, let alone ask for help. You just had to behave properly and get the answers to the tests right.

Mr Kennel was different, though. He'd seemed a bit scary at first because he was so impatient, but his impatience was mostly with himself. Things seemed to be just as puzzling for him as they were for children, even though he was quite old. Abby wondered if it was like that for all adults, though they pretended it wasn't. Somehow she rather hoped so. If it was all right to go on being puzzled about things, she'd never have to turn into a different, efficient kind of person when she grew up. She could go on being herself for as long as she lived.

The next day was a Sunday, and there was a Victorian Day at the Castle. Abby would much rather have gone back to Sue's house to talk some more about Mr Kennel and his book, but her mother had asked her to be a flower girl, and she couldn't get out of it now.

Wearing a long dress and a white apron, with her hair pinned up under a straw bonnet trimmed with violets, Abby spent the day selling posies of flowers to the Castle visitors, and they beamed at her and said how lovely she looked. "A real Little Nell," one lady said, and then explained that Little Nell came from a book by Charles Dickens. "Written over a hundred and fifty years ago," she added.

Abby thought about it as she went on selling her flowers. Over a hundred and fifty years ago.

Everything would have been different then. No cars, no aeroplanes, no radio or TV or computers, no jeans or trainers, just these heavy clothes, with bonnet strings that cut under your chin. She was glad it had all been left behind. And yet the woman had talked about Little Nell as if everyone must know her. Charles Dickens had invented a girl who was still alive.

No wonder Mr Kennel was hooked on writing books. It would be so terrific to dream up a story that people would remember for years. And if it was that great, you could see why he was upset about not getting started.

One of the staff walked past dressed as a cook, with her sleeves rolled up and her hair tucked into a mob-cap. "Cheer up," she said. "Only half an hour to go."

Abby smiled back, trying to make it clear that she didn't mind being a flower seller. It was just that she'd been thinking about something else.

Chokker was kicking an empty Coke can along the shore road. After a bit, it hit a stone, jumped sideways and fell into the stream that ran out to the beach between the DIY shop and the post office. He watched it get swept away in the hurrying water, and wondered whether to go and retrieve it from the other side of the shops. Then he shrugged. It didn't matter that much.

He paused, looking at the post office window with its notices handwritten on postcards. Someone had lost a cat; someone else wanted to sell a boat; there was a family dance in the hall on Friday night. A newer one, computer-produced, with sharp letters in black and purple, reminded anyone interested that the post office cyber café was now open. Except it wasn't, of course, because this was Sunday.

Not much of a café, anyway, Chokker thought. *Not much of a post office, come to that.* It was dead old-fashioned, with a brass rail along the top of the grille, and sacks of dog meal and pony nuts standing about, because the Robinsons who ran it did animal stuff as well. Anything to make a bit of money – that was why they'd started the cyber café, he supposed. He wandered on, thinking about the cramped little room with a couple of PCs and a grotty coffee machine. He went in there and played a computer game against himself sometimes, if no one else was around. He didn't like it when other kids came in; they just mucked about and laughed. Games were good practice; they gave you quick reactions. Luma needed to move fast – he never knew when something might happen.

Chokker stopped dead as an idea hit him. For a moment he didn't quite know what he was thinking, only that it could be a way to extend power beyond the reach of the swift kick and clever footwork. *Cyber-attack.* Scare the enemy; let him know someone was on to him. Could it be done? He wasn't sure. He didn't even know if the summer-house had a computer in it. The kennel man was pretty ancient – he might still use an old-fashioned typewriter.

I should have gone into the summerhouse with the others, Chokker thought, *then I'd have known.* As he walked on, he felt a bit breathless at the thought of getting that close to the enemy.

Would the Grand Master mind the use of mod-ern weapons? The hooded face and the deep voice always sounded calm and loving, not like the frantic voices of the cyber-games. The Master belonged to something much older. He gave tough instructions, though. *Never shrink from the first attack. If an opportunity presents itself, take it.* No, he probably wouldn't mind. The computer might count as an opportunity.

But this isn't Luma. It's me. It's real.

Chokker pushed the idea away. He went down to the beach. The Coke can was lying in a pool of sea water between some rocks. He dipped the toe of his trainer under it and flicked it out, then chipped it neatly over the weed-covered rocks to land on the sand. He took a run at it and booted it high and clear along the beach. *Anyone watching wouldn't look twice,* he thought. *They'd reckon I was just an ordinary boy.*

🌿

Mr Kennel looked more rumpled than ever. His grey hair stuck up wildly, and he held his glasses in his hand, frowning as if he had forgotten all about his promise.

"What is it now?" he demanded.

They had stood back politely after Sue tapped on the door, but Fraser said, "You said we could come again if we had some ideas."

"Written down," Neil added. "And we have."

"We've got five," said Sue.

Mr Kennel didn't seem particularly pleased. "Five." He ran his fingers through his hair. "Good Lord."

"So can we come in?" asked Fraser.

"I suppose you'll have to."

"They're not very good," Abby said as she trooped in with the others. After all, he was a proper writer. He'd probably find their ideas silly and useless – but he wasn't looking impatient.

"Whatever they are, you've done better than me," he said.

Sue and the boys had gone to look at the parrot.

"Can I give her a Polo?" Sue asked.

"No," said Mr Kennel. "Bad for her teeth."

They all looked at him, and he looked back, with his eyebrows up but not smiling. Then Sue giggled, and Neil joined in.

"Parrots don't have teeth," said Fraser, then he looked at Mr Kennel again, and laughed.

"What was the other noise?" Sue asked. "Not the parrot – there were weird voices."

"Bulgarian choir," said Mr Kennel. "Music from other countries is great. Shakes you up. What about these ideas, then?"

Sue produced her piece of paper and read out the list, and he listened carefully.

"Pretty good, really," he said when she had finished. "I like the dogs turning into dragons. In fact, I like all of them. You've got some pretty cracking inventions – the bad hair day ride and the chocolate that's waiting to do you in. Dead inventive."

"So are you going to put it in your book?" Fraser asked.

Mr Kennel took the list from Sue and sat down on the sofa, looking at it. Sue stood beside him and Neil perched on the sofa's arm. Abby and Fraser stayed where they were. After a few moments, Mr Kennel glanced up. "Thing is, it's all a bit so-what."

"I don't see what you mean," said Fraser.

"There's a so-what test. It's like, you watch a television programme all the way through, and sometimes you enjoy it. Other times you think, *Yeah, but so what?*"

"Right." Fraser nodded.

Neil was nodding as well. "You mean, was it worth bothering with?"

"Exactly," Mr Kennel agreed. "Books are the same, only more so. Watching television is pretty easy, so I guess you don't care much if it's so-what. But reading a book takes a bit of effort, so it needs to be worth the effort."

"Yes," said Neil.

Abby thought all books were worth reading. It was the one way you could get into a different world of your own. But she didn't say anything.

"Do you ever get bored with writing?" asked Sue.

"I daren't," said Mr Kennel. "If I'm bored with what I'm writing, the readers will be bored too. And that's fatal."

"It can't be so-what," said Neil. "And our ideas are." He didn't seem to mind.

"Not all of them. You've got some real crackers here."

Abby started to feel a bit braver. "We could have a hero," she said. "Someone that things happen to."

"Or a heroine," said Sue.

"Or both," said Neil.

"Yes," Mr Kennel agreed. "That's essential."

"When do we start?" asked Fraser.

Mr Kennel turned to look at him. *"Start?"* he said. "What do you mean, *start*?"

"Writing the book," said Fraser, as if it was obvious.

"We can go on helping you," Sue explained. "We can think up some more ideas."

"I can't have you lot in here, writing a book."

"Why not?" asked Neil.

"I don't know what I'd do with you. I mean, I need peace and quiet. You'd drive me insane."

"But we wouldn't be here all the time," Sue pointed out. "We're at school all day. So you could get on with writing the book, and we'd just come and give you more ideas. If you wanted them," she added.

Mr Kennel stared at her, pulling thoughtfully at his lip. "I wonder," he said. "Maybe this ought to be a book for people your age. It would make a change."

"You said you needed a change," Sue said encouragingly.

He nodded. "The thing is, though, writing a book is real, solid work. I can't have you wandering in and out of here just for a laugh. If you're going to join in, you'll have to do some real thinking."

"Course we will," said Neil.

"But wouldn't you mind?" Abby asked.

"I'll chuck you out if I start minding," said Mr Kennel. "But it could be all right. I've got a bit out of touch, I suppose. Haven't seen anyone for weeks, only my wife and the dogs."

"What do we have to do?" asked Fraser.

Mr Kennel fished under a pile of papers for a notebook. He flipped it open at a clean page and found a pen. "First thing, we'll need some idea of what this book's *about*," he said. "Is it supernatural

– ghosts and all that – or a fantasy adventure, or what?"

They all looked at each other blankly. Nobody knew.

"I wanted a princess who's shut up in a tower," Sue said, "and gets rescued. It's on our list of ideas."

Fraser rolled his eyes, but Mr Kennel wrote it down. "Rescue. Yes. Someone can get rescued."

Neil said, "I like it when bad things happen, and you think it can't come out right, then it does."

"Happy ending," Mr Kennel agreed. "OK. Or at least happyish. I'm not in for anything gooey. Heart-rending, yes; gooey, no." He was jotting things down. "Hero and heroine. We'll have to think about them. Where they live; what they're like. We need wild things to happen."

"Like going into a different world," said Neil.

"Or something frightful happening in this one," said Mr Kennel.

Abby's mind flew back to her nightmare. "I thought the dogs had turned into black lizards," she heard herself say. "And they were at the windows. They wanted to kill the children."

Mr Kennel looked at her. "That's a very strong idea," he said. "Could be quite a tough one to handle. You sure you don't mind?"

"It's all right," said Abby. *There's no need to get upset,* she told herself. *It's only happening in a book.*

"Tell you what," said Mr Kennel, putting his notebook on the desk. "You lot go and do some more thinking, right? Think who's going to be in it. Try and get to know them. Imagine what's going to happen to them."

"Can we draw pictures?" asked Sue.

"Sure. Draw pictures, write poems, jot down your dreams. We need to build a darn great compost heap of ideas. We won't use all of them, but that doesn't matter. Books are like icebergs: there's more hidden underneath than you ever see."

"Can we come back tomorrow?" asked Sue.

"Um – I'd rather you left it for a couple of days," said Mr Kennel. "I need to do a heap of thinking as well, and a bit of p and q would come in handy."

"P and q?" asked Neil.

"Peace and quiet," said everyone else.

"The actual writing of this book will be down to me." Mr Kennel was thinking again. "When we've got some sort of plan I'll send it to my publisher, see if she likes it. But you're going to be essential. If we do get a book out of this, I'll put your names in it as co-authors. I'm not pinching your ideas and passing them off as mine, OK?"

"OK," said Fraser. "When do we come again, then?"

"Thursday," said Mr Kennel. "And what about your mate outside?" he added. "The Tarzan guy in the tree. D'you reckon he'd help?"

They looked at each other, then Abby said, "I'll ask him." But somehow she didn't feel that Chokker would.

"You must be joking," said Chokker.

Abby shrugged, and went on walking beside him along the rough grass at the top of the beach. It was the next day, after school. He looked at her and felt irritated. She was quite thin, and with her grey eyes and the long, fair hair that hung down over her shoulders she seemed ridiculously defenceless.

"You can't trust him," he told her. "When people get murdered, it's nearly always by someone they know. It says so in my SAS book."

"Mr Kennel isn't going to murder anyone," said Abby. "He's all right."

"How do you know he's all right?"

"I just do."

"Huh." *Never waste your time with the uninitiated. They may cause you to lose your way, because they do not know their own.*

"See you," Chokker said. He ran across the road only just in front of a passing car and was away up the track to the hill. He didn't slow down until he came to the place that people called the Fairy Glen. It was always wet up there, the stream spreading out sideways through the soft grass. You had to move carefully, or you could put your foot into a boggy bit and go right down. Besides, the cattle didn't like it if they thought you were running after them. They were the Highland sort, with enormous horns. The Master hadn't said anything about how to deal with cattle-attack.

Go undercover. The idea dropped into his mind, complete and perfect. He would pretend to be interested in this stupid book. Play along. That way, he'd be on the spot, in a better position to defend Abby and the others. If anything happened, they'd have someone to fight for them.

But there was something else. Chokker came to a halt, thinking about it as he kicked a white toadstool to pieces in the grass.

The bloke will know I can't do book stuff.

They'd given up bothering at school. As long as he didn't cause any trouble, it was all right. He just sat there, looking as if he was interested, and that worked pretty well. He was good at drawing. He knew every detail of the fighting costumes and masks and helmets, and the great sword the Master held. It had an engraved hilt with dragons all over it. He'd paused the video lots of times, so as to have a proper look at it.

The writing bit was something else. Reading the book by the SAS man had been really hard, because there were so many long words. It had seemed totally impossible at first. He'd started with the bits of description round the pictures, and that gave him a clue about some of the words, and he'd worked the rest of it out because he wanted to know what it said. He wasn't bothered about the school stuff; it was never interesting anyway. Abby was in his group, so he mostly copied from her – she didn't mind. Nothing wrong with that. People had secretaries, didn't they? And the computer was good because the spell-check did everything.

This bloke and his book, though – dead tricky. Was he going to want great chunks of writing from all of them? Would he make them read things out? Reading out loud was the worst. He'd look at Chokker with that kind smile that made you feel like an idiot.

But Abby might need me.

Chokker scowled fiercely, squaring his shoulders. She was such a soft girl. So nice to everyone, and so quiet. He couldn't let her down.

🌿 Three

Chokker joined them when they gathered outside the summerhouse after school on Thursday.

"Hi," said Sue. "Are you going to come in with us?" She was holding a bundle of the drawings they had done, as well as a piece of paper with a few more ideas on it.

"Might do," said Chokker.

Abby caught his eye and almost smiled, but she didn't say anything.

Mr Kennel opened the door. "The gang's all here, then."

Fraser said, "Chokker's here as well."

"Fine," said Mr Kennel. He looked at Chokker and added, "That's you, is it? From the tree?"

Chokker nodded, and followed the others in. He saw the computer at once, a whacking great thing with a big screen. Its tower had two slots for CDs as well as the usual one for floppies, and there was a colour printer as well as a black and white one, and a scanner. So the guy wasn't as old-fashioned as he looked. Well clued up, in fact. *So be careful.*

"HELLO!" shrieked the parrot. "HELLO, HELLO! SHUT UP, AGATHA!"

"Yes, shut up," said Mr Kennel. "Honest, one of these days I'll stick that bird's beak up with Sellotape."

Sue said, "We did these drawings."

"Great." Mr Kennel looked through the pictures and held up Sue's drawing of a tower with black clouds all around it. "Is this where your princess is a prisoner?"

"Yes. Only the window cleaner comes, and he rescues her. I wrote the idea down."

"Towers don't have windows," Fraser said. "At least, the one at the Castle here doesn't." They'd had an argument about this, but Sue had been firm. Her tower had windows, she said, so there.

Mr Kennel took the same view. "If you *invent* a tower, it can have as many windows as you like," he said. "The whole thing could be glass, come to that. Why not?"

"People could throw stones at it and break it," Fraser said.

"Armoured glass," said Mr Kennel promptly. "Tough as steel. The stones just bounce off and smack into the people who threw them."

Neil looked amazed. "Can you get glass like that?"

Mr Kennel shrugged. "I've no idea. But if you

can dream up a tower and a princess, you can have bouncy glass as well, can't you? Who's this?" He held up Abby's drawing of a girl by a dark window.

"It's the girl in the story," Abby said. "She's in her room. And the dogs are outside."

"Ah, yes. The dogs." Mr Kennel put the drawings down. "They really started me thinking." He looked at Abby. "What's your name, by the way?"

"Abby," said Abby. The others told him their names as well, all except Chokker, who didn't need to because it had already been told.

"Mine's Stanislaus Proschynski," said Mr Kennel. "You'd better call me Stan; it's a lot easier."

Sue smothered a giggle. "We've been calling you Mr Kennel."

"Very reasonable. But on the whole, I'd rather be Stan."

Abby thought it was a scrappy sort of name for such a peculiar, interesting person, but it was nice and plain. Yes, it suited him.

"This girl of Abby's is a good person to start with, I think," Stan said, staring at the drawing again. "We'll have to get to know her – see things from her point of view. She looks to me like a rather private person who doesn't always say what's going on in her head."

Abby had an uneasy feeling that the girl was herself, and she didn't want her to be. "She's got dark hair," she said. "Wavy." Not like her own, which was long and straight.

"Fine," said Mr Kennel. "You could do a more detailed drawing of her. Maybe the house she lives in too. And we'll need to decide what she's called."

"She could be Emma," said Abby. She'd been thinking of the girl as Emma, but it sounded a bit prim, now she said it aloud.

"Boring," said Fraser.

"Couldn't we call her Kylie?" Sue asked.

"Or Louise," said Neil. "Our mum's called Louise."

Stan wrinkled his nose. "Nice names. Nothing wrong with them. But none of them really grabs me, know what I mean?"

Fraser frowned, thinking hard. "It doesn't have to be an ordinary name, does it? I mean, we could make one up. Like they make up names for cars. Astra, and things like that. Montego."

"Ford," said Neil, and snorted with amusement.

"Don't be such a prat," said Fraser. "You know what I mean."

"Thing is, it needs the right sort of sound," said Stan.

Everyone looked puzzled.

"Names are words, aren't they?" he went on. "*Pick* sounds sharp. *Rose* sounds round and sweet. We need something that's right for this girl by her window. Put it on your list of things to do."

"Is there a boy as well?" asked Neil.

"Yep, got to have a boy," said Stan. "The heroine can't do it all on her own. So think about him as well."

Strong, Chokker thought. *Quick on his feet. Tough. Kind.*

"Strong," said Neil.

"But he's got to be nice," said Sue. "The sort of person you really like, even if he is tough."

"Yes, that's important." Stan thought for a moment. "I think he should be a bit special. He might have been longing for ages to do brave, exciting things, only there's never been a chance."

"Well, there isn't, is there?" said Fraser. "So what's *his* name?"

"I don't know." Stan shook his head. "Any ideas?"

"It ought to be a made-up one," Abby said. "Like the girl."

Unusual. Special. "Luma," Chokker said aloud.

He heard his own voice like an electric shock, and his face flushed with fury. What an idiot, coming out with it like that! He hadn't meant to. But the summerhouse man was looking impressed.

"Luma," Stan repeated. "That's rather good. I like the way it's quite close to Luna, which means the moon. It really does give the boy a touch of something strange. We can use that, if you're all happy with it."

Sue wrinkled her nose. "It's a bit weird," she said.

"Why would anyone call their child that?"

"He might have changed it," said Abby. "My auntie's name is Elizabeth, but she couldn't say it when she was small; she just said Liffy. And she's still called Liffy."

"Could be Luma was called Lewis or something, and the same thing happened," said Stan.

Everyone nodded. Chokker's panic was starting to fade. After all, nobody knew who Luma was. They just thought he'd had a good idea.

"That's great," said Stan. "We've got our hero now, ready to do amazing things. The girl needs to be a contrast. More thoughtful or something. A bit magic, maybe."

"What sort of magic?" asked Sue.

Stan shrugged. "I'm just thinking aloud. Thinking is like fishing. You bait a hook and drop it in the water, but you don't know what you're going to catch. It could be a fine, fat trout, or an old boot, or nothing at all. But if you don't throw a line out, you'll never know."

"So we have to think about magic," said Neil.

"Yes please," Stan agreed. "And a name for the girl."

"Cat," said Abby, then blushed. "No, that's silly."

"Not silly at all," Stan said. "Short for Cathleen?"

"Or just on its own," said Abby. The girl was dark-haired and sort of private. "Like a cat."

Stan nodded. "They like to find things out, don't they?"

"Our cat packed herself in one of the bags when we were going on holiday," said Sue. "Mum picked the bag up and felt it move."

"Good thing she did," said Fraser. "Bit late if you'd found out at the airport."

Stan was still thinking about the names. "Cat and Luma. I like the way they fit. Emma and Luma sounded awkward."

"What d'you mean?" asked Fraser.

"They've both got two beats," Stan explained. "Em-ma. Lu-ma. Cat and Luma sounds a lot slicker. Cat 'n' Luma, yeah. There's a better swing to it."

"I didn't think writing was like this," said Neil.

"All writing gets said in your head first," said Stan. "You hear the words before you write them down. Whoever reads them is going to hear them too, so it matters what they sound like. I read my stuff out loud to myself, to check there's nothing that's awkward or difficult to say."

"So it's going to be Cat and Luma?" Fraser asked.

"I'm happy with that," said Stan. "If we think of something even better, we can always change it."

Chokker watched the others smiling and nodding. *Cat*, he thought. A slinky black figure flitted past the edge of his vision and vanished behind the Master's cloak. She could have been there all the time, so quick on her feet that nobody saw her.

"So what's going to happen?" Fraser asked. "In the book, I mean."

Stan looked at Abby. "I keep coming back to your dogs turning into these black lizards," he said. "Or dragons, or whatever they are. Somehow it links in my head with all this stuff in the papers about GM crops. Do you know what I mean?"

"Genetic modification," said Fraser. "We did it at school."

"Changing plants and animals to make them more useful," said Neil. "Bigger crops and things."

"Only it might change things in ways you don't want," Sue put in. "And once it's started, nobody can stop it."

Abby nodded in agreement. "My dad says it's really dangerous, because it'll make super-weeds you can't get rid of. And there are plants that have been grown for making medicines. You shouldn't eat them because they're sort of drugs, but if they mix with other plants, you might, and you wouldn't know." She didn't often say such a lot, but she had a feeling it was important.

"People have trampled GM crops down because they think it's wrong," Sue added. "I saw it on telly."

"So did I," Stan agreed. "That's what started me thinking. If we set the book in the future, the whole thing could have got completely out of hand.

There's crazy changing going on."

Fraser got the idea. "That's why the dogs are turning into lizards!"

"Exactly," said Stan. "Cat and Luma suspect it's changing humans too. Maybe they find out something. Or Cat knows about the danger because she's a bit special."

"Magic," said Sue, nodding.

"What sort of danger?" Neil asked.

Stan was thinking fast. "If GM spreads to humans as well, we might end up with designer babies, all the same as each other. Designer people. Quiet and hard-working, who never argue, never get into any trouble. Whatever they're told to do, they'll do it."

"Even if it's killing someone?" asked Sue.

"Oh, yes," Stan said. "If we're going to have a danger in this book, it needs to be a big one."

They were all staring at him. Sue and Abby looked worried, and Neil glanced at his older brother. Fraser was frowning uncertainly.

He must be a scientist, Chokker thought. *He understands all this GM stuff. People think scientists work in laboratories and wear white coats, but they don't have to.*

"It is only a story, isn't it?" Sue asked.

Stan smiled at her. "Don't worry. When you write a book, you can frighten yourself half to death, but you know you've made it up. You're always in control. If it gets a bit heavy you can change it. We don't have to do this GM business," he added. "We can pick something quite different."

Fraser had gone on thinking. "The scientist in charge might want to change the world so he can control everything."

"There's a bit of that going on already," Stan said. "But we don't have to stick with what's real. We could make these dogs really weird. They could have forked tongues like snakes. They could breathe fire."

"Scary," said Sue.

It's only a story, Abby told herself. But it was horribly close to her nightmare.

"It's quite good to read scary stuff," Stan said. "You're going to meet a whole lot of tricky things in real life. Everyone does. They don't come as such a surprise if you've already met them in a book."

"How's it going to end?" Abby asked. She still felt very uneasy.

"We'll have to work that out," said Stan. "The scientists might realize they've made a mistake."

"They'll try to undo it all," said Fraser.

"Take the dogs away, for a start," Chokker said. *Send out a hit squad. But a trained fighter could see them off.*

"Cat and Luma will have to kidnap a dog, and hide it," said Neil excitedly, "so they can prove what's going on."

"Yes, great. But where are they going to keep it?" Stan asked. "A fire-breathing dragon isn't like a hamster."

Everyone laughed. The parrot laughed too, and walked about upside down on the bars of the cage roof, shouting, "COME IN! COME IN!"

"Someone will have to help them," said Abby. "They can't manage on their own."

"You're right," Stan agreed. "They're going to need someone or something on their side. With real power."

The Master, Chokker thought, but this time he didn't say anything.

Neil was looking bothered. "It couldn't really happen, could it? I mean, not *really.*"

"I hope not," said Stan. "But this is fiction, remember. We're making it up. It has to seem real to us, though, so I'm glad you're kind of believing it. This story has to happen to us as if we were there, part of it. We'll have to look at it from outside as well, to check that our readers will understand what we've put, but the vital thing is to get it true in our own heads. Otherwise the readers won't feel it's true either. Then our book's a dead duck."

"Cat and Luma will have to find a grown-up," said Sue, who hadn't really been listening. "Or a friendly wizard."

Stan seemed reluctant. "Grown-ups tend to be so dull. They stop kids from having adventures, because of this safety business. And I hear that children's books have been a bit full of wizards lately, so we might need to look for something else."

There was quite a long silence, then Abby asked, "What do we do next?"

"Go on thinking," said Stan. "Don't struggle with the problems – they'll get sorted later. Just keep open to new ideas – and write them down, in case they slip away. They do sometimes, and it's so annoying. More drawings would be useful too."

"OK," Fraser said. "I can't come tomorrow, though – I've got football practice."

"Fine," said Stan. "I'm going to need some thinking time myself. I'll write some sort of beginning for this book, just to give us the flavour of the thing. I'll read it to you next time we meet. Then we can change it or move on. Decide what comes next."

"How will we know when you've done it?" Fraser asked.

"I'll hang a sign out."

"What sort of sign?" asked Neil.

"I don't know. I'll think of something. Just keep your eyes open, right?"

"Right," everyone said. Even Chokker nodded.

"You can keep the drawings if you like," Sue said.

"Thank you very much. They'll be a help." Stan went across to the door and opened it. "Now, off you go. And bung down some more ideas. I'm not doing all this on my own."

"GOODBYE!" shouted the parrot as everyone started to go out. "GOODBYE, GOODBYE. SHUT UP, AGATHA. GIVE US A PEANUT!"

"Oh, be quiet," said Stan.

"QUIET! QUIET!" Agatha screamed.

"I think she's really funny," said Sue.

"You don't have to live with her," replied Stan.

Chokker went out last, making sure the others were safely in front of him. He had to pass quite close to the summerhouse man.

"All right?" Stan asked him.

Chokker nodded. He wasn't willing yet to exchange words with the enemy.

On Saturday morning a yellow balloon floated above the summerhouse, tethered by a long string. Abby saw it from the garden behind her house, and ran past the kennels without a thought for the dogs, to find Sue and tell her Stan had done the first bit of the book. Sue phoned Fraser and Neil. By the time they got back to the summerhouse, Chokker was there as well, watching from behind the walnut tree. Abby wondered if he'd been there all along. You could never tell with Chokker.

Stan draped a green cloth over the parrot's cage. "Don't want any chat from her," he said. "She's rubbish at thinking."

Sue giggled. They were all sitting about on chairs and the sofa, waiting to hear what Stan had written.

"NIGHT-NIGHT, AGATHA," the parrot said from under her cloth. She already sounded sleepy.

"Night-night," said Stan firmly. He turned his desk lamp to shine on the piece of paper he held, and it made a glowing patch in the dimness of the summerhouse. The daylight outside still filtered through the closed blinds, but it was hardly bright enough to read by. Stan glanced at his listeners and put his hand to his head. "I must be mad. I don't read unfinished stuff to people."

"But you said you would," said Neil.

"I know. It's all right; I'm going to. Just don't expect too much, that's all." Stan cleared his throat, still frowning a bit. Then he began to read.

Cat glanced through the wire netting that surrounded the Jordans' garden. She'd hoped the puppies would be about, but there was no sign of them today, just the pigeons strutting and cooing on their roof. They were the racing sort, so they had to fly back from all sorts of places. The high netting was to keep cats out. Mr Jordan was sure they were after his birds. He didn't mind dogs, but then, dogs couldn't jump and climb – especially fat dogs with short legs, like his. She was called Beauty, though Cat didn't think she was particularly beautiful.

Beauty was sitting in the sun, scratching. She nibbled at the front of her leg, then turned sharply to bite at the fur above her tail. Perhaps she had fleas, Cat thought. She turned to walk on. The dog looked up at the movement – and made a sudden rush at the netting. She hit it so hard that she yelped and staggered back; but she charged again, trying to get at the girl on the other side, barking and snarling, scrabbling furiously at the wire.

Cat had jumped away in fright, but she was so puzzled that she approached again, staring down at Beauty. She didn't actually like dogs very much, because they seemed so rough and heavy, not flexible and soft like cats. *Cat and dog,* she thought. Maybe her name made her a cat person, whether she liked it or not. But the Jordans' dog had never behaved like this before. She'd always seemed too fat and lazy to move much.

"Beauty?" Cat said. "What's the matter?"

The dog snarled again, backing away. A wisp of steam came up from her breath, which seemed odd on a warm day. You could only see your own breath when the weather was frosty. There was something odd about her fur too, Cat thought. The hair looked matted, as if it was sticking together in clumps. She came closer, trying to see what the matter was – and Beauty leaped at the wire again. This time her breath scorched across Cat's bare legs with the heat of a blowtorch.

Cat gasped with the pain of it. For a moment she stood as if stunned, while the dog raged on behind the wire, then the horror of what had happened swept over her, and she turned and ran.

She didn't stop until the Jordans' house and the wire and the demented dog were left far behind and she was in the safety of the woods. This was the place she always came to when in need of comfort, where the shaded stream ran down the hill between rocks and ferns. Panting for breath, she sat down in the grass by a clump of tall foxgloves, and looked for the first time at her injury. The skin on the front of her legs was red and shiny, and it still stung fiercely. She pulled off her sandals and waded carefully into the cold water until she was standing knee-deep in the stream.

She looked up at where the sun sparkled like shards of diamond through the green beech leaves above her, and closed her eyes against the brightness. Slowly, calmness came, as it always did when she got away from houses and human activity. Her legs began to feel soothed, though the shock of the dog's scorching breath still jabbed at her mind.

What was it? she asked silently. *Tell me.*

No answer came at first, and Cat knew why. Her mother could never be doing with anxiety.

Be happy, sweetheart, she would say. *Life's too short to waste it in worry.* Cat let herself dwell on that memory for a few minutes, then she let go of that thought as well, and knew nothing but the wash of the stream's water against her burnt legs and the warmth of the sunlight that beat down on her head.

Stan looked up as he finished the first page, and Sue said, "Ooh, great. Ever so creepy."

"It's not too creepy, is it?" Stan asked. "I don't want to put people off. But Cat needs to be a bit magic, like we said. So I thought she might be in contact with someone who's not really there. At least, not for anyone else. Like a kind of hotline to someone secret. Someone amazing."

Like the Grand Master. Chokker nodded without meaning to, then wished he hadn't, because Stan caught his eye and said, "*You* see what I mean, don't you?"

"Sort of," Chokker said. *Be careful,* he told himself. *Don't get sucked in.*

"So is Cat's mum a ghost?" Fraser asked.

"Yes," said Stan. "In a way. She died when Cat was small, only she's still in contact." Then he looked worried again. "Could be a bit gloomy, though."

"I don't think it's gloomy," said Sue. "If my mum had died, I'd rather she was around. Better than going away completely."

But people *did* go away completely, thought Abby. Nothing was left of them except a wish that the awful thing had never happened.

Neil asked, "What's a shard?"

"A bit of broken glass," Abby told him, glad to think about something else. "Like a shattered splinter."

"That's where the light's coming through the trees, isn't it?" said Stan. He looked back at what he'd written. "Here we are: *shards of diamond*. Maybe I should change it. What do you think?"

"Diamonds are small already," said Fraser. "So they can't be shattered. Not without a hammer or something."

"True," Stan admitted. "What if I put *shards of bright glass* – would that be better?"

"Yes," said Neil.

Chokker wasn't interested in shards. The thing about Cat's mother being dead had sparked off a terrible idea. *What if the Grand Master's dead? The video could have been made years ago.* The man in the dark robes might not be there any more, walking through the screens of his Japanese house. *People get old and ill. They lean on sticks or stay in bed all the time.* But the Master could never be like that. He'd always be quick on his feet, as strong as a big cat.

His voice would always be deep and warm.

No, he's alive. Got to be.

"I want to know what happens next," Sue was saying.

"OK," said Stan. And he started to read again.

The answer came in words that had no sound. *You'll have to be careful, Cat. Something very dangerous is starting. A great evil.*

Cat felt a flinch of fear. *What is it?*

I don't know yet. There are powerful men, in a big building. They want to change everything.

What must I do? Cat asked.

But nothing more came filtering through the leaves that broke the sky's brightness, except a repeated warning.

Take care, my darling.

Abby shivered, crossing her arms to hug herself as though she suddenly felt cold, and Stan glanced at her in concern. "OK?" he asked.

She nodded. Part of her mind was with Cat, feeling the cold water wash past her burnt legs, and it seemed weird to be also here in this room, with the daylight faint behind the closed blinds.

"Why doesn't Cat's mother tell her what to do?" Neil asked. "I mean, if she's magic, she must know."

"Cat's mum is only as magic as we make her," Stan said. "And we'll have no waving of wands and changing people into toads, thank you very much. I'm not into all that."

"Oh." Sue sounded disappointed. "Why not?"

"Too easy," Stan said. "It gives you instant answers. Abracadabra, and they all live happily ever after."

"I think that's nice," said Sue.

"It's rubbish," said Fraser. "There's no such thing as magic."

"I wouldn't go that far," said Stan. "I mean, there's luck, isn't there? Good luck and bad luck."

"Yes, but magic's something you do on purpose," Fraser argued. "And you can't be lucky on purpose."

"I'm not saying you can. But would you agree that one chance thing can lead to another?"

"Well, yes," said Fraser.

"So there could be a pattern of chance accidents, all connecting with each other," Stan went on. "A bit like the Internet, only bigger and stranger. Some people are hardly in touch with it at all, and others can work it really well. They're the people I think of as magic."

"Because they know things other people don't?" asked Sue.

"Yes." Stan pushed his fingers through his hair, leaving it standing up like the crest on his parrot's head. "We're so afraid of magic now. People think accidental things are dangerous and frightening."

"Sometimes they are," said Abby.

"But you can't be totally safe," Stan argued. "Even if you lock your doors and do nothing but watch the television, you could die of a heart attack on your horrible old sofa because you've got so fat and unhealthy. So you might as well be out in the magic world, letting things happen to you."

Abby tried to imagine talking to her parents about the magic world, and knew she couldn't. "Have you written any more?" she asked.

"Yes, quite a bit. Sorry, we got sidetracked." Stan picked up his papers and found his place.

Cat waded to the bank and climbed out onto the dry earth, then sat down on a rock and dusted bits of sandy grit from the soles of her feet. The burning was still sore, and the skin on the front of her legs was bright pink and unnaturally glossy. Aunt Madge would look exasperated when she saw it, as if Cat had damaged herself through perverse stupidity. And Cat could imagine what would follow if she should be rash enough to mention the dog and her scorching breath. Pursed lips, a tired look. *I've told*

*you before about these stories. You want to be careful,
young lady.*

No need to ask what that meant. It was years
now since the first, huge row, during which her aunt
had shouted, *You'll end up like your father, whoever
he was, good for nothing.* Cat had never known
her father, but her idea of him was very precious
and private, so she had attacked Aunt Madge
with flailing fists. Uncle Arthur had bundled her
upstairs, slapped her hard and locked her in her
bedroom.

Wriggling her toes in the warm sunshine, Cat
thought back, as she so often did, to the older scraps
of memory that were her treasures. Tendrils of dark
hair touched her face as she was lifted from the
bath and wrapped in a warm, white towel. *This little
piggy…* Fingers pinched gently at each toe then ran
like a mouse to tickle her under the arm and cause
fits of laughter. Stories. Lots of stories that faded into
dreams.

Then the awfulness.

One morning it was Mrs Parsons from next door
who came to get her up. She'd been babysitting
the night before, but she was usually gone the next
morning. She helped Cat to put her clothes on,
and wouldn't answer when she kept asking where
Mum was. There were more neighbours in the
kitchen, Mrs Hodge and Mrs Field, and both of them
had red eyes as if they had been crying. Mrs Parsons

tried to make Cat eat up her cornflakes like a good girl, but she didn't want to. Then at last she took Cat on her lap and told her there had been a car accident last night, and she wouldn't see Mum any more, because she was dead.

Cat tore herself away and rushed to the back door. She tugged it open and ran out into the garden, certain her mother would be out there somewhere. But she wasn't. Cat put her arms around the trunk of the cherry tree and stood there with her cheek pressed against its cold bark while she screamed and cried. The neighbours were talking to her and trying to take her hands, but she didn't understand what any of them were saying, and after a while they left her alone.

The sobbing gave way at last to a feeling of utter tiredness. Cat's arms dropped to her sides and she leaned against the tree in exhaustion. In the next moment her mother was all around her. Cat could smell her particular scent and feel the closeness of her arms.

I'll never leave you, sweetheart, she said without sound. *When you need me, I'll be there.*

Stan put his papers down. "That's as far as I've got."

"It's ever so sad," Sue said.

"I know," Stan agreed. "I'm sorry about that.

But it's only a start. Nothing's fixed." He pondered a moment, then shook his head. "Anyway, that's enough for now. You probably ought to be doing your homework or something – I don't want trouble from your parents."

"I like Cat," said Sue. "She's really nice."

"And her mother," said Abby.

Stan smiled. "I must admit, I'm rather pleased with Cat's mum," he said. "The great thing about her is, she can't be killed or injured, because she's already dead. *Dead* handy, you might say."

Everyone groaned.

"I reckon the Jordans' dog did have fleas," said Fraser. "And Mrs Jordan bought one of those animal shampoos, only it was a new sort and it started changing the dog."

"It couldn't," said Chokker. "They test all new stuff before it goes in the shops."

Fraser frowned. "Well, what else could it be?"

"He could have got it off the Internet," said Neil. "Dad got some stuff off the Internet to make his hair grow. It didn't work, though. He's still bald."

Stan stood up. "Right," he said. "That really is enough." He pulled the cloth off the parrot's cage, and Agatha took her head from under her wing and opened her grey-lidded eyes. "GOOD MORNING," she said, and everyone laughed.

❧

Chokker walked back to the village alone, feeling irritable. He'd stood with the others on the road, talking about the book, and they'd all thought Luma and Cat would know each other from school. They were wrong, of course.

Luma didn't go to school. He didn't walk along the shore road or live in a house with a slate roof and a smell of boiling potatoes and a fuchsia bush by the gate. He belonged in a place far up a mountain, with temple gongs and cool courtyards and a volcano with smoke coming out of the top. Luma worked with the Grand Master every day. He knew things you could never see on the video. He saw the face that was hidden by the dark hood, and felt the touch of the strong hands. He and the Master ate together at a low, square table and talked together and practised together, and sometimes the practice hurt, but that was all right, because it was never meant to be unkind. At night, the tall figure would look through the painted screens around Luma's bed and say, *Sleep well, my son.*

Every night after he had turned the light off, Chokker listened to the deep voice saying those words. He could hear them even if the video wasn't running. Thinking of it now, he felt a wave of sleepiness although he was walking along the road in the cold wind. It was a pattern, like the fight movements. It was the way he left the real world behind and went into the better one of his dreams.

"Where have you *been?*" asked Abby's mother. "Lunch has been ready for ages."

"Sorry," Abby said.

"Sorry isn't good enough. I want to know what you've been doing all this time." Her mother tucked up a strand of the fair hair that was dangling across her glasses. "I phoned Sue's mother, and she said Sue wasn't in either. What have the pair of you been up to?"

"It's just – we were writing something," said Abby.

"*Where* were you writing something?"

Abby had the feeling that her mother wouldn't approve of her being in the summerhouse. She'd never said anything against the foreign people, but nobody knew them very well. It was going to seem odd that Abby and the others had spent so long with Stan. "We were with Neil and Fraser," she said evasively. "And Chokker Bailey."

"Chokker – you mean Charlie? The boy who lives with the Finbows?"

"Yes," said Abby. With a stroke of inspiration she added, "He doesn't have many friends."

Her mother sighed. "Well, I suppose … what were you writing?"

"It's a sort of story," said Abby. "About genetic modification."

"For school?"

"Sort of. We did GM in science." That, at least, was true.

"Well, all right," said her mother. "But you could have let me know. Another time, if you're at Neil and Fraser's, ask if you can phone me."

Abby gave a sort of nod. Was it a lie if you let someone believe something wrong? Yes, probably. But children weren't supposed to go to places with strangers, and it might be hard to explain that Stan wasn't a stranger; he just needed a bit of help.

Abby's mother sighed and said, "We really will have to get you a mobile."

"You don't have to worry," Abby said. She didn't want a mobile. With one of those in her pocket, she'd never be properly on her own again.

"Go and wash your hands," her mother ordered. "And do please hurry up."

Abby stared at her face in the mirror above the washbasin. She had the same sort of hair as her mother, straight and fair, though she didn't wear it bundled up with strands escaping. Abby loved her mother more than anyone in the world, but there was always a tight, unhappy feeling when she thought about her. She loved her dad as well, of course, but she didn't have to worry about him. He had the gardens to look after, and he was always the same, even if he didn't smile much – sort of steady.

Abby's mother wasn't steady. She was like the

weather, filling the house with sunshine or else with storm and misty confusion. Her dad didn't seem to notice the weather of the house much, perhaps because he was outside such a lot.

Abby dried her hands and went to join them at the table.

🌿 Four

"I want to know how Luma comes in," Neil said as he, Fraser, Sue and Abby were walking home on Monday. "It's all been about Cat so far."

Abby had been wondering the same thing. "I was talking to Chokker at break," she said. "He doesn't think Cat and Luma would know each other through school. It's too ordinary."

Load of rubbish, Chokker had said when she suggested it. *Luma doesn't go to school.*

"So what's his brilliant idea?" asked Fraser.

Abby ignored the sarcasm. "He didn't say."

"Perhaps they don't know each other at all," Sue said. "Cat's mother could tell her where to find him. Because she's magic."

"So where *will* she find him?" Neil asked.

"I don't know," said Sue. "I haven't got that far."

Abby said, "Luma might be a traveller or something, like Stan. He could live in a caravan."

"He's not grown up, though," said Fraser. "He can't live on his own."

"No, he'll have parents or someone," said Abby. "Only, they mustn't take him off on a journey. We need him here for the book."

"They don't *have* to move around," Neil pointed out. "They could live in a caravan for some other reason."

"Like what?" asked Fraser.

"Maybe they just don't have a house."

"Why don't they?"

Neil shrugged. "They're broke or something. I don't know."

Sue thought of something else. "We thought Cat and Luma were going to kidnap a dog, didn't we, to save it from the GM people. Is that why Stan did the bit about Beauty and her pups, do you think?"

"Expect so," said Neil. "Cat got burnt because Beauty is turning into a dragon. So her puppies might be dragons as well."

"That's what Stan said," Abby remembered. "A fire-breathing dragon isn't like a hamster." She found the idea quite scary.

Sue said, "It might set the house on fire."

"They'll have to keep it somewhere else," said Fraser. "An old garage or something. There might be one near Luma's caravan." Then he was struck by an idea. "What if it's made of asbestos? That doesn't burn. They used to use it for roofs and things, only it's not allowed any more."

"It gives you cancer," said Sue.

Abby fished in her school bag for a pen. "I'm going to write all this down, or we'll forget it."

They sat on the bench behind the paper shop, where the grass sloped down to the sea, and Abby tore a scrap of paper out of her notebook. "Garage," she said, writing. "Caravan. What else?"

"Cat's mum," said Neil. "Telling Cat how to find Luma."

"I don't think she can," said Fraser. "Cat's mum's a ghost, isn't she? Ghosts don't do stuff like that."

"She's not just an ordinary ghost," said Sue. "She's kind of – energy or something." Then she had an idea. "Perhaps when someone dies, all their feelings spill out and go drifting around. So Cat picks up the feelings from her mum."

"Could be," Fraser admitted. "Like radio waves."

Abby tried to concentrate on the spelling of *asbestos*. Her fingers were managing the pen quite well, but her mind was jumping about uneasily. The thought that a dead person could leave her last feelings floating around was oddly upsetting. Had that happened to her lost sister? And if so, who had picked up those feelings? Was she, Abby, partly Sylvie as well? She stopped writing in mid-word and stared at the purple-flowered thrift that grew in the grass. How could you know that what you saw was real? How could you know that you were absolutely *you* and not someone else?

Abby pulled her mind back to practicalities. *I mustn't be late home*. She folded the paper and pushed it back in her bag. "I've got to go," she said. "Mum gets worried."

"Did you tell her we'd been at the summerhouse?" Fraser asked.

Abby shook her head. "She thinks I was at yours. I didn't exactly say I was, but…" She still felt uneasy about it.

"We didn't tell ours either," admitted Neil. "But we're often late, with football and stuff."

"I just said I was with you and Fraser," said Sue.

They looked at each other, then Fraser spoke. "There's this thing about strangers."

They all knew what he meant.

"But it would be awful if we had to stop," said Sue. "And Stan isn't a stranger."

"Well, he is, but he's all right," Neil said.

"He didn't *ask* us into the summerhouse," Sue pointed out. "He wanted us to go away and leave him alone. And if we stop giving him ideas, he might tell us not to come any more."

"That would be awful," said Neil.

"We'll say where we've been if Mum asks, though," Fraser went on. He sounded very firm about it.

"So will I," Abby agreed. But the thought of being questioned by her mother made her freshly uneasy, and she scrambled to her feet. "See you tomorrow," she said. And she set off across the grass, almost at a run.

Chokker was at the chip shop. The Finbows didn't like him going in there. They said it wasn't hygienic – just because an inspector dropped in one morning and found a rat in the chip fat. The place got closed down for a bit after that, but it was all right now. People still asked for rat and chips sometimes, but Jimmy, who ran it, didn't raise an eyebrow, just ignored them and turned to the next person in the queue.

Chokker walked along behind the boatyard, where a couple of big yachts were already out of the water, resting high in their iron cradles for the winter. The smell of the sea mingled with the warm waft of vinegar from the nest of greasy paper in his hands, and he blew on each hot, salty chip before putting it in his mouth.

This was the best time of the day, when school was over and he was free to do what he wanted. He sometimes wished some huge disaster would happen so that all the ordinary stuff would have to stop. There'd be no more turning up to meals with your hands washed, no collecting your clean clothes from where Dorothy put them in the utility room. The whole household would be blasted into nothing; there'd never be another family meeting to send peaceful thoughts into the world. No putting a voluntary contribution from your pocket money into the Helpful Box; no setting out for school at the right time. No school, just piles of rubble. The TV news showed a lot of stuff like that, people getting bombed and kids in hospital with blood all over them. The Finbows thought it was awful. Chokker couldn't see why they worried. The world was over-crowded anyway, and some people didn't even want their kids. They just wanted each other. Voices echoed in his head. *Do we have to have that brat around? Go on, shove off.* Whack.

He crumpled the chip paper and chucked it into the sky. A gull dived towards it hopefully, then wheeled away and settled on a lamp-post, dropping a splatter of white muck on a car's windscreen. *Take that,* Chokker thought, and grinned.

No point in going back to the house yet. The younger ones would be having their tea. The whole place would stink of boiled eggs and Marmite and nappies. Chokker set off along the beach the other way. *May as well see if there's anything happening at the summerhouse.* The writer guy was off his head, but he was clever, you had to admit that. He knew a lot of stuff. He could be tougher than he looked.

As he came to the putting green, Chokker saw Abby ahead of him, hurrying along the road. He followed her, keeping a good distance between them. He didn't want to catch her up, only to see what she was doing. *Good practice.*

As he expected, Abby turned off the road when she came to the kennels, and ran quickly past the dog pens and up the path. She reached the summerhouse and paused there, and he wondered if she was going to tap on the door. She didn't. She bent down, as if she was putting something on the doorstep. Then she was off again, up the hill to her house.

Chokker frowned. *What's she up to?* Watching carefully for any signs of the man looking out between the drawn blinds, he trod quietly up the path. There was a heavy stone on the summerhouse doorstep, with a piece of paper underneath it. He stood still, sheltered from view by a straggly bush, and listened for any sound. The rapid clicking of a keyboard came faintly to his ears. It paused, and he shrank back behind the branches, but then it began again. Chokker crept closer. He was safe as long as the man kept typing. He reached the doorstep and lifted the stone quietly, easing the paper out from under it. Then he straightened up, staring at the words Abby had written.

Garage.
Caravan. Luma could live in it, only not moving about.
The dragon-puppy could burn the house down.
Assbestoss won't burn, good for shed.

80

How does Cat find Luma?
Does Cat's mum tell her where he is?
~~*When someone dies*~~

The last three words were crossed out, but Chokker could still see them. He frowned over the list, trying to make sense of the short lines. He didn't often bother with what writing actually *meant*. When Mrs Long heard him read, he just ran the sound of each letter into the sound of the next one and hoped they made words she'd recognize.

He put the paper back where he had found it, and replaced the stone without making a sound. Then he went on up the hill. He skirted around the fence of Abby's house and went through the Castle gardens and out of the far gate, into the forest above the village. It was a much longer way home, but that was the good thing about it.

Unwillingly he found himself thinking about the story. If Luma had to be in it, the caravan wasn't a bad idea. *Better than some ordinary house.* And he knew where there was a caravan too, quite near here. He went on through the trees, then came to the cart track and started down it.

The caravan had a hedge between it and the field where a brown horse and a Shetland pony lived. It was very neat and tidy, with a knocker shaped like a horse's head on the narrow door. There were plastic gnomes among the geraniums in the small patch of

81

garden. *Luma wouldn't live here,* Chokker thought.

An old lorry container stood in the field. It was the length of a big truck, with double doors at one end. Rust was coming through the coat of dark green paint someone had given it, but it was solid and fireproof. Just the place to keep a dragon-puppy.

Chokker shook his head, impatient with himself. *Dragons don't exist.* It was all rubbish, and he wasn't going to get sucked into this stupid story. He stared across at the slanting field and the moor beyond it. The sun was going down behind the hill.

Luma would like the horses, though. Chokker stood with his hands pushed deep in his pockets, thinking about the boy who was almost himself. Luma was mostly in the Japanese place, with the Master, but the others didn't understand that. It was going to be weird, having him in this stupid book. There'd be questions about where he came from and who his parents were, and Luma wasn't cluttered up with all that stuff. He was just himself.

The brown horse was grazing quietly, with the pony at its side. *Brown's the wrong colour,* Chokker thought. *Luma would ride a white horse. He might have worked with horses before he met the Master. Ridden ever since he was small. That's why he's so strong.*

Chokker walked on, and the pictures in his mind walked with him. The white horse with the boy on its back was moving fast across the hill, and clouds flew in the darkening sky.

"Thanks for the ideas," said Stan a couple of days later. "And for leaving the list on the doorstep without disturbing me. Very considerate. I like the caravan a lot: that can go in the book. And the shed idea is useful. Only it can't be asbestos or we'll get letters from parents, saying we're endangering their little darlings." He glanced at Abby's list. "Difficult word to spell, isn't it? Just one *s* each time: *a-s-b-e-s-t-o-s*. Not that it matters – the meaning's clear."

Chokker said, "You could use a lorry container. There's one up in the field."

"Is there really?" Stan looked impressed. "That's perfect. I might shift the litter of pups out of the Jordans' house and have them in the container instead."

"Is it always like this when you write a book?" asked Sue. "I thought you'd begin at the beginning and go on until you got to the end, but you keep going backwards and forwards."

"Oh no, it's a to and fro affair. Once the characters are real and solid, it gets easier, because you know what they'll do, but even then, you have to organize the thing, get all the bits and pieces into the right place. Hence the clutter." He indicated the untidy pile of papers on his desk.

"Don't you work on the PC?" asked Fraser.

"Once it's planned I do," said Stan, "but I still print stuff out all the time and go through it in hard copy. The screen only shows you a bit of a book, and I like to have the whole thing in my hands. Computers are useful, but they're just machines; they don't understand about thinking. Pencils are better. You can't beat a nice pencil. Anyway," he added, "I've got a lot to do now, thanks to you, so I'd better get on with it. See you tomorrow, OK?"

"OK," they all said, and left him to it.

They were back the next day.

"Shall I cover up the parrot?" Sue asked.

"No, she'll be all right; she's getting used to you. We'll shut her up if she's noisy. OK, Agatha?"

"OK, AGATHA," said the parrot, and gave a raucous laugh.

Stan started to read.

Cat's feet were dry now. Reluctantly she pushed them into her sandals and did up the buckles. It was time to go back to Aunt Madge and Uncle Arthur. She climbed the short slope back to the path, and put her hand on the bark of the tall ash that grew there, for a last touch of comfort.

Suddenly her mother's presence was strong again.

Look for the boy. He'll help you.

How will I find him? Cat asked. But even as she spoke the silent words, she could see in her mind a white horse with a boy on its back, moving fast along the edge of a hill.

He's been up to look at the lorry container, Chokker thought. *He's seen the horses. But there's only a brown one and a pony there; the white horse was my idea. I didn't tell him, though.* He had an odd sense that his mind had been invaded.

Unwillingly, he went on listening.

Cat walked on through the wood, her thoughts still taken up by the half-dream of the boy on the horse. She came out on the track that led down to the village, and started along it, between the hawthorn hedges. The clouds were blowing across the sky.

The hedge gave way to Davey Gowan's place – a plot of land with a ramshackle caravan in one corner, fenced off behind barbed wire. The caravan stood in a junkyard of assorted stuff: mowers, tools, buckets, a rotting armchair, a sink unit, a chest of drawers with no drawers in it and countless unknown objects roped down under blue plastic sheeting. Could the boy be here? Cat gazed around her, puzzled.

A rusted steel container, the sort hauled around as part of an articulated lorry, stood in the corner of the field with its doors open. Beyond it, horses were grazing, and Cat had a flash of understanding. That was why she had seen a boy on a white horse. Davey spent most of his time doing odd jobs and selling whatever he could lay his hands on, but he dealt in horses as well, so they came and went. And today there was a white one among the others.

Is he here? she asked, and the warm silence told her that he was.

Very quietly, she climbed the gate into the field and walked towards the open doors of the container, which faced away from her. Hay was spilling out of it into the sunshine. And a boy whose hair was the same pale colour as the hay all around him lay on his side, fast asleep.

Cat stared at him. He wore jeans and a dirty white T-shirt, and his mouth was slightly open. One hand was under his cheek, but the other lay palm up, the fingers loosely curled and containing nothing. It was a hard hand, grubby and strong, though it looked defenceless now in the quiet sunshine. The boy's eyes were flickering behind his closed lids, and Cat knew he was dreaming.

A wisp of half-forgotten nursery rhyme came back to her mind.

> *Where is the boy who looks after the sheep?*
> *Under the haystack, fast asleep.*
> *Will you wake him?*
> *No, not I.*
> *If I do, he'll be sure to cry.*

This boy would not cry. His sleeping face was thin and tough, and he looked as if he had not cried for years. Cat sat down on the edge of the container with her feet in the long grass. Her legs were still an angry red colour, and they stung afresh in the warm sun, but she did not mind. She leaned her head back against the door frame, and waited.

After a while, one of the horses came ambling across the field, followed by several others. Cat put her finger to her lips in a futile effort to hush the noise of their treading feet, then realized how useless it was. One of them whinnied with shocking loudness – and the boy was on his feet in a flash, fists up in front of him, his face tight with concentration although the pink-printed pattern of the hay still marked the right-hand side of his cheek.

Cat flinched from his fast movement but he came no closer. He stared at her and lowered his hands. Then he turned to the horses and said, "Shove off."

They walked obediently away.

The boy looked back at Cat as if in wonder. "You were in my dream," he said.

Stan glanced up. "I'm going to start a new chapter here. The kids have got more to say to each other, but I want a pause after Luma says that about Cat being in his dream."

"Can they talk to each other in dreams when they're apart?" asked Sue.

"I think so," said Stan. "It's the only place where they're safe. Enemies can't get into your dreams."

"Yes, they can," said Chokker.

"Go on?" Stan looked interested. "I've never had that happen to me."

Then you've been lucky, Chokker thought.

"What happens next?" asked Neil.

"Sorry – shouldn't keep stopping, should I!" Stan picked up his papers and began again.

✿Five

"How did you get in?" the boy demanded. "What
were you doing in my dream?" He sounded angry.

"I'm sorry," said Cat. "I didn't know I was there.
I didn't mean to be." She stood up to face him.
The boy's dark eyes stared at her through long
strands of rough, strawy hair.

"The woman told me," he said, as if talking to
himself. "She said I had to help you." He frowned.
"But I can't; it's too difficult. Why should I?"

Cat didn't understand what he meant, but
somehow she knew he was only cross and confused.
He was odd, certainly, but he didn't seem dangerous.
She stood very still, waiting for him to settle down in
his mind.

The boy turned his attention to Cat, inspecting
her carefully. When he saw the redness of her
legs below her cotton skirt, his lips tightened.

"Dragon breath," he said. "She was right."

Cat shook her head. "It wasn't a dragon; it was a dog. Her name's Beauty and she belongs to some people called the Jordans. Only there's something wrong with her."

"Mutating." He ran a hand through his tousled hair, looking worried. "It's started happening."

"What has?"

"The madness. A great evil, like she said."

Cat stared at him. *A great evil.* Her mother's words were clear in her mind, and a weird certainty took hold of her. "This woman in your dream," she said. "What's she like?"

"She's dark. She laughs quite a lot, but she's sad sometimes. She misses you." He looked at her. "She's your mother, isn't she?"

Cat nodded. She looked down to hide the tears that had sprung to her eyes.

The boy was angry again. "Why does it have to be me? I didn't choose this; it's not my fight."

After a few minutes, Cat asked, "What's your name?"

"Luma."

"Luma," she repeated, trying out the sound of it. "That's nice. Do you live here?"

He nodded. "With Davey Gowan. He brought me up. He calls me Lew. It's Lewis, really."

Cat wondered had happened to the boy's parents.

"They were travellers," Luma said as if understanding her question. "There was a fire, and their caravan was burnt. Davey found me under the wreckage. He thought I was dead, and I had been, for a while. I can still move into that other world."

Cat nodded. *So that's why he knows my mother.* There was a kind of logic about it. But what did he mean about the great evil? "Luma, what's happening?" she asked. "It's something serious, isn't it?"

The boy stared away at the edge of the hill, where the red sun was going down. He sighed.

"Yes, it's serious. I didn't want to know, but she said I had to understand. There are powerful men who aim to rule the whole earth. They're marvellously organized, like ants are. They're going to turn everything we know into an ant world." Luma was looking at Cat, but his eyes saw something else. "We'll go on behaving like people. We'll even look like people, she says, but in our minds we'll be ants, totally obedient to our ant masters. We'll have ant babies because no other sort will be possible, and we'll eat ant food that looks like proper food but it isn't. The whole earth is turning into an ant earth, and nothing real will grow any more."

Cat's hands were over her mouth in horror. *No,* she protested silently, *it can't be true.* But she knew it was. *What can we do?*

"Nothing," Luma said, as if in answer to her unspoken question. He had turned his head to look at the hill again, and Cat knew why she had seen him riding away on the white horse. He wanted to escape from this.

"But we can't just stand by and watch it happen," she said. "We must do something."

"No! Leave me alone!" In the next moment, he had leaped out into the field and was running across the grass. He jumped the gate at the end and ran on, veering to his left so he was hidden from Cat's sight behind the hedge.

She waited for a few moments, but she knew he would not come back. The red sun was cut in half now by the dark shoulder of the hill, and the air was turning cool. She turned away.

"Are the ant men the GM scientists?" asked Sue.

"That's right," said Stan. "We need villains in our book, and I reckon the GM lot are the most likely villains around at the moment. This is all happening in the future, remember."

"Why was there a fire?" asked Fraser.

"I haven't worked that out," Stan said. "Davey's a bit vague at the moment, though the horses seem right. I'm not sure about Luma's traveller parents either. Maybe we need something else."

Chokker wasn't sure about any of it. Luma wouldn't want to go away. He'd be there, ready to fight.

"I like the bit about the white horse," said Sue. "Perhaps Luma came from a circus."

"Now there's a thought," said Stan.

Neil said, "His parents might do an act with elephants or something."

Abby shook her head. "Horses." It was obvious.

Stan had pushed his fingers through his hair. "I can't see Davey in spangles and tights."

"He might have been a stable man," said Fraser, "looking after the horses."

"Yes!" said Sue. "Luma's parents could have left him with Davey while they were doing their act."

"He could be Luma's grandad," Neil put in.

Stan said, "I thought about that. If he is, he'll know all about Lew, as he calls him. So we'll have to know too, before we can write him in. And at the moment, we don't. So it might be better to leave that question until we're further on."

"OK," agreed Fraser.

Chokker nodded too. Nobody could know much about Luma.

Stan picked up his papers again. "Any more to say about this, or shall I go on with the next bit?"

"Go on," they all said.

"Right."

When Luma came back to the caravan, Davey's mates had dropped in, Pat Jordan and Terry O'Hagan. They'd parked their truck just inside the gate, and were drinking beer with Davey.

"Where's it all going to end? That's what I want to know," Pat was saying. "Walking into innocent folks' homes and taking their animals away. They've no right."

"Ah, but they have," said Terry. "I was talking to a farmer in the pub, and he said this disease is like foot and mouth. They're trying to stamp it out before it gets any worse."

"I was round at my mum's this afternoon," said Pat. "Her dog's got it. Beauty. I went and had a look at her – breath's as hot as Hades. I said I'd take her to the vet tomorrow, in the van. Couldn't put her in an ordinary car – she'd melt the plastic. Mum's hoping the vet can cure her, but I don't reckon Beauty's going to come back."

"Got a litter of pups, hasn't she?" asked Davey.

"They're all right," said Pat firmly. "Lovely puppies, they are. They look fine to me, but they'll most likely have to go as well. Mum's dead upset. She's blaming Dad for using that new stuff for his pigeons."

None of it made sense to Luma, but the names caught his attention. *Beauty,* he thought. *Jordan.* The girl with burnt legs had mentioned them only half an hour ago. Her dark hair and anxious eyes were sharp in his mind, and so was the warning of evil that had come in his dream life. *But I'm not ready,* he protested. *It's happening too fast.*

"What new stuff?" asked Davey.

"Something they developed at Massa," Pat said. "They should shut that place down, if you ask me."

"Ah, come on," said Terry. "We do all right out of Massa. Trucking stuff in." He winked. "And out. I'd a couple of good poultry cages last week, no questions asked. Michael's a good lad. He's got to check the van, of course, because of the security cameras, but he turns a blind eye. I always see him right for a drink if there's anything useful."

Pat shrugged. "Yeah, I know. We've both done OK out of the place. And Dad was glad enough to be one of their testers for the new pigeon stuff. Free food for six months, and his birds winning every race. Can you blame him? But I reckon Mum's right. This thing with the dogs has come from Massa."

Luma didn't usually bother with what Davey and his mates said to each other, but things were different now. Whether he liked it or not, he was involved. "What is Massa?" he asked.

"That big factory, out past Sumbury," Davey told him. "Research institute, they call it. Funny kind of research. First it was the crops, all these altered strains so no farmer for miles around could grow the old kinds they were used to. Now it's the animals."

He took a drink from his can and gave Pat and Terry a baleful glance. "You know what I heard yesterday? They've cows up there with udders so big, the creatures have to wear a bra, stop the teats from dragging on the ground. Now, that's not natural."

"None of it's natural," said Terry. "That's the whole point. They're after improving it. Higher yields, more profit."

"Well, I want nothing more to do with it," said Pat.

"They've a load of sugar beet ordered for next week," Terry remarked, and after a short pause, Pat shrugged.

"One last load wouldn't do any harm, I suppose."

"There speaks a man of principle," said Terry, and passed him another beer.

Luma sat down beside Davey. "What d'you mean about taking people's animals?" he asked.

"There's these hit squads," Terry explained, "going round inspecting all livestock, dogs and cats included. I don't know what they're looking for, but if they find it, they just take the animals away."

"Where to?" asked Luma, though he could guess.

"Back to Massa," said Pat. "They've a van with cages in it. And the Lord knows what happens to the poor beasts when they get there. But there's one they won't have." He smiled.

Davey looked at him suspiciously. "What are you up to?"

"I'm keeping one for Mum – promised I would. If the vet doesn't put them down, Massa will have them once they find out the dog was ill. And they *will* find out. The guy who brings the pigeon feed has to fill in a report each week. He checks the dog as well as the birds."

Luma could see what was coming next.

"And where are you going to keep this pup?" asked Davey, though he could see too.

Pat and Terry exchanged a glance. "We thought you could find it a corner somewhere," Pat said. "Just for a week or two. We brought it with us – it's in the back of the truck."

"Oh, no, you don't," said Davey. "I am not having a dog with some crazy disease in my caravan. What if Massa come sniffing round? What about my horses?"

"They're not interested in horses," Terry said.

Davey was not convinced. "How d'you know? Anyway, I'm not having it, and that's flat."

"We weren't thinking of the caravan," said Pat. "You've that container in the field. We could make a pen for the pup inside there, right at the back, behind the hay; nobody would know a thing about it. And think of my poor old mum."

"Poor old mum be blowed," said Davey. "You just want to have a smack at authority – I know you."

Pat smiled. "Don't we all?" He handed Davey another beer. "Come on, though – you're not telling me you're happy with this Massa thing? Tell you what, just keep the pup for a day or two until we find somewhere better. You're safe as houses. Nobody knows it's here, not even my mum. And she'll be so chuffed to get one of Beauty's puppies back. If Massa ask, we'll say it was a stray."

Davey sighed, then took a drink from his new can. "All right, then," he agreed. "But if anyone asks me, I don't know the animal's there."

"Fair enough," said Pat. He reached out and slapped Davey on the shoulder. "You're a good pal, so you are. I'd do the same for you, any time."

"Sure you would," said Davey with disbelief.

They all went out to the truck. Luma watched as Terry undid the tarpaulin that was laced down over the tailgate. A snuffling noise came from inside, and Pat reached in. "Come on, then," he said. "Good dog, where are you? Ah, there you are."

He straightened up with a wriggling black puppy in his hands, and turned to Luma. "Here, hold it a minute while we go and sort out a pen. We've a couple of hurdles in the truck."

Luma stared down at the puppy that had been thrust into his arms. It was panting and excited, and as its breath licked across the back of his hand, he could feel that it was more than usually hot. *A great evil.* And he was standing here, holding a part of it.

Stan looked up.

"Is it going to burn him?" Abby asked. She almost regretted her idea of dogs becoming lizards or dragons – it was turning into a very alarming story.

"No," said Stan. "It's still quite young. But there's going to be trouble later. Hang on before we talk about that – there's one more bit to read."

"Oh, good," said Sue.

That night, Cat dreamed she was staring at a vast screen. It occupied the whole of a white wall, and it showed a field of wheat growing under a cloudless blue sky. Every stalk of the wheat was exactly the same length, like a bristly floor you could walk across. The camera zoomed in and showed that every ear of wheat was bursting with fat grain. Music played, and the picture changed to bulging sacks being handed down from a lorry to grateful African children. Then it was back to the wheat field again.

In her dream, Cat stared around and saw that she was in some sort of factory, as white as an operating theatre but filled with strange, grey machinery. Monitor screens stood on every bench and hung from the low ceiling, and each one showed the wheat picture. Then the music stopped and a red exclamation mark filled every frame.

Be vigilant at all times, a man's voice said. *We need our workers to be as straight and honest as our Massa Nugrane wheat. Those of you who are less than wholehearted must be discarded, just as imperfections in our grain cannot be tolerated. The intelligent among you will understand this.*

The blades of a combine harvester sliced through the wheat towards the viewer, so huge and sharp that Cat involuntarily ducked.

Do not imagine that your dreams are private, the voice went on. *Our researchers are able to penetrate that privacy; we can detect anything in you that is less than faithful to Massa. While you sleep, the truth of your mind is known to us, so be sure that your thoughts are empty of all undesirable elements. For the health of all, deviation of the few cannot be tolerated.*

The slicing blades swept forward as though they were leaping from the screen, and Cat gasped in terror. In that same instant, someone put a hand on her shoulder. She tried to scream, but could make no sound. Then she saw it was Luma.

Come away, he said. *There's nothing you can do.*

But Cat went on staring at the screen as though it had hypnotized her. The wheat was pouring into a vast silo. Slices of bread popped up from a toaster. Children bit into their toast, smiling and looking healthy.

Luma took Cat's hand. *Come on,* he said – but she could not move. She looked down and saw that a great nail had been driven through each of her feet, pinning her to the floor.

Sue gave a frightened squeak, and Stan looked up. "Don't panic," he said. "There's a mighty leap coming up. Change of scene." He read on.

Cat woke to find her legs stinging. She was entangled in the duvet, and rolled over to free herself. Her aunt's angry words sounded again in her ears. *You fell into some* nettles? *Stupid girl. Running around like a hooligan – aren't you* ever *going to grow up? Go and have a bath; that'll cure it.* But the hot water had made the burning worse, not better.

Cat pushed the duvet aside so that the air could cool her scorched legs, and after a few minutes she drifted back into the dream.

Luma was tugging at her hand. *Come away,* he insisted.

The nails had gone. They had never been there; she was free to move her feet if she wanted to; but a new certainty had grown in her mind.

I have to be here, she said. *There is something I have to do.*

Not yet, her mother's voice said. *Wait for the time to come.*

Luma echoed the same words. *Not yet. Come quickly – they know we're here.*

A single eye had filled every one of the screens. From every bench and every high-mounted monitor, Cat and Luma were being watched. On the big screen that took up the end wall, the eye was so huge that Cat could see every vein in the yellow-tinged white that surrounded the circular blue iris. In the centre of its staring black pupil she could see the small reflections of Luma and herself.

Close your eyes, Luma said urgently. *Dream your way out.*

Cat was too scared to move. *But they can see us, standing here.*

No, they can't. They know something is here, but the Eye can't read what it is. They just want you to think it can. You're seeing your own image, that's all. But we must go. The alarms are going to ring.

As he spoke, a deafening scream of electronic noise broke out. Cat put her hands over her ears, but the metallic voice that rang through the building was too loud to be excluded.

SECURITY ALERT: ACTIVATE ALL SYSTEMS. SECURITY ALERT...

The warning was repeated incessantly, and lights blazed throughout the building.

Luma was holding Cat's hand; they had leaped away. They were being carried through the sky and the night wind was blowing in her face. Something solid was supporting them, and Cat found she was sitting behind Luma on a white horse.

If they couldn't see us, why was it dangerous? she asked.

He turned his head. *Because they are constantly upgrading their computers' ability. I thought it was all right—*

But you weren't sure, said Cat. Her arms were tight around him in case she should fall off, and she felt him give a quiet bark of laughter.

Nothing is ever sure, he said.

The dream shifted.

She was lying on soft grass where small white daisies grew. She looked for Luma, and saw him in the distance, riding a white horse along the edge of the moonlit hill. She could not call to him, and neither could she wake up.

"That's your lot for the moment," Stan said.

"I have dreams like that sometimes," said Sue, "when I think I've woken up, but I haven't."

"Funny, isn't it?" Stan agreed. "But what do you think? Is it too frightening?"

"No," said Chokker.

Abby thought it was, but she didn't like to say so.

"What's a mighty leap?" Fraser asked. "You said there was going to be one."

Stan laughed. "It's an old saying. There was a strip-cartoon writer once – Dan Dare stuff, you know the sort of thing. The writer went on holiday, and left enough adventures to last a couple of weeks, but he was late back, and they'd run out. The editor was frantic. He rang the guy up and said, 'Look, you've left the hero tied up all on his own in a burning building – what are we to do?' 'No panic,' said the writer. 'I'll be in tomorrow.' And when he came in, he sat down and wrote: *With one mighty leap he was free.*"

"Oh, I see," said Fraser. "So when Luma took Cat away on the dream horse, it was a mighty leap?"

"You've got it."

"Whose is the Eye?" asked Sue.

"I need to do a lot more thinking about that." Stan ran his fingers through his hair. "I just thought this outfit was desperate to control its workers, so it's got this supervision system. Only, of course, you can't stop people dreaming."

"Perhaps it's not a human eye at all, just a computer-generated one," Fraser suggested.

"That would be good," said Abby. She was glad of any explanation that would make the Eye less scary.

"Only someone's got to program it," Fraser went on.

Stan looked at him thoughtfully. "So there has to be a Mr Big in the background, whatever the computer does."

Everyone nodded.

None of that mattered, Chokker thought. "Luma wouldn't have run away," he said.

"But he had to rescue Cat," Abby pointed out.

He frowned. "He didn't have to. He could have stayed there and fought the security guards. He's good at fighting."

"You can see that," Sue agreed, "the way he jumped up when the horse woke him. He was ready to fight straight away. How did he learn all that?"

"Davey might have taught him," Fraser said.

"But it's a different world, isn't it?" said Abby, still thinking about the Eye. "Luma couldn't fight them, because he was only there in a dream."

Chokker shrugged. He didn't want all this dream stuff. He wanted something the Master could deal with.

"How did Luma know the Eye couldn't really see them?" asked Fraser.

"Because he's partly in the dream world," said Sue, as if it was obvious.

Fraser wasn't convinced. "What if there *isn't* a dream world?"

Stan shrugged. "We're not saying there is. Just

that we've got one in this book."

Abby's mind had jumped to something else. "Nugrane wheat. It sounds like a headache." Her mother quite often complained of migraines.

"Sure does." Stan made a note. "I'll change that. If you can think of a better name, please do. We need a name for Cat's mum too."

He held up a hand as they started to offer suggestions. "No, don't tell me now. My brain will collapse if I don't have a cup of coffee and a quiet sit-down."

"PEANUT," said Agatha from her cage. "GIVE US A PEANUT."

"Oh, all right," said Stan, getting to his feet. "Bossy old brute, you are."

"BOSSY OLD BRUTE!" shouted Agatha.

Stan put his hand over his eyes and shook his head. "This parrot has learned all the wrong things. Just as well I'm not in charge of children – heaven knows what they'd end up saying."

"Children are not parrots," said Sue with dignity. And then they all went home.

Six

Dorothy Finbow looked up from the table as Chokker came into the room. "Charlie, we were just saying, you seem to be very late coming home these days," she said. "You're old enough to do some things for yourself, of course, but—"

Her husband interrupted. "To put it briefly, where have you been?"

"Let him sit down first," said Dorothy. She doled out a helping of shepherd's pie and put it in front of Chokker. "You've washed your hands, have you?"

"Yes," said Chokker, though he hadn't. "Sorry I'm late," he added. With any luck, a quick apology would shut them up.

Dorothy nodded kindly. "I'm sure you are. But do remember that Gerald and I are responsible for you. Try to be a little more thoughtful."

Chokker started eating. After a few minutes, Gerald said, "I'm waiting for an answer to my question. Where were you?"

"With some of the others."

"Where?"

Chokker took another mouthful and wondered what to tell him. Chances were, Gerald already knew. It would be just like him to set a little trap. *You were playing football? But someone saw you at the summerhouse behind the kennels. How do you explain that?*

Better to play safe. "There's this man who's writing a book," he said. "We're helping him."

Gerald closed his eyes for a moment, as if praying for patience. "And who exactly is this man?"

"He's called Stan." Chokker was cursing himself. Gerald didn't know after all. He could have got away with a football story.

The Finbows were looking at each other in concern.

"Where does he live?" asked Dorothy.

"In this summerhouse. At least, that's where we go to help him."

"What summerhouse?"

"It's behind the dog pens," he said reluctantly.

"Along the shore road, you mean? The kennels?"

"Yes."

Gerald was looking astounded. "And you've been doing *what*?"

Adults were so stupid sometimes, Chokker thought. You had to tell them things again and again before they got it. "We're helping him write this book," he repeated.

"Is there any other adult with you?" Gerald demanded.

"No." *Only the parrot. Better not say that, though.*

"Dear heaven," said Dorothy faintly, "what on earth is going on?"

Her husband was looking grim. "I don't know," he said, "but I certainly mean to find out."

Chokker lost his temper. "There's nothing going on," he said. "We were up there, mucking about outside, and the guy asked us in, that's all. He was stuck for ideas, so he said we could help."

"Let me get this straight," said Gerald. "You are the person who gets terrible reports from school and never reads a word if he can help it, and you're telling me you are helping some foreigner to write a *book*?"

Chokker shrugged. He didn't care much if Gerald believed it or not. Stan wasn't *some foreigner*, anyway. Things had changed. It was all right, up there in the summerhouse. The book was none of Gerald's business. If he started interfering he'd spoil everything.

"It does sound a little odd," Dorothy admitted.

"It's more than odd," said Gerald. "Can you imagine how we're going to look if—" He didn't finish the sentence, but Chokker knew what he meant. *If the man in the summerhouse turns out to be some lunatic rapist or a serial killer.* Gerald was a social worker; he took these things seriously.

109

"Um – this man," Dorothy asked carefully. "Did he – touch any of you?"

"Course not." The idea was stupid. And anyway, if Stan had started anything like that, Chokker would have flattened him. He was older now, and the Master had taught him well. Nobody would knock him down now. Nobody would lay a finger on him.

The Finbows didn't ask any more. As soon as he could, Chokker escaped to his room. *They're loving this,* he thought. *Like they love being concerned about drugs and teenage mothers and starving children in Africa. They think the man in the summerhouse is a Problem, capital P.*

He stared out of his window into the dark. There was going to be trouble, he could see that a mile off. The Finbows were going to make a fuss. A week ago he wouldn't have minded, because Stan was still the enemy. But he wasn't the enemy now. Stan never set mean little traps like Gerald, and if he was impatient he said so. You knew where you were with him.

And besides, he had Luma.

I shouldn't have mentioned Luma, Chokker thought. *It was a mistake. Stan's going to get it all wrong about him, because the blasted Finbows are going to muck everything up, and I won't be there any more to keep him straight.*

He turned away from the window and slumped down on his bed. The Finbows were the enemy

110

now. Why did they have to be so stupid? He'd liked them at first, especially Dorothy. They were better than most, except for their total sense-of-humour gap, but they took everything so seriously. Did they really think you could be completely safe and cosy, with nothing nasty ever happening? *Get real. Grow up.* Sometimes he felt as if he was the grown-up one and they were the kids.

The evening yawned ahead, an ocean of boredom. No way would he sit downstairs in that lounge. He thought of watching the video, but somehow he couldn't be bothered to reach out for the remote. Why couldn't people mind their own business?

Chokker sat through the hours of school the next day in a state of dread and fury. The Finbows hadn't mentioned Stan at breakfast, but he'd caught them exchanging a glance as he was pushing his arms into his jacket sleeves, and Dorothy had said, too casually, "You won't be late tonight, Charlie, will you?" He hadn't answered.

At the end of the afternoon, he was out of the school before anyone else, running across the road and down between the shops to the beach. Most people stumbled around when they tried to move over the shifting stones, but Chokker knew how to do it. *Keep your heels down so your feet can't twist, and move fast. If you slip, go with it and put in a couple of quick steps so you're still balanced. Keep moving.*

A piece of paper was taped to the door of the summerhouse by the middle of its top and bottom edges, and its corners fluttered in the breeze. The large printed letters of the message could be read even from where Chokker stood.

Sorry, folks. Bad case of restless natives, I'm afraid. It's been nice knowing you, but bye-bye. Thanks for the help.

Stan and Agatha.

From inside, Chokker could hear the quiet clicking of the keyboard. He stared at the paper, reading the words again and again. He didn't know what *restless natives* meant, but he got the general message. No more summerhouse. Gerald had put a stop to it.

He didn't hang around, did he? Like the Master says, the first strike is always the best. Chokker struggled to think straight. *When you are attacked, keep cool; don't panic.* But coolness evaded him. His fists were clenched in his pockets.

The others came pounding up the path, then stopped beside him.

"What is it?" asked Abby.

Chokker stood aside to let the others see the notice, and they crowded round it. Fraser read the words aloud.

"What's a restless native?" Neil asked.

"It means there's trouble," his brother told him.

"Someone's complained," said Abby. "It must be one of our parents."

"I told my mum, and she said she didn't mind," said Sue.

"We haven't told ours yet," said Neil.

"Neither have I," Abby said. She felt uneasy. *I ought to have told her.* But she might not have understood. She'd never liked the foreign people, ever since they came. *All those dogs.*

Fraser looked at Chokker, who was scowling darkly. "Was it you?" he asked.

"I didn't mean to," Chokker said.

There was an awful silence.

"They made a fuss about me being late," he explained. "They said I had to tell them where I'd been, and I thought they knew, so I said. They get to know about most things."

"You never liked it, did you?" said Abby bitterly. "You said we shouldn't go in."

"That was at the beginning." Chokker couldn't explain what he meant. He hardly understood it himself, but in a weird way, Stan and the book had started to matter quite a lot. And now it was gone.

"It's not my fault," he said. But it was, he knew it was. He turned away from the others and bolted down the hill, crashing through bushes, careless if anyone heard or not. His enemies weren't here.

"Oh, poor Chokker," Abby said. "I shouldn't have said that."

"Yes, you should," said Fraser. "He didn't have to tell."

The others weren't watching; they were talking among themselves.

"Can't we go in and see Stan?" said Sue. "Just to say goodbye?" She looked as if she was going to cry.

"We could try," said Neil.

Fraser tapped on the summerhouse door. From inside, the parrot shouted, "HELLO, HELLO, COME IN!" The clicking of the keyboard paused – but then it began again. And the door stayed shut.

By the time he reached the village, Chokker had shaped his murderous rage into a plan. He paused outside the post office, calculating carefully. He'd thought of a cyber-attack on Stan when the thing had just started, but that seemed like a game now. This was real.

As far as he knew, there was no way an email from a cyber café could be traced, but he'd have to be careful. Any stupid mistake might make the post office people remember him as the boy who'd got in a muddle. Not that he'd ask for help; he'd never do that. He walked slowly down to the sea's edge, mentally going through the procedure. He'd mucked about on the Internet lots of times with the other kids; he knew how to log on and all that. There shouldn't be any problem. He fished in his pocket to see if he had fifty pence. Yes. OK, then. He just needed to think of a name.

The obvious one flashed into his mind. *Luma*. No, that was too close to the truth. But he could put the letters the other way round, like a code. Then he shrugged. Why was he bothering? If they found out it was him, well, tough. He made his way back up the beach, opened the post office door and went into the warm smell of dog biscuits and chicken meal.

Abby's mother tapped on her door. Abby sat up quickly, rubbing her eyes on her sleeve.

"What's the matter, sweetie?" her mother asked.

She couldn't answer. It was stupid to be so upset when they'd only been involved in the book for a while. But...

Her mother sat down beside her. "Come on. Tell me."

"It's – the summerhouse."

"At Neil and Fraser's?"

Abby shook her head. "It wasn't at Neil and Fraser's."

A bit at a time, the story came out, and at the end of it Abby's mother looked reproachful. "You didn't tell me the truth, did you?"

"Not all of it. I'm really sorry. But I didn't want it to be spoiled," Abby blurted. "And now it is."

"Oh dear," said her mother. "But I can see how Chokker's foster-parents feel. Taking care of other people's children, they're specially responsible. And ... we all want to keep our children safe."

"I know." *But what about Cat and Luma?* Abby thought. They weren't safe; they had terrible dangers to face. *Nothing is ever sure,* Luma had said. Life was going to seem small and dull without them. "It was only a story," she said. "But I really miss it. I'll never know what happened now." Tears threatened again.

"Well, we'll see," said her mother. She thought for a moment, then stood up. "Tomorrow is Saturday. We'll go to the library and find something nice for you to read. There are lots of other stories about."

Abby nodded. *But other stories are written and finished,* she thought. *Ours has only just started. And without us, it might die.*

The next morning, Chokker sat at the kitchen table, trying to look calm and ordinary. Gerald was in the other room, checking his emails as he always did before breakfast. Then he opened the kitchen door and came in. He had a printout in his hand. "Look at this," he said to Dorothy.

Chokker helpfully wiped a dribble of milk off Rosie's chin. Rosie was the youngest of the children, a messy eater. He took another bite of toast.

Dorothy read the message and looked at her husband, aghast. "Heavens," she said. "Who on earth is it from? Who's this Amul?"

"A code name, obviously." Gerald shook his head. "Can you believe that?"

"What does it say?" Chokker asked innocently, and the Finbows turned on him together and said, *"Never mind."*

He was careful not to smile. The words of the message were as clear to him as though he still sat before the screen.

You have maid a big mistake. The man in the summerhouse is OK. It was good and you have spoiled it. Those who do evil things will be judged and punished.

The last bit came from the Master. Chokker wished he could have added a lot more, but it had taken him a long time to put that much together. Words weren't easy to manage.

Dorothy was frowning over the paper. "It sounds a bit deranged," she said. "And whoever it is has got the wrong kind of *made. M-a-i-d* instead of *m-a-d-e.*"

But I put it through the spell-check, Chokker thought. *It must be right.*

"I'd think it was a child, only the language is so sort of biblical," Dorothy went on.

"Could be a foreigner," said Gerald. "Amul doesn't sound English."

"A foreigner," Dorothy repeated thoughtfully. "Well, I wonder."

They exchanged one of their private glances, and Gerald said, "We'll talk about it later."

Chokker was hardly listening. *It worked,* he thought. *They're really rattled; it's brilliant. I'll send them another one this morning.* Only he'd need some more money. He finished his toast, wiped his mouth and stood up. "Do you think I could have my pocket money?" he asked. "Please?"

"What's the hurry?" asked Gerald. "It's Saturday, you know you'll get it."

"Sometimes I've got some left," Chokker said, inventing wildly. "But I haven't this week. I had to buy another pencil for school. Mine got pinched."

"You mean you lost it."

"Well, yes." *Think what you like.*

"I'd always rather you told me the truth." Gerald fished a small fold of banknotes out of his pocket and peeled one off. "There you go. And do try to use it sensibly."

"Yes, I will," said Chokker, straight-faced. "Thank you very much."

Abby went down to the summerhouse late that afternoon. It glowed in the drizzling rain as if it had come from some other place and was just perched there for a while, ready to take off again. She could see it in her mind's eye, getting smaller and smaller as it soared away, up through the clouds to some place where the light was brilliant all the time. And where people were not suspicious and things didn't get spoiled.

One of the blinds was half up. Abby stooped and stared in under it. She didn't know what she wanted, only that it would be good to see Stan just once again. He turned from his desk as if he felt her looking at him, and got up.

When he came out, he pulled the door shut behind him as if to make it clear that he wasn't asking her in. "Hi," he said. "All on your own?"

"Yes," replied Abby.

Stan frowned. "Look, I'm really sorry about this." He ran a hand through his untidy hair. "It was great having you around. Will you tell the others? Give them my apologies? Seems a bit rude to let you go off without a word."

"But – can't we do some more of the book?" Abby begged. "Please!"

"Not if I've got to have minders standing around," said Stan.

"Minders? What do you mean?"

Stan looked at her thoughtfully. "You don't happen to know some people who look after a boy called Charlie, do you? There wasn't a Charlie among you lot, as far as I remember."

"That's Chokker."

"Oh, I see," said Stan. He nodded a couple of

times and Abby waited, but he didn't say what he had seen. Then he went on. "Chokker's a great kid. You're all great – but there's a limit to what I can put up with. I'm not having some other adult in here. So it's curtains, I'm afraid." He gave Abby a smile. "Keep writing. You never know, you might do a book of your own one day. You and the others."

Abby nodded unhappily. It didn't seem very likely.

"Mustn't keep you standing in the rain," said Stan. "See you around, OK?"

"OK," Abby said. And Stan went back into his summerhouse and shut the door.

Walking back up the hill, an idea flashed into Abby's mind. *Keep writing*, he'd said. Maybe they could write ideas down and post them to him. Nobody could object to that, could they? Stan might even send new bits of the book back to them, the same way. She quickened her pace. As soon as she got in, she'd phone Sue.

Later that evening, when the younger children were asleep, the sound of the television downstairs stopped and a murmur of voices replaced it. Chokker guessed that the Finbows were talking about the emails. He'd sent the second one this morning, and when Gerald brought it to show Dorothy, she'd put her hand to her head and said, "I can't bear it." They'd exchanged looks that meant a lot, but they hadn't said anything else. *Not in front of the children*.

Chokker crept quietly down to the kitchen, knowing from past experience that anything said in the lounge could be heard through the serving hatch. He got a bottle of Coke out of the fridge and poured some into a glass. If they came in, he'd say he just wanted a drink. There'd be a fuss about cleaning his teeth after the Coke, but that didn't matter.

He was in luck.

"I'm still not sure," Dorothy was saying. "This one's got two mistakes. *Rough* is spelled *r-u-f-f*, and he's got the wrong sort of *die*, with a *y* instead of an *i*. I don't think Proschynski would do that. He seemed quite an educated man, even if he was rather rude to us. And after all, he is a writer."

"He's a *Pole*," said Gerald. "I grant you, his English is perfectly fluent, if a bit Americanized, but people often learn to speak a language without understanding its finer points. And writers have got editors who do half the work for them."

Dorothy didn't seem to be listening. "Spell-check," she said, and Chokker heard her snap her fingers as if she'd just realized something.

"What?"

"These mistakes," she explained. "They're all ones that will get through a spell-check, because they're proper words. They won't get a red line underneath."

There was a pause, then Gerald said, "Yes, I suppose you're right. That's not the point, though, is it? We're looking at the possibility of some maniac child abuser with a taste for biblical-sounding threats. And if that person exists, we need to do something about it."

"There's no proof that there's been any abuse."

"There's never any proof at the beginning of these cases," Gerald reminded her. "And as long as we insist that a second adult is present at all times it should be fine."

Dorothy interrupted him. "Time for a cup of tea, I think."

She'll be coming in here to make it. Chokker fled soundlessly, taking his glass of Coke with him.

Abby, Neil and Fraser met at Sue's house the next afternoon. It was much harder to think about the book without Stan.

"You know that place they dreamed about," said Neil, "with the Eye and everything – was it a factory?"

"I thought it was a laboratory," said Fraser.

"Could have been," said Sue. "I don't know. But anyway, what are they going to do next?"

There was a long pause. Nobody seemed to know.

Abby said, "We've got to think of a name for Cat's mother."

"Mrs Magic," said Neil, but everyone groaned.

"She doesn't seem like Mrs anything," said Sue. "Can't she have just one name?"

"Like what?" asked Fraser.

"Polly," said Sue. "Poppy. Nasturtium."

Mother, Mum, Ma, Abby thought. *Mama.* What else sounded a bit the same? She ran through ridiculous names – *Mata, Maga, Mala, Mara* – then stopped. "Mara?" she said aloud.

"That's nice," said Sue.

Fraser wasn't much interested in names. "They've got to find this place where the Eye is. Not just in a dream, I mean *really* find it. And do something about it."

"Pat and Terry know where it is," said Abby. "They can take Luma there."

"And lots of awful things happen," Sue agreed, "but they muck up the computers and stop it all."

"How are they going to get in?" asked Fraser. "There'll be security and stuff."

"Mara will have to help them," Abby said. "If that's what we're calling her."

"But there's got to be someone behind it all," said Neil. "They'll have to meet him, and then there'll be a big fight."

"How are they going to win?" asked Sue.

There was silence again.

"I wish Chokker was here," said Abby. "He's good at things like fights. He'd know."

But Chokker wasn't there, and it all seemed hopelessly difficult.

Chokker was walking along the edge of the sea. The water that came rippling in washed over his trainers from time to time, and his feet were soaking wet, but he didn't care.

He would have to stop sending the emails. That had gone wrong as well. The Finbows had this stupid idea that Stan had sent them, so things were even worse. Gerald was seeing Stan as some maniac who lured kids into his summerhouse and then sent threatening messages when they stopped coming.

An unwelcome thought was nagging at him. He didn't want to put it into words, but it wouldn't go away.

I'll have to tell them it was me.

He stood still, frowning at the water as it swilled across the rocks. It licked around his feet as if it would like to carry him away. Standing here with cold legs was like a punishment, but it didn't make it all right.

I can't tell them, I just can't.

The Finbows would go on and on about it. They'd be terribly patient. Gerald's face would be tight, as if he was boiling inside like a kettle, but he'd be careful not to shout. In his very even voice, he'd go through all the usual stuff about self-control and seeing things from other people's point of view.

The tide was rising. Chokker turned to move off the rock he was standing on. His foot slipped on a piece of seaweed, and he was in the water up to his knees.

Stupid, stupid. He could have wept with the failure of it all. He floundered up the beach and sat with his back against the sea wall, hands dangling across his sodden jeans. It would be better to run, and get some warmth back into him, but he couldn't be bothered. It didn't matter. Nothing mattered. He went on sitting there.

There was nothing much to tell Stan, Abby thought as she walked past the dog pens on her way back up the hill. Three short words weren't worth posting. She stopped at the summerhouse, which was in darkness, and put the folded piece of paper under the stone. It said: *Cat's mum: Mara.* And it seemed very useless.

🌿 Seven

At the end of Monday afternoon, Mrs Long said, "Abby, can you stay behind for a few minutes?"

When the others had gone out, she went on. "Your mother phoned Mr Grant this morning, and he asked if I'd have a word with you. It seems you're involved in something to do with a book. Is that right?"

"Yes," said Abby. Why had her mother phoned the headmaster? There was no need for that.

"Don't look so worried," said Mrs Long. "It sounds an interesting idea. Can you tell me a bit about it?"

She listened while Abby stumbled through the tale of what had happened, ending with the note on the door that said it was all over.

"Did the note explain why?" she asked.

"No. It just said: *Bad case of restless natives.*"

Mrs Long laughed. Then she said, "There must have been some reason why they were restless. Did somebody object?"

Abby felt her face redden. "I don't know," she said. "But Chokker – I mean Charlie – told Mr and Mrs Finbow. He didn't mean to." She wasn't sure if she should say this.

"So they went to see him?"

Abby wasn't sure about this either. They might have phoned. "He said something about having to have other people there, so he couldn't go on letting us in."

"When did you talk to him, Abby?"

"Yesterday. He came out of the summerhouse. He said would I say goodbye to the others for him. Then he asked if I knew some people who looked after a boy called Charlie. He didn't know Chokker was called Charlie."

"Why did he ask?"

"I don't know. He didn't say."

"Thank you, Abby, that's a big help," said Mrs Long. "Is there anything else you would like to tell me?"

Abby shook her head. Then she added, "Stan's really nice; we all liked him."

"All four of you?"

"Five, with Chokker. He didn't want to do it at first, but then he kind of got interested."

"Chokker was actually *working* on the book?" Mrs Long looked surprised.

"Yes. He had some really good ideas. He thought of Luma – he's the boy in the story."

"Goodness. And this writer – Stan – is he willing to let you go on helping?"

"Oh, yes," said Abby. "He really needs us. Otherwise he might run out of ideas again."

Her teacher smiled at her. "That would never do. All right, Abby, run along. I think Sue's outside, waiting for you."

Chokker was sitting on the wall at break-time the next day. Abby went up to him. "Why don't you come round to Sue's on Saturday? We're still trying to do some more ideas for the book."

"No thanks," he said.

"Why not?"

Chokker shrugged. It was no use her sounding friendly. They knew he'd told the Finbows, and nobody forgives a traitor. He didn't belong with them now. Never had, not properly.

"But we need you," said Abby. "You know about Luma. He's your idea; you suggested him. We don't know what he's supposed to do."

Chokker stared at her. Then he said, "I don't know either." In the next moment, he had run off to kick a loose ball into the game it had escaped from, and he didn't look back.

That evening, going up the path past the summer-house, Abby stopped dead, and stared. On the doorstep, where she had left her note, there was a flat package in a plastic bag. And it had her name on it.

She picked it up and looked inside. It contained a sheaf of papers, fastened with a paper clip. The front sheet said in Stan's flyaway handwriting: *Thought you'd like to look at this. Thanks for Mara. Brilliant. Courage to all the comrades. S.*

Abby took her treasure home in a glow of happiness. Upstairs, she read the pages with greedy attention. The scene had changed, she found, but she thought it was happening in the Massa factory.

The meeting was not going well. Magnus Chip was in a filthy temper, and the engineers and managers sat in grim silence.

"You mean to tell me a couple of intruders just *walked in* here?" Chip's Chicago accent sounded more pronounced in his fury. "What in hell's going on?"

"They were not *real* intruders, sir," Eddie Molotov explained again. "They were, as we say, virtual. They came in through the process of dreaming."

Chip glared at him. "You're supposed to be head of engineering, right? And you let these two turn up in the Eye room like they own the place. Do we have security or do we not?"

"We do, sir," Pete Crabbit of security promised. "As you know, the whole system is fully alarmed."

"So how come it couldn't pick up two total strangers?"

Eddie tried not to sigh. "Our current state of technology is not proof against dreaming, sir." *Not yet. And thank God for that,* he thought privately.

"Then damn well get it proof," said Chip. "I've had it up to here with you Britishers pussyfooting around."

Glances were exchanged across the vast mahogany table. Archie Rutherford of diplomatic relations took a sip of water. He replaced the glass on the table very precisely, and everyone except Magnus Chip knew it was a sign of protest.

"Permission to speak, sir?" asked Jack Potts, an elderly technician who had been in the army.

Chip's hot blue eyes shifted to him. "Go on."

"The problem is, sir, dreams don't obey the rules of logic. Everything else has its physical laws. The speed of light—"

"I know what the speed of light is," Chip interrupted. "It's damn fast. Whaddaya trying to say?"

"Dreams have no known speed, sir. And no substance. We can't measure them."

"You mean they're like some kind of virus?"

"Not exactly, sir. Viruses are pretty well understood these days."

"You take me for an idiot?" spat Chip. "I didn't say they weren't understood; we're talking about measuring. And you can't measure viruses. These goddam hackers still get into the computers. It ties up half my staff, working out how to see 'em off."

Jack managed to go on looking respectful. "Absolutely, sir." He started to say something else, but Magnus Chip interrupted again.

"What's known about these invaders?"

"Not a lot, sir." Caroline Petty of human relations took over. "We have not discovered them to have any real existence. It seems likely that they are, as you say, some kind of infection."

"A virus," said Chip. "Didn't I say so?"

"You did, sir." Brian Timms, junior engineer and, in Eddie's opinion, prize creep, nodded respectfully.

"Our difficulty is," Caroline went on, "we cannot protect ourselves against dreamers. Our systems are based on logical reasoning, but these people work with no reason at all. They jump from one thing to another, sticking ideas together much as children do, regardless of whether they make proper sense. In fact, we're beginning to suspect that last night's invaders may have been children."

"You're kidding," said Chip.

Nobody smiled. Magnus Chip's father had put a huge amount of money into Massa, so his son got away with a fair amount of idiocy.

Jack Potts said, "We've put in a lot of work on the security software, sir. It now picks up the presence of non-physical intruders. Dreamers, in other words. It can detect a thought vibration."

"So when's it going to catch these people?" asked Chip.

"It can't do that yet. But it did record that two persons, probably children, dreamed their way in here last night. As soon as they became aware of the security measures, they dreamed their way out again."

"Nobody went through the alarm doors," Crabbit said. "I've replayed all the security camera videos, several times. Not a trace."

Magnus Chip stared at him, and a slow understanding dawned. "Well, hey," he said, "how about that! They got through the alarms. We're looking at a real system out there. If we can get to understand how these dreamers do it, we'll have a hotline right into the way they work. From then on in, the hackers can go chase themselves. Right here at Massa, we'll be doing kangaroo leaps into folks' minds." The brilliance of this idea excited him. "Hey, we can stop all this protest about GM before it even starts. The first sign of someone objecting – zap! They forget they even thought it."

"Amazing," said Brian Timms.

Simon Witter of publicity smiled. Like everyone else round the table, he knew the engineers had been working on this very thing for months. "Just think of that," he said admiringly. "What a story."

"It's under wraps," Chip warned him. "Until we come up with the goods." He sat back in his chair, tossing his electronic notepad onto the table. "And we'll do that, lickety-split. Right, Molotov?"

"Yes, sir." Eddie's face was expressionless though a shock of dismay had lodged itself in his mind, waiting to be dealt with. "Is that to take up all available resources, sir?"

"You bet."

"And we'll keep the existing work running as well?"

"Yeah, of course."

"Can I ask for additional staff?"

"I don't deal with details," said Chip. "Go and talk to personnel."

Eddie nodded wearily. This was what he'd expected. Perhaps he didn't want extra staff. Perhaps he wanted to walk away from the whole thing. He asked the routine question. "What is the job description to be, sir?"

Chip shrugged massively. "Hell, I don't know. You guys want me to do all the work? Call it the Dream Machine or something."

"The Dream Machine," repeated Simon. He smiled at Magnus. "That's absolutely brilliant."

Powerful idiots like Chip were like engines, Eddie

133

thought, observing Simon's smile. They had to be kept well oiled and supplied with fuel.

"Where's the coffee?" demanded Chip. "My cup's empty."

"Sorry, sir," said Caroline, and got to her feet. Cautious conversation broke out.

Eddie Molotov entered the words *dream question* into his own notebook. He pushed it back into his pocket, and closed his eyes for a long moment. A headache was building up. In his department they were already closer than Chip knew to breaking into the minds of other people. As an engineer, the idea had fascinated him. It could be a huge breakthrough, a completely new understanding of how humans felt and thought. He hadn't stopped to think what the biology boys were up to. He'd accepted that they were doing their own peculiar thing, seeking to improve crop yields and animal stocks – it wasn't his business. Engineering was a pure thing, undertaken for the pleasure of solving problems, but other people wanted to use it for weird purposes, and the joy of pure thought was getting spoiled. Eddie didn't like it. He didn't like it at all.

"Abby, tea's ready," her mother called. Reluctantly, Abby laid the pages on her bed. The story had gone quite grown up, she thought. She felt pleased that Stan assumed she'd understand it.

She didn't get any more reading done that day. It was the first evening of an art exhibition in the Castle, and she'd promised to help her mother with the refreshments.

The place was packed with artists and their friends, helping themselves to little sandwiches and cocktail sausages on sticks from the big tables in the café. Their pictures hung on the wall, but Abby could hardly see them through the crowd. She collected empty wine glasses and took them through to the kitchen where helpers were washing them, and by the time the last artist had gone, it was late.

In bed, Abby turned to the next page of the story, but she was too tired to make sense of it. She put out her light and slept.

She took the package of papers to school the next morning, and told Sue what had happened in the bit she'd read.

"What have you got there, Abby?" asked Mrs Long.

"It's some more of the book. He left it outside," she added quickly.

Mrs Long smiled. "Isn't that exciting." She glanced at her watch. "We've a lot to get through this morning, otherwise I'd love you to read it out to everyone. Is there much of it?"

Abby showed her the sheaf of pages, and the teacher shook her head. "We'd never fit all that in," she said. "Such a pity. Perhaps you can tell us about it this afternoon in verbal expression."

"Yes," said Abby. She was longing to know what the rest of the pages said, so she kept sneaking a look at them, in between doing other things.

At break-time they trooped off to the bicycle shed where they'd be sheltered from the wind. They passed Chokker sitting on the wall, and Fraser said, "We've got some more of Stan's book – d'you want to come and listen?"

"No thanks," said Chokker.

Abby lost her temper. "Yes, you do," she said. "I've been reading the next bit in class, and Luma comes into it, so we need you. I think there's going to be a fight or something."

Chokker shrugged, but when they moved on, he got up and followed.

"Why don't you read it out?" Neil said to Abby. "We can't all see it properly; there's too many of us."

"All right," agreed Abby. She got the pages out and turned them back to the first bit. She read that, then went on.

The Massa building was strangely quiet after the meeting. People sat hunched in thought before their computers, and conversation around the coffee machine was even more muted than usual.

"What's *muted* mean?" asked Neil.

"Very quiet," said his brother. "Don't interrupt; you can ask me after."

"All right," said Neil, and Abby continued. Some of the long words were difficult, but she managed most of it all right.

Eddie Molotov still had a headache. He pressed his fingers through his wiry grey hair, trying to ease the pain, and knew the Eye on the monitor relayed his movement to the Eye room. He had set up the system. He didn't like what the security people were doing with it, but there was no going back.

Briefly he thought about Dennis Kidd, who had been head of engineering before him. Dennis had walked out after some enormous row at high level. It was simply an accident, of course, that he was run over by a car on a dark night very shortly afterwards.

No connection, Eddie thought carefully, aware of the technical set-up that was now so close to detecting any thoughts expressed in words. The Administrator upstairs was very pleased with it.

Eddie sighed. Magnus Chip's Dream Machine brainwave was nonsense, of course. He couldn't see why the Administrator let him come up with these stupid ideas, as if they were original. Probably to keep him sweet because of the money his father had invested in the place. Everyone knew it was absurd, but with the Eye watching and listening, nobody dared to admit that. Except, of course, in the private code that existed between them.

Bill Conroy caught Eddie's eye. "All geared up, then?" he asked cheerfully.

"Absolutely," said Eddie.

They looked at each other with unspoken questions. *What are we going to do? What's the Administrator up to?*

"Unusual, isn't it?" said Bill.

Eddie nodded. Unusual was their word for anything ridiculous. "Highly innovative." *Utterly insane.*

"Such a challenge," Bill agreed. *Plain impossible.*

"Exciting," said Eddie. *A total pain in the bum.* "It'll demand concentrated thought." *I'll need at least two days off sick.*

"Me too," said Bill, forgetting the code for a moment. "Thinking, I mean," he added quickly.

"This is something truly demanding." *Nervous breakdown time.*

They both laughed in desperation, hoping the Eye would see their faces as exhilarated.

Sue said, "What's *exhil*—"

"Ssh!" said everyone.

"Being pleased and excited," Abby told her, and turned the page. "It changes to a new place now. There's three dots, then it starts again." She went on reading.

I don't know what to call you, said Luma. *Do you have a name?*

The dark-haired woman smiled. *You can call me Mara. You found Cat as I asked. Thank you.*

I didn't find her, said Luma. *She found me.* He had been in some dream place when the girl came, and had woken to find her sitting there, between him and the sun. He'd thought for a moment that she was an enemy.

She will need you, said Mara.

Luma liked the dark-haired girl who made so little fuss over the burns on her legs, though they seemed to be getting worse every day, but he still wished he hadn't been dragged into it.

Why me?

Because you can see things that are hidden to her.

He knew this was true. *But so can you.*

I am not in the real world. Dangerous things are going to happen, and Cat will need someone brave. Someone real.

There was no point in protesting.

What will I have to do? Luma asked.

Mara's smile warmed him. *Ride your horses; run across the fields; be happy in your living days. What you do will be right.*

But how will I know?

The question was not answered. Luma was awake, lying in his bunk in Davey Gowan's caravan. Davey was snoring, and the early morning light was coming in through the small window.

The next afternoon—

The bell went. Everyone got up.

"You're not to go on reading it without me," said Sue.

"Or me," Neil agreed. They were both in a younger class.

"We'll keep it till lunchtime," Abby promised.

In the bike shed after they'd eaten their packed lunch, Fraser took over the reading.

The next afternoon, Luma found Cat staring through the wire into the Jordans' garden.

"How did you know I'd be here?" she asked, and he shrugged.

"I just did."

Cat nodded. Her mother's smile was close in her mind.

The pigeons fluttered and cooed on the roof of their shed, but there was no sign of the dog. Pat would have taken her to the vet, Luma remembered. But what about the pups?

Mrs Jordan came out and put some rubbish in the dustbin. She was wearing rubber gloves and old trousers, and her frizzy hair was tied up with a flowered scarf.

"Hi," said Luma. "Have the puppies gone to new homes?"

Mrs Jordan didn't answer straight away. She came across and looked at them through the wire. "Why do you want to know?"

"Just wondered," Luma said. "I live with Davey Gowan; he's a friend of Pat's. Pat was saying Beauty wasn't well."

"The vet put her down," Mrs Jordan said. "He said it was kinder. And we had to take the puppies in as well." Her face was set in determined lines, not making a fuss. But then, Luma thought, she knew about the pup Pat had saved. He wondered if she knew where it was.

"I saw Beauty," Cat said. "A couple of days ago. She was very hot, wasn't she?"

Mrs Jordan looked up quickly. "How do you know she was hot?"

"I was standing by the wire." Cat glanced down at her legs, which were blistered and weeping now.

The woman followed her gaze, and caught her breath in concern. "Did Beauty do that?"

"She didn't mean to. It was just her breath."

Mrs Jordan frowned. "Something's gone wrong," she said. "All these improvements they're making – some of them are good, but I reckon something's got out that shouldn't have."

"What improvements?" asked Cat.

"Like the pigeon food. My husband's pigeons are homers, you see. He puts them in for races; the first bird to get back from wherever they've been taken wins a prize. It wasn't Pat's fault," she added. "He's a good boy. He meant well, but he told his dad about this new feedstuff."

Luma nodded. "He was telling Davey. What's the feed supposed to do?"

"It improves their brains," Mrs Jordan said. "Most pigeons, you see, when they're let out of the basket, they fly up then circle a few times, getting their bearings. Well, that takes time. But once Eric's birds were on this brain food, they had the whole thing in their heads, like it was imprinted there, he said. The minute they were out, they were off like a shot, no circling, no nothing. It gave them a good ten minutes' start on the others."

"So they won all the races?" Cat asked.

"Yes, they did. Eric won a lot of money; he was dead chuffed. But the other breeders can get the stuff now, so he's lost the advantage."

"Why was he the first?" asked Luma, though he had a fair idea already.

"Pat tipped him the wink," said Mrs Jordan. "He delivers stuff to Massa, see, where they make all these animal foods, and a friend of his who works there told him. They test anything new on a few outsiders before they put it on the market. It's what they call a field trial. So Pat thought his dad would like to be on it. He brought the stuff over for him. It was a kind thought," she went on. "I'm not saying anything against Pat. But I reckon this dog illness is an infection that came with the pigeon food."

"Did the vet think so too?" Cat asked.

Mrs Jordan looked alarmed. "We couldn't tell the vet," she said. "Eric had to sign these papers Massa gave him, something about industrial secrets.

He didn't mind; he was dead pleased with the stuff."
She glanced back nervously at the house, then took
a step nearer the wire and lowered her voice.
"Between you and me, I wish he'd never set eyes on
it." She stared again at the reddened, weeping skin
on Cat's legs. "I'm sorry Beauty did that to you," she
said. "Really sorry." Then she turned and went back
to the house.

"We must go and see the vet," said Cat. "We've
got to find out what he knows about Massa."

Luma nodded. He thought about the pup
stashed away at Davey's place, remembering the
heat of it in his hands. He wasn't at all sure that
Mrs Jordan would ever get it back. But if it had the
illness, what were they to do with it?

He and Cat walked on, side by side, as if they had
known each other for a long time, and Luma felt a
moment of something like panic. He did not want to
be mixed up in all this, but there was no choice.

🌿Eight

Fraser looked up. "That's all there is."

"Hasn't he put what the vet's going to say?" Sue looked disappointed.

"He's probably writing that bit now," said Neil.

Chokker got up and walked away. Then he broke into a run, crossing the grass to where some kids were looking for conkers under the tree that leaned across the fence. Luma wouldn't stand around talking. This Massa place had to be attacked, that was obvious. Cat was going to need proper fighters on her side, not just ghosts and dreamers. Stan hadn't got it right.

Fighting. *Yes*. Chokker felt a rush of new energy at the thought of it. He picked up the hollow case of a conker from where it lay in the grass, and hurled it into the air. There was something very good about the way it soared above the tree and landed somewhere on the other side of the road. He heard a squawk of surprise from a passing woman, and grinned. *Scored a hit there*. That was what Stan's stupid book needed – some real action.

And then an idea came into Chokker's head that surprised him.

He couldn't use one of the school computers, not without a lot of explanation, and writing the note was difficult because he had to hide it whenever Mrs Long came to his table. There was no way of checking the spelling either.

"How d'you spell *fight*?" he asked Mandy, who was sitting beside him.

"*F-i-g-h-t*. What are you writing?"

"It's private," said Chokker.

He laboured on, angry that it was so hard. Mandy wasn't clever; she just did as she was told. It wasn't fair that she was better at words than he was. He looked at what he had written.

Yo got it rong abat Luma. He isent just a kid, he can fight. Hes difrent and... The next word was a tricky one.

"How d'you spell *special*?"

"I'm not sure," said Mandy. And before he could stop her, she had her hand in the air. "Mrs Long, Charlie wants to know how to spell *special*."

Mrs Long came to their table. Chokker put his arm over the note, but she asked the same question as Mandy. "What are you writing, Charlie?"

"Nothing," he said.

"Well, whatever it is, you don't need to worry

146

about spelling just now. Where's your worksheet?"

He slid it out from under his elbow. He hadn't ticked any of the boxes.

"Now, come along," said Mrs Long. "Put your name in the corner. On that line, look."

Chokker wrote his name, mentally cursing Mandy.

"Good. Now think about the first question. *Is a rainforest wet or dry?* What does this word say?"

"Wet," said Chokker.

"And this one?"

"Dry."

"So which box do you tick?"

Chokker thought for a moment of ticking *Dry*, just to wind her up, but decided he'd better not.

"*Wet*. That's right. Good. Now try the next one. I'll come back and help you in a minute." She gave him an encouraging smile and moved on to Kevin Dobb's table, where they were mucking about.

Chokker retrieved his note. He'd just have to guess about the spelling.

...*speshl*, he wrote. *He can do things. It needs mor stuf hapning. Thers to much dreming.* He nibbled the end of his pencil, thinking. Mara was dead, so she couldn't be much use. *I dont think pepel go on living after ther ded,* he wrote with reckless speed. *Cat has got to get propper* – he wondered how to spell *soldiers*, then saw he could add a bit to the word Mandy had spelled for him – *fighters.*

He sat back. Mandy was ticking boxes as if she really liked them. How were you supposed to finish a letter? Mrs Long glanced across from where she was helping Danny Parsons, and Chokker leaned forward again quickly. He'd just sign it. *C. Bailey,* he wrote, and put a squiggle underneath.

After school he ran all the way along the shore road to the kennels. He ran past the bungalow, making for the path to the summerhouse, but the back door opened. A woman shouted after him, "Excuse me!" Several dogs had come out with her, but they seemed friendly.

He stopped. "I was only—"

"Listen, we have enough trouble with you children." She had curly, greyish hair and was wearing a rather unravelling jersey over trousers that were tucked into brown boots. "What you want?"

She must be Stan's wife, Chokker thought. "Nothing, I just—"

"Then, please…" She waved a hand. "I'm sorry."

"I just have to leave a note," said Chokker. He showed it to her, and felt rather superior. He'd never written a note to anyone before.

"OK. You give it to me."

"But it's for—"

"Stan, yes. I'll tell him. What is your name, please?"

"Chokker."

She looked interested. "Like chocolate?"

"Um, sort of." But, yes. That had been one of his first words, his mum had said. That was why he got his nickname.

"So it's easy to remember," Stan's wife said, and smiled. "Very nice. I am Anastasia. Stasi. It's easier."

Chokker gave her the piece of paper. "The spelling might be a bit..."

"Stanislaus will understand. I spell very terrible too, in English." Then she looked worried. "You better go, Chokker. I like to ask you in but..." She shrugged. "People are very stupid; they think crazy things. I give him the note." She smiled at him, then whistled for her dogs and shut the door.

"No interesting emails?" Dorothy asked as she doled out mince and potatoes.

"No. We were evidently right in our diagnosis," said Gerald.

Chokker particularly hated the way they talked to each other in this code of long words. Did they think he was an idiot? He started eating.

"The treatment had the desired effect," Gerald continued. "Stopped him dead, didn't it?"

Chokker mashed a potato very carefully. So Gerald still thought Stan had sent the emails. *The treatment* must mean whatever he and Dorothy had said to stop him seeing the kids any more.

"I'm not entirely convinced," Dorothy said.

"Those messages don't sound right to me."

Gerald wiped Rosie's face with a piece of the kitchen roll that always stood on the table. "Never mind what they sound like," he said. "There's a possibility that something undesirable is going on, and we have to deal with the person concerned, before he goes any further."

"It could be very unwise unless we're sure."

"Obviously. But do you seriously think anyone else could have sent those messages?"

"Yes," said Dorothy. "I do."

Gerald looked annoyed. "Then you'd better prove it."

Rosie hurled her spoon to the floor, and Dorothy bent down to pick it up. "I might just do that," she said. Which was as near as they came to having a row.

There was apple crumble and custard to follow. Chokker kept his eyes on his plate, but a terrible uneasiness was stirring in his mind as he ate. Did Dorothy suspect that he had sent the messages? He tried to imagine confessing to it, and flinched away from the thought.

I can't tell them it was me, I just can't. They'd go on and on about how disappointed they were. But, worse than that, they'd know he'd been thinking of them as the enemy. They might even send him back to the home like the others had, and that would be a downer, because they were better than most.

Hating them had to be very private.

After the meal he trailed up the stairs to his room, thinking about the problem. Maybe he'd better send one more email. Just a short message from Amul, telling them he was someone really respectable. A doctor or something. But it couldn't be anyone real; he'd have to make it up.

Chokker's brain ached with thinking. He reached for the remote and switched on the video, for the first time in several days. The warm voice came to him like a comforting arm round the shoulders, and he lay back on his bed with his wrist across his eyes.

Sorry for being away, he said silently.

And, as always, he felt forgiven.

Abby caught him outside school the next morning.

"This is for you!" she said, and thrust a letter into his hand. "It's from Stan! It was on the summerhouse door."

Chokker stared at the bold capital letters on the envelope. MR C. BAILEY. There was a bit of sticky tape on the top edge.

"Aren't you going to open it?" asked Abby.

"Yeah, sure." He turned it over and pushed his finger under the stuck-down flap. He'd never had a letter. Envelopes had Christmas cards inside them, or a birthday card from Dorothy and Gerald.

Abby watched him, and he knew she was dying to know what the letter said. So was he, but he managed to stay cool.

"I sent him a note," he said. "About the book."

"*Did* you?" She looked really impressed. "So what does he say?"

"Have a look if you like." He handed the letter over, and Abby read it aloud:

"Dear Chokker,

Thank you very much for your helpful comments. You are quite right: the book does need to move faster. I'll have to think a lot more about the plot.

I'm very interested in what you say about life after death. You may be right in thinking there's nothing at all — we just end, and that's it. Back to the state we were in before we were born. But it's interesting to think about, all the same, since nobody can prove it one way or the other. And I do think dreaming is vital. Private imagination is the most important thing about us. Without it, we might as well be jellyfish."

Abby laughed. "I like that, about the jellyfish."

"Yeah," said Chokker. He waited for her to go on.

"That's why it's so useful to have Luma. He's the only one who can go between the real world

and the other one. He lives as an ordinary boy
– or at least, fairly ordinary – but, as you say,
he is special. He is the connecting link.

I like your idea that he is a fighter. I haven't
worked him out very clearly yet, so any ideas
about him are extremely welcome. I don't know
much about fighting either. I'll have to do some
research on that.

Best wishes to a fellow author,
Stan."

Abby looked up as she finished reading. "Aren't you clever," she said, "sending him all that stuff." Her voice held a new respect.

Chokker shrugged modestly, but he felt warm inside.

"Will you write to him again?"

"Yeah. Expect so."

And then the bell went.

Now that he knew what the letter said, it was easier to make out the words. He wanted to read them again and again. This was proper business, one person to another, none of that crap about being kind and making allowances. He gave it his full attention, absorbed in feeling his way through each word, while Mrs Long took the register and read the morning thought. Then she said something about number puzzles, and Mandy handed out worksheets.

Chokker didn't take any notice. *Special,* he read. So that was how it was spelled. Good. He'd remember that.

A kind of silence made itself felt, and Chokker looked up to see Mrs Long approaching. He rammed the letter into his pocket, but she held out her hand.

"I'll have that, thank you," she said. "Whatever it is, I'd rather you paid some attention. With tests coming up, you can't afford to be wasting your time."

"I'm not wasting it." He kept his hand on the letter.

Mrs Long changed from cross to firm but nice. "You can have it back at the end of the day," she promised. "What is it, anyway?"

"It's a letter," he said.

That surprised her. "Really? Well, how lovely. May I see?"

"It's mine," Chokker told her.

"Yes, I know it's yours." Then she added with an edge of menace, "Perhaps you'd rather show it to Mr Grant?"

Being sent to the head would start all sorts of trouble. Mr Grant took things seriously. He'd probably get in touch with Gerald and Dorothy. Chokker sighed. "OK," he said.

He put the letter in the teacher's hand. She ran her eyes over it, then looked at him in astonishment.

Abby chipped in. "It's from the man I told you about, who's writing the book. It was on his door this morning, for Cho— for Charlie. So I brought it to school."

"Goodness. Well, how very interesting." Mrs Long turned back to Chokker. "I wonder if we could have a photocopy of it to keep in the school?"

Chokker scowled doubtfully, and she said quickly, "Don't worry, it'll still be yours. Look, take it down to the office yourself and ask them to copy it. All right?"

After a moment he nodded. It sounded safe enough. *And anyway,* he thought, *the other kids are going to be dead impressed.*

Chokker left school that afternoon as quickly as he could, and headed for the post office. It was more important than ever now to defend Stan against Gerald and Dorothy. The summerhouse man was a bit wacky, but his letter was like one reasonable person talking to another, and there wasn't much of that about. So the email had to be sent.

As he ran, Chokker grappled with the problem of what to say. Maybe he could just tell the Finbows that Stan was an OK person. But would that make it clear the message came from someone else? Perhaps not. He slackened to a walk, more bothered than ever. They might still think Stan had written it. He had to make them understand that Amul wasn't

155

Stan. Perhaps the best thing would be to add a bit at the end. *By the way, I am a doctor*. Yes, that would do. He felt for the money in his pocket and pushed open the post office door.

Small children rushed at him. "Hi, Charlie!" they said merrily. Rosie flung her arms around his legs. And Dorothy smiled at him from where she stood with the buggy beside the birthday cards.

"Hello," she said. "I thought you might be in."

Chokker felt as if he had stepped into a lift that was dropping very fast. The blood seemed to rush into his head then vanish, leaving him with a faint buzzing and no thoughts at all. He wanted to turn and run, but Rosie was still wrapped around his knees and he couldn't.

"It's all right," Dorothy said quietly. "Don't worry, nothing awful is going to happen." She disentangled Rosie and turned the buggy round. "Could you open the door for me?"

Chokker opened the door. They started along the pavement, and he fell into step beside Dorothy, because he couldn't think of what else to do.

"They were your emails, weren't they?" She sounded matter-of-fact.

After an agonized pause, Chokker gave a very small nod. Then panic hit him again.

I've told her, I've told her. Oh God.

"I thought it must be you. I nearly asked you, but I'd have felt so awful if I had been wrong."

They went on for a bit, then Chokker managed to ask, "Does Gerald know?"

"Not yet. Mr Grant phoned me this afternoon, you see. He read me the letter you had from your writer friend."

So that's why they wanted the photocopy. Chokker felt betrayed.

"He was very impressed," Dorothy went on. "He's wondering if Mr Proschynski would visit the school and give a talk about writing books."

Oh, brilliant, Chokker thought bitterly. *One minute he's the big no-no, and now they're treating him like the famous writer.* Why couldn't they have stayed out of it?

Dorothy glanced at him. "I'm really sorry we got the wrong idea. But such terrible things happen to children. It's constantly in the papers."

Chokker nodded. He wondered if visits to the summerhouse were on again now.

"I just wish you'd been able to talk to us about it," she continued. "That's a bit disappointing."

"I told you he was all right," Chokker said. *And you didn't believe me.*

"Yes, you did. Just – if we'd understood what you were doing."

You might not have approved. He was at it again, arguing with them silently. Funny how there could be words in your head, but you couldn't say them. It seemed safer that way, but perhaps it wasn't.

After a bit he asked, "Shall I push the buggy?"

"Thanks," said Dorothy. "That would be great."

And they walked on in the sharp sea wind.

Nine

Abby smiled at the sight of Stan being ushered into the Annexe Hut by Mr Grant. He had obviously made a big effort to look respectable. He was carrying a briefcase and wearing dark trousers instead of his usual baggy cords, and he'd combed his hair. Two classes had been crammed in, Mrs Long's on chairs at the back and the younger ones sitting on the floor. A hush fell.

"We are very lucky in having a real, live writer with us today," said Mr Grant. "We know him as Mr Proschynski..." He raised his eyebrows at Stan. "Am I pronouncing that right?"

Stan gave a polite shrug, as if to say mistakes didn't matter.

"But he uses a different name for his books," Mr Grant went on. "Stan Bassett."

Kirsty Baker gasped and said, "Hey, my mum reads them!"

Stan smiled at her and said, "That's nice."

"What are they about?" asked Ian Kerr.

"There'll be time for questions at the end," said Mr Grant. "If that's all right, Mr … shall I call you Bassett?"

"Easier to call me Stan, really," said Stan. "Yes, questions at the end. And at the beginning, if you like."

"What are your books about?" Ian asked again.

Stan moved closer to the children and said, "You know what a thriller is?"

Mr Grant sat down, looking as if he'd had more to say.

Ian nodded. "Like, exciting."

"Thrilling," put in Sue, and giggled because school suddenly seemed a bit like the summerhouse, and everything was peculiar.

"Look, I'll show you." Stan opened his briefcase and got out a lot of his own books. People gasped at the idea of doing all that writing. Then he started explaining how each one was set in a place he knew through travelling around. He was very good, Abby thought. Everyone could hear him at the back, and he wasn't boring. He told them what some of the stories were about, then went on to what was happening now – how he'd been stuck for ideas until "some people sitting here today" had come along and helped him.

"Can we help too?" Kirsty Baker asked.

Chokker hoped Stan would say no. *It's ours; it's special.*

Stan gave him a quick glance, then went on smoothly. "Tell you what, I'll read some of the stuff we've done so far, so you'll know what the book's about. Then we can discuss what happens next. New ideas are always welcome. But I can't have sixty people in my workroom," he added, "breathing down my neck while I'm trying to think. I need a bit of peace and quiet. That's reasonable, isn't it?"

Everyone nodded. *Good,* thought Chokker.

"We could do it at school, though," said Mandy.

"And you could come in lots of times, and see how we're getting on!" Sue added.

The headmaster shifted uneasily on his chair, and Chokker could see he wasn't happy about that idea. It wouldn't fit in with the timetable and tests.

Stan smiled at Mandy and Sue, but made no promises. He fished a sheaf of printed pages out of his briefcase. "Anyway, here we go," he said.

He explained what had happened in the first chapters, then started on a new bit. Everyone listened intently.

Cat and Luma sat in the vet's waiting room. Nobody else was there, but they could hear a murmur of voices from the surgery next door. Cat tried not to think about her legs, which were stinging badly. The skin was blistered and broken now, and the burning seemed to be eating its way ever deeper. Aunt Madge said she must have been scratching. She'd given her some cream to put on, but it hadn't helped.

Luma was frowning. He wished he wasn't here, but there'd been no choice, really. When he'd seen Cat at the bus stop on her own, he knew he had to join her.

He was worried about the pup that Pat and Terry had smuggled into the lorry container. It had grown fast in the last few days, and he didn't like the look of its red eyes and harsh, spiky fur. He was sure it had the Massa disease. He had fed it last night because Davey was busy with the horses, and it'd snarled at the food, snatching it out of the bowl as if it was killing an enemy. He felt it might kill him too, given half a chance.

A young woman put her head round the door. "Hi," she said. "Come on in." Then she looked again and said, "No animal?"

"No," said Cat as they followed her into the surgery. An older woman in a white overall was typing at the keyboard on the bench. Cat wondered where the vet was. She said, "We wanted to ask Mr Morris something."

"Mr Morris isn't well," said the young woman. "I'm Angie McIver. I'm standing in for him. What they call a locum."

"Oh." Cat wasn't sure if this could be a proper vet.

162

She had a fringe of dark hair almost to her eyebrows, and she didn't wear a white coat, just a white T-shirt and jeans.

Angie laughed. "It's all right, I've got the letters after my name. What did you want to ask him?"

"It's about Mrs Jordan's dog," said Luma. He didn't really want to talk about this. If anyone found out about the pup hidden behind the caravan, it could mean big trouble for Davey.

Cat took up the story. "She had to be put down last week, and her puppies. We think there was something funny about it."

"What sort of funny?"

"Something weird was wrong with Beauty," Cat said. "I was standing the other side of the wire, but she burned my legs."

The nurse who had been typing turned to look at her.

"How did she?" asked Angie.

"Just with her breath. And her coat was sort of matted. All sticking together."

The young vet looked puzzled. She pulled a chair out from the wall. "Sit down here for a minute, and let's have a look." She crouched in front of Cat and examined her legs carefully, and when she glanced up, her face was concerned. "Have you seen a doctor?"

Cat shook her head. "Aunt Madge said it was nettle-rash."

"This isn't nettle-rash," said Angie. Then she added, "What does your mum say?"

"I don't have a mum. Aunt Madge looks after me. And Uncle Arthur."

"Did you tell them about the dog?"

"No."

Angie went on staring at her for a moment. She had light brown eyes with dark eyelashes, and they were very steady. "OK," she said. She got to her feet. "What did you say the owner's name was?"

"Jordan," said Luma. "Mr and Mrs Jordan."

The vet nodded. "Isabel, can you find that for me?"

The nurse scrolled through patients' records, and Angie stood behind her, watching. Then she put her finger on the screen. "Jordan. Here we are. He's a pigeon breeder. And Beauty, yes. The pups were born eight weeks ago, right?"

"Yes," said Cat.

The young vet looked at her seriously. "Before we go any further with this – you're absolutely sure it was the dog that caused these burns?"

"Yes, it was," said Cat. "Honestly."

"Just her breath – she didn't lick you or bite you?"

Cat shook her head. "She couldn't. I was the other side of the wire."

"Right." Angie turned back to the screen. *"Euthanasia,"* she read. "OK, the dog was put down. And the pups as well, the next day. *Special disposal.*

Isabel, what does that mean?"

Isabel glanced uneasily at Cat and Luma. "It was a Massa case," she said. "I don't know if Mr Morris would like me to—"

"Never mind Mr Morris," said Angie. "I'm in charge now. What's Massa?"

Luma said, "It's the big factory, or laboratory or something." He almost added, *We've been there,* but stopped himself.

"It's a research institute," Isabel said.

"And what's that got to do with this dog and her pups?" asked Angie.

The nurse frowned. "There have been one or two problems," she admitted. "They're working on mutant strains, as far as I understand. Mr Morris knows more about it than I do."

"Mutant strains?" asked Angie. "GM? Genetic modification?"

"Well, yes."

The young vet stared at her. "Oh, I see," she said. "And it's been escaping, right? Wind-born particles or something. Mice, birds, whatever. So now there's mutation in domestic animals. Does Mr Morris get a lot of these cases?"

"I shouldn't really—"

"Talk about it?" Angie interrupted. "Why not? Have you signed the Official Secrets Act or something?"

"Not exactly."

"What do you mean, *not exactly*?"

"There's a form," Isabel admitted. "All the local vets have signed it."

"Part of a special arrangement?" enquired Angie. "A nice little fee for keeping quiet?"

"It's nothing to do with me," said Isabel. "It's not my business; I just work here."

"OK." Angie took a moment to control herself. "But you know what *special disposal* means, I presume."

The nurse nodded reluctantly. "A Massa case animal that's died can't be returned to the owner for burial."

"So what happens to it?"

"Massa supply their own body bags. We put the animal in one of those, and seal it. Then we phone them and they come and collect it."

Angie whistled soundlessly. "How come I don't know this?"

"I expect they'll be on to you once they find out you're here. You're new to the district, aren't you? We have a different locum usually, but he was away. We didn't know we were going to need one. Mr Morris was kicked by a horse, you see. Broken ribs."

"And I've only just qualified, so these Massa people haven't got round to me yet," said Angie. "But why the hot breath? What are they trying to produce?"

"Guard dogs," said the nurse. "I asked the man who came last time, and he told me. They want really effective guard dogs."

"Do they follow up these cases?" Angie asked.

"Oh, yes," said Isabel. "They've been round the whole area, inspecting dogs. Any that failed their tests were taken away. There's been quite an outcry about it – people are upset, as you can imagine."

"I've seen nothing in the papers," said Angie.

"There hasn't been anything," the nurse told her. "Someone wrote to the local paper, but Massa wouldn't comment. And there were no more letters after that."

Angie nodded slowly. "Interesting," she said.

Cat and Luma did not glance at each other, but they shared the same thought. Even to this nice vet, they must not mention the puppy that was shut in the lorry container behind Davey's caravan.

Stan put his papers down. "That's it, folks. The story as far as I've got."

A buzz of conversation broke out and hands shot up with questions, but Mr Grant started to clap, and everyone had to join in.

"Thanks," Stan said when it died down. "Who's first?" He picked Ian. "Yes."

"What's going to happen next?" Ian demanded.

"Cat and Luma will have to attack Massa and stop it working," said Stan. "But they can't just march into the place, because it's all top security. They'll need to find some other way."

Sue's hand was up. "They got in once already, but it was in a dream," she said, in case the others hadn't understood this. "So they can do it again. And Cat's mother can help them. She talks to Luma, so they can make a plan."

Stan nodded. "Luma's special." He glanced briefly at Chokker. "He's got one foot in the world of spirit people. Cat hasn't, except through her mum." He forgot he was trying to look tidy and ran his fingers through his hair. "I've been thinking – it might be more useful to the book if Cat died as well. As the result of the burns or something."

"Why?" asked Mandy. She looked horrified.

Sue didn't mind the idea. "Then she'd be in the other world," she said. "She could move around in a way that living people can't."

"Go in and out of Massa when she wants," Neil agreed. "Yes, that would be great."

Abby's face had turned pink. Talking about death in that casual sort of way was awful.

Stan looked at her and said, "It's only an idea. We can do something else if you hate it."

Kevin Dobb was looking puzzled. "But she can't do anything if she's dead, can she?"

"Course she can," said Kirsty. "She's alive in a different world, isn't she?"

"Suppose so." He didn't look convinced.

"I just don't want her to die," Mandy said obstinately.

"It's a book, remember," Stan pointed out. "It's not real life. When you write a book, you get to feel you know the people in it really well, but the fact is, *you made them up*. Have you heard of a writer called Charles Dickens?"

Quite a lot of people nodded.

"Well, Dickens made up a character called Little Nell," Stan said.

"Oh, yes!" said Abby. A woman at the Castle had called her a real Little Nell on that Victorian Day.

Stan smiled at her and went on. "She was a kind of saintly child, totally good and sweet. But she got left behind in the story – I guess he didn't give her much to do except sit there looking beautiful – so she was a problem. She hadn't been mentioned for about ten chapters, and dragging her in again was going to be difficult. So he killed her off. And he was so upset, he cried for three days."

"You're kidding," said Neil.

"No, I'm not; it's perfectly true. It turned out to be a good move for him," Stan went on. "Half of London went into mourning for Little Nell, and it did wonders for his sales."

"Do you sell lots of books?" asked Kevin.

"Not as many as I'd like," said Stan.

"I think we should stick to questions about writing," said Mr Grant.

There was a pause, then Danny Nicoll asked, "Have you always been a writer?"

"No, but I got fired from everything else I tried. So there was no choice, really. I just had to write."

"How old were you when you started?" asked Kevin.

"About thirty. I was a slow learner, I guess."

Mr Grant said, "Do we have questions about this particular book?"

Everyone thought.

"If they get into Massa, there'll be a fight, won't there?" said Danny.

"Yes, there will," Stan agreed. "But I'm not sure what sort of fight. We'll have to work all that out."

"Ray guns," said Kevin, firing something imaginary. "Ker-pow."

Chokker shot him a glance of contempt. "Swords," he said. Big double-handed ones, with hilts in the shape of dragons' heads.

"Massa will have all sorts of stuff," said Fraser. "Poison gas. Chemicals."

"Yes." Stan looked thoughtful. "Maybe some of the workers might fight on the other side, because they don't agree with what the firm is doing."

Fraser shook his head. "They won't risk their jobs."

"They need the money," Mandy agreed.

Stan asked, "You mean they'll defend Massa, no matter what it's up to?"

Most of the children nodded, but Abby said, "Some of them could think it's wrong. Massa can't control everything."

Chokker frowned. "Someone's got to be in charge." *Someone strong, that you can really trust.*

Stan looked at him thoughtfully. "You and I may have different ideas about that," he said. "I think the world is in charge of itself, you see. It knows what it's doing, and we have to trust it. But we can't start on that, or we'll be here all night."

Chokker nodded.

Kirsty put up her hand. "What about the vet? Will she do something about the dogs?"

"She could ask the other vets what they know," said Mandy.

Ian was bouncing up and down, hand in the air. "She might find another dog that dies, and when the people from Massa come to get it, she could follow them and get into the factory. Only the guards won't let her, and they start beating her up."

"She could call the police on her mobile," said Kirsty.

"What if the police are on Massa's side?" asked Stan.

Kirsty stared at him. "They wouldn't be, would they?"

Stan shrugged. "The top police might be pals with the Massa boss. Drink at the same club; get nice holidays on his yacht."

"That's awful," said Mandy.

"Yes, it is," Stan agreed. "But we're writing a kind of thriller. Or, at least, an exciting fantasy story. Things are likely to get tough."

Mr Grant looked at his watch and said, "Maybe our visitor could give us one or two professional tips." He turned to Stan. "We keep telling the children their work has to be drafted and redrafted before it's right. Would you like to say something about that?"

Stan frowned. "There's a risk they'll get terribly bored," he said. "And that's the kiss of death for a writer. There's no hard and fast rule about the way people work. Some writers nit-pick over every sentence, others think the whole thing out while they're walking round the garden, then bung it down in a more or less finished state. If you look at the manuscripts of people like Dickens, you'll find there are not many changes – but then, he was writing by hand. Working on a screen has made it so easy to amend things that we've stopped trying to get it right first go. It's led to a kind of sloppiness, I think."

"Do you use a computer yourself?" asked Mrs Long.

"Yes, for the final stage. Publishers expect it. But

I put the book together in a patchwork sort of way, a bit here and a bit there, with a lot of pencilled notes on bits of paper. Once I've got the whole thing assembled, I do fuss over every word, but these people" – Stan waved a hand at the children – "aren't writing for publication. They're learning their craft. Practising. Like they practise football, though they're not going to play for a Premiership team, because they're not grown up yet. So I wouldn't expect them to fiddle about with every detail unless it's for some special purpose." He turned to the children. "The really important thing is to get your ideas straight. Know what you want to say. Though you'll need the technical stuff sooner or later."

"What technical stuff?" asked Ian.

"Grammar, spelling, all that."

One or two people made a face, and Stan spread his hands impatiently. "Come on," he said, "they're essential skills. If you've got something worth saying, you want to make sure people understand it, don't you? So you need a bit of craftsmanship. How many of you expect to drive a car when you're old enough?"

Every hand went up, though some rather slowly, as if they hadn't thought about it.

"There you are, then," said Stan. "You'll take expensive driving lessons, because you need to drive. You'll work hard and get your licence, then you can go wherever you want. Writing's the same. It's something you need, something worth working for. And don't be put off by all these tests and exams," he added. "You're not doing it for the sake of passing tests; you're doing it for yourself, because your thoughts deserve proper expression. Don't sell yourselves short."

Mrs Long put her hand up from where she sat beside her class. "I think this is all very exciting," she said. "We don't have much time for creative work, unfortunately, but is there any way we can go on helping with the book?"

"Keep exploring ideas," Stan advised. "Draw pictures of the characters. Cat and Luma, Angie the vet, Cat's awful aunt and uncle – we haven't met them yet, but believe me, they are truly horrible. Drawing helps you see them clearly. You could draw the Massa building, and the dogs that are turning into dragons."

"The scientists," said Fraser.

"Yes. Cat's mother and the dream people. Davey Gowan's caravan, with horses in the field. Davey's the old guy Luma's lived with since he was small. Write down anything you can think of. Try and see the story as if you're part of it."

"What about writing poems?" asked Mrs Long.

Stan nodded. "Poems would be great. They're like chocolates – small, but full of flavour."

Mrs Long nodded and smiled. "We'll do that."

Mr Grant asked, "When you start a book, what comes first? Is it the plot? Or should we be thinking about character and description?"

"It's the central idea," Stan said patiently. "What the book's *about*. You can't separate the different elements from each other; there's no writer in the world who does it that way. You have to get familiar with your characters and the place they're living in, and have a rough idea of what's going to happen. It's a sort of carrier-wave. Once the people you've invented come alive in your mind, they'll start writing the plot, even though you're still in charge. If you plan too tightly, it can turn out that the people in your book simply won't do what you want. Then you're in trouble. Drives you insane," he added.

Mr Grant looked at his watch again, then stood up. "I'm sure we all agree, Mr Bassett has given us a lot to think about," he said. "We're most grateful to him for giving up his time. Mandy?"

Mandy stood up as well, and read from a piece of paper. "Thank you very much for coming to talk to us and answering our questions. It was very interesting, and we all enjoyed it very much. We hope your new book will be a great success."

"Let's say a big thank-you," said Mrs Long.

The applause was more enthusiastic than it had been at the beginning. When it died down, Kirsty asked if she could have Stan's autograph for her mum, and he ended up writing his name sixty-three times, on scraps of paper that got very small towards the end, as people tore them in half then in half again so that everyone had a bit.

Walking home with Sue, who was chattering non-stop, Abby couldn't help thinking about Stan's idea that Cat should die. She saw what he meant about her joining her mother in the dream world, and she had to agree that it might be useful for the book, but all the same, she found it worrying. Cat seemed so real. And death…

"What's the matter?" asked Sue. "You've gone quiet."

"Sorry."

"What were you thinking about?"

"Just – Stan and everything."

"It's great, isn't it!" Sue said happily. "We'll be able to go to the summerhouse again. I can't wait."

"Neither can I," Abby agreed. "There's such a lot to decide." And some of it was going to be scary.

Chokker went up the hill, for no purpose except just to be out and running around after a day between the walls of school. He came down the track that led past the horse field and the neat and tidy caravan, and stopped to look at it. This wasn't where Luma lived. Trying to think of that messier place run by Davey Gowan in the story was like trying to slide a transparent picture on top of the one he was seeing now.

Real things get in the way, he thought. Davey was easy to imagine, because there was no real Davey to compare him with. He'd be a wiry old man with a brown, deeply grooved face and probably one or two missing teeth. He'd have a lot of scruffy mates like Pat and Terry, only older. He'd meet them in the pub. *He's the sort who likes a drink, must be.* But Davey was OK; he wasn't like anyone real. He'd never come down from his room in that very smooth way that made you know he was taking care to keep his balance. He wouldn't smell of whisky; he wouldn't have that stupid smile that could so quickly turn into something else. He'd never—

Chokker pushed the rest of it away. *Davey lives in a caravan.* Not even a real one, just a pretend caravan. Safe ground. He went on thinking as he walked. Pat and Terry were the sort who had friends all over the place. They knew this guy, Michael, who worked at Massa, and they were knocking stuff off on the side. If Luma wanted to get into the place – really get in, not the dream business – they could probably fix it. Under sacks or something, in their truck.

But Stan wanted Cat in the other world, with her mum.

An idea came from nowhere.

It's Cat who goes in, not Luma. And the Eye sees her, and she gets grabbed by the security people. Magnus Chip says she has to die, so they take her down

177

to the lab, and give her an injection that kills her. Yeah, brilliant. He smiled to himself, and the story ran on in his mind. *Luma gets worried when she doesn't come back, so he tells the vet girl. She'll help him find out what's happened. She'd be good in a fight too; she's quite tough. And, at the end, she and Luma can be in charge of everything, with someone like the Master to help.*

Must tell Stan.

Chokker wondered if Gerald and Dorothy would let him use their computer to write the idea down. They were being particularly nice to him at the moment, so there was a good chance they might.

🌿 Ten

"HELLO!" shrieked Agatha. "HELLO, HELLO! GOOD MORNING!"

"It isn't morning, you daft old bat," said Stan. "It's nearly teatime."

Several days had gone by since his talk at the school and there had been no sign from the summerhouse, but today Abby had brought news of the yellow balloon flying again, and they'd rushed up the path after school. Sue had a drawing of Luma holding the puppy beside Pat and Terry's truck, and Abby had done one of Angie inspecting the burns on Cat's legs. Chokker, in his mysterious way, was already inside, sprawled in an armchair.

Stan liked the drawings. "Brilliant," he said. "We'll need more about the pup in the lorry container but I've jumped ahead a bit. Chokker sent me some really good ideas, so I've been working on those."

Chokker managed not to smile – he didn't want to look smug. His second note to Stan had been rather good, he thought. Gerald and Dorothy hadn't minded him using the computer. They'd seemed dead keen, in fact. And Stan had said it was terrific.

"This is about Cat's big adventure," Stan said. "See what you think." He started to read.

Cat lay in the back of the lorry, under a pile of sugar beet. The tarpaulin that covered the load was close above her and she sweated in the airless space. The heavy, dirty roots, the size of big turnips, were caked with dried mud and their earthy smell filled her nose and rasped at the back of her throat. But the voice in her mind was insistent. *It's time, my darling. Be brave. Do the thing you fear. It will be all right. Believe me, it will be all right.*

The stifling weight of the sugar beet made it hard to breathe, but the fear was the worst thing. It had stayed at a distance while she'd burrowed her way into the lorry's load, almost as though it watched her in amusement, but it kept creeping closer. When she heard Pat and Terry coming towards the lorry, she almost wished they would look in and find her, so she wouldn't have to do this thing, but they didn't. They climbed into the cab, talking to each other cheerfully, and started the engine. And then the fear rushed into her heart and made it beat at a fluttering, unsteady speed, as if a captive bird was struggling there.

The journey didn't last very long. Before she was ready – but would she ever be ready? – the lorry was slowing down, and she felt it turning off the road. Then it stopped.

"Hi, Terry," a man said. "How's yourself?"

"Never better," replied Terry. "Got a load of sugar beet here. Don't ask me what they want it for, but that's what it is."

"Better have a look, I suppose. Security cameras and all that." Footsteps trod their way round to the rear of the lorry, and Cat sensed that light and air were coming in as someone hitched up the tarpaulin from the tailgate. She held her fluttering breath, and felt sick with fright.

"Sugar beet, right enough," the man said. "OK, Terry, on you go. Barn number three. You know where it is." Then he added quietly, "Fancy a game of darts tonight?"

"Sure," said Terry. "See you there."

The lorry started up again.

How am I going to get out? Cat thought desperately. *And where should I be? What's the right place?* She wished Luma was with her. She had waited for what seemed a long time in the muddy farmyard while Pat and Terry were in the house. A smell of steak pie had been drifting from the kitchen, but she could not have eaten anything, though it was a long time since the breakfast toast with her aunt and uncle.

She'd been relieved when Luma hadn't turned up. The whole thing had been his idea, so she wouldn't have to go. *Thank goodness,* she'd thought. She'd been about to creep back through the gap in the hedge, when her mother's voice had sounded clearly in her mind.

The boy has other things to do. This is ours, my darling, just for ourselves. It's time. Trust me. Trust me.

Firm hands had seemed to guide her as she scrambled up and got a knee over the tailboard, pushed her way in and crawled over the sliding, lumpy roots to the front end of the truck, then began her burrowing. There had been no anxiety in those moments, just a sense of absolute rightness – but it had ebbed away during the journey. Now, as the lorry came to a halt, Cat was close to utter panic. Some distance away, dogs were barking and howling.

She heard Terry say in the cab, "Not a soul about, would you credit that."

"Your pal at the gate hasn't rung through to control, then," Pat said. "Or they're taking their time about sending someone down."

"So we can take a look around, can't we? Never know what might be lying about." Terry gave a chuckle. "Michael and me, we understand each other."

"You old devil," Pat said in admiration. Then the engine was switched off and the doors of the cab slammed. A few moments later there was a louder outburst of barking from the dogs, then the noise settled back to the usual level of dismal howling.

Move now. The voice nudged her gently. *Don't be afraid, sweetheart; it's all right.*

Cat floundered her way out of the sugar beet and crawled to the tailgate. Turning round, she put one leg out, feeling for a foothold. The edge of the truck rasped against her weeping skin, but she hardly noticed. Now that Pat and Terry had gone, she was alone with her mother, and she felt strangely sleepy, almost as if her brain had shut down. She was being taken care of by this most beloved person, who would manage everything.

Cat slithered out of the truck and found herself standing on a concrete floor in a covered space with enormous sliding doors on either side of it. Pale blue bags that looked as if they were full of dirty laundry were piled on a pallet, and Cat went towards them, as she knew she had to.

It was so easy. They weren't tied, and the top one was almost empty.

Yes. The voice was perfectly calm. *In you get.*

Cat was hardly settled in the cotton bag when a noisy machine approached, and she felt the pallet being lifted up and trundled away. Doors opened and shut, and the outside air gave way to a smell of washing powder. The pallet was dumped on the floor, and the machine moved away. After a final, metallic bang of a door, there was silence. She could not even hear the dogs outside.

For several minutes, Cat dared not move. She listened intently, and the silence hummed in her ears. A tiny bit at a time, she twitched the edge of the bag down from her face until she could see out. She smothered a gasp, thinking for a mad moment that huge eyes were watching her, then she saw they were the circular windows of large washing machines. All of them stood silent. Very cautiously, she turned to look behind her. The big room was empty. The strip lights in the ceiling glared, and the white tiles and bare tables offered no shelter where anyone could be hidden.

Cat wriggled out of the bag and got to her feet. There were double doors in the wall to her right, each with a circular window in the middle, and beside them was a row of hooks on which hung pale blue overalls and white hats, each on its own peg. With absolute certainty she walked over to them and put on one of the overalls. She buttoned it up, then reached for a hat. It was made of white plastic straw, and it was a bit too big, coming down to her eyebrows.

You look fine. Her mother was smiling. *They'll never guess. Go through the doors now. Into the building.*

The doors did not move at Cat's touch.

There's a card in your pocket.

Sure enough, the overall contained a plastic card on a fine chain, the end of which was clipped to the pocket's edge. INTERNAL SECURITY, it said, with a bar code and an arrow to indicate which way to use it.

Cat swiped the card through the slot beside the door, and found herself admitted to a pale grey corridor. The walls, the ceiling and the floor were made of shiny grey plastic, and so were the doors that opened from it. A high-mounted camera at the far end of the corridor stared along its length, and Cat was glad of her over-large hat and anonymous blue overall. If anyone was watching her on some screen, they'd think she was just a laundry worker.

As if in a dream, she went quietly along the plastic floor to the lift at the end of the corridor. She used the swipe card, and the grey doors slid open. Inside, the row of buttons gave her no information, so she pressed the first one.

The lift rose smoothly to the next floor, and when the doors opened again, Cat found herself gazing into a huge laboratory. White-coated figures bent over their work at benches, some at computers, others dissecting things that had been animals. There was a strange chemical smell, and beyond the big windows a brilliant yellowness shone from fields of rape that seemed to reach to the horizon.

One man glanced up and saw her, but he took no

notice of the overalled figure in a white hat. *Great,*
Cat thought. *I'm getting away with it.* Suddenly she
was excited by this mad adventure, which was
turning out to be so much easier than she'd
expected. She pressed the next button in the lift.

A vile-smelling heat rushed in as the doors
opened. Cat flung her arm across her eyes to stop
them watering, and when her vision cleared a little
she saw there was a wide space in front of her, then
a wire-mesh fence that reached from floor to ceiling,
with a second one a metre or so inside it. She took a
couple of steps forward.

Behind the fences were stainless-steel pens, each
with a metal kennel at the end. And in the pens
were black creatures that made her skin crawl with
terror. They had the heads of dogs, only with longer
jaws like small crocodiles, and their thick tails
tapered to a point. Their blackness looked almost
like armour, and she saw that instead of fur, they had
overlapping scales. As she watched, one of them saw
her. Its scales rose as it hurled itself at the pen wall,
and a rush of flame came from its mouth with a
roar like a blowtorch. The others roared as well,
becoming instantly excited. A roasting heat blazed
out from them, and the metal walls were scarlet with
their reflected fire.

Bells rang with a shatteringly loud noise as Cat
staggered back, and two men rushed in from a door
on her right. They were holding large cylinders that

looked like outsize spray cans, and they wore black rubber gas masks.

One of the men pointed his cylinder at the animals and released a hissing cloud of vapour while the other rushed at Cat and pushed her back into the lift. He was shouting frantically inside the black rubber mask with the ridged breathing tube connected to a pack on his chest, and she caught the muffled words: "Get out, get out!"

Cat stabbed at the top button, wanting to be as far away from the fire-dogs and the clouds of gas as she could. She was coughing as the lift rose, and her chest hurt. *Guard dogs,* the nurse at the vet's had said. *Really effective guard dogs.* Well, they had them now, all right. Any one of those creatures could burn an intruder to death.

Cat was still strangely calm in the centre of her mind, though she noticed that various things were wrong with her. A dizziness was affecting her sense of balance, and her stomach was queasy. The pain in her chest was quite severe, and breathing was becoming difficult. These ills were on the outer edge of her awareness, but her injured legs hurt so much that the pain broke through her tranquillity. The heat in the dog place had inflamed them to a raw redness that was almost unbearable, and she bent down, laying her hands over them to try to soothe them. She was still in that position when the lift doors opened.

Outside, there was another grey plastic corridor, though a shorter one this time. Cat lurched a little as she tried to stand up straight. Her eyes didn't seem to be working well, and she rubbed them as she looked up at the screen that stared from a high corner. Fuzzily, she saw the illuminated notice on the door ahead of her change its message from KEEP OUT to ENTER. The door opened as she approached it, admitting her to a waiting room with leather armchairs and glass-topped coffee tables.

The door on the far side of this room said, in dark, old-fashioned letters: THE ADMINISTRATOR. It too swung silently open as Cat limped towards it as though in a dream. The light in the huge room she entered was blue and brilliant – was it the sky? The air was cool and fresh; it smelled of flowers. Plants with huge leaves were growing in tubs. She took a few steps forward from the lift, and raised her head to stare at the bright glass above her, sparkling between big, green leaves. Happiness flooded through her whole being, dispelling all its pains. She wanted to lie down and sleep.

Soon you will, my darling, Mara said. *Soon, soon.*

A man's voice spoke from somewhere in the brightness. "Do come in," it said. "I've been expecting you."

Stan looked up.

"Oh, no!" said Sue. "Don't stop there – I can't bear it! What's going to happen?"

Fraser flapped an impatient hand at her. "We'll find out. There's more, isn't there?"

Stan nodded, turning over a page. "We're leaving Cat on a cliffhanger for a moment, while we duck back to Luma. You'll all be wondering why he didn't turn up. There's got to be a proper, solid reason. So I put this in." He started reading again.

Luma and Davey sat in an office that had a lot of filing cabinets. A pot plant drooped on the windowsill. Luma looked at it with sympathy, feeling its thirst and growing weakness. This was not a place where people would understand the needs of plants. He wondered if he and Davey had been brought here for another official telling-off, or if this was going to be something worse. They'd never been collected without warning before, let alone in a car with no handles on the inside of the back doors so you couldn't get out. Perhaps they'd been arrested.

The woman in a black suit who sat behind the desk looked at them through glasses that had a chain going round the back of her neck. Luma wondered if she was afraid people would try to steal them. "You have had repeated warnings," she was saying to Davey. "But your whole way of life remains extremely irregular. Why, for instance, is this boy not at school?"

"He's learning," said Davey defensively. "He's a good lad with the horses."

The woman sighed. "Being good with horses is not an education. And all our reports confirm that you are not a suitable person to be in charge of a child."

"I'm not a child," Luma protested.

"You are twelve," said the woman. "That is not adult."

Yes, it is, he thought. *If you feel adult, then you are.* He scowled at the desk and its plastic sign that gave the woman's name: MRS P. PIMM.

The two men who had brought him and Davey to this place sat on chairs by the door. Luma had assumed at first that they were policemen, but their navy blue uniforms had no badges or shiny buttons. They looked more like caretakers, except that one of them had a stud through his eyebrow. Both of them were overweight. They were tough, Luma recognized, but they might not be too quick off the mark. He had to get out of here. The window was no good – this room was on the second floor. Too far to jump. It would have to be the door, then. Tricky.

Cat wouldn't have gone to Massa without me, would she? He was trying to fend off the scraps of dream that showed her in that place. An awful certainty was growing in his mind. *She's there, I know she's there.* Every time he shut his eyes, the images came rushing back – grey plastic walls, Cat on her own. A man in a huge room with a glass roof. Sparkling light, the scent of flowers and evil.

Mrs P. Pimm was still talking to Davey and writing things down. Luma made up his mind. He took a deep breath and said, "I need to go to the toilet."

One of the guards got to his feet. "Come on, then."

He escorted Luma along the corridor and came into the gents with him, standing there and watching while Luma had a pee and did some rapid thinking. They'd come up from the car park in the lift, but he'd spotted a door labelled EMERGENCY EXIT.

They started back the way they had come, Luma walking quietly beside the man. His heart was beating fast, and that was good. Fear made you faster, as long as you were in control of it.

Now, do it now.

He turned to the man and held out his hand, palm up, with the fingers lightly closed as if they contained something. "Seen one of these?" he asked.

It was an old trick, but it worked.

"What?" The man looked down. In that instant, Luma jumped sideways and kicked him hard behind his right knee. He didn't wait to see the man pitch

191

backwards – the first seconds were the vital ones. He was through the emergency exit like a shot, and out onto an iron fire escape. He clattered down it with reckless speed, and was well on the way to the ground by the time he heard people starting after him. He jumped the last five steps and ran, dodging round parked cars and square beds with rose bushes in them, down the drive and out of the gate.

He crossed the road, risking his life in the traffic, and ran on. A bus was about to pull away from a stop but he jumped through its closing doors, showed his pass – out of date but the driver didn't notice – and sat down beside a fat woman. She was so big that she totally filled the window, and nobody looking in from the outside would see a boy on the inner seat.

Luma had no idea where the bus was going, but he stayed on it until his breathing had settled and he'd had time to think. Then he got off and looked across the road at the sun that was setting behind some tall trees in a park. *That's west, then*. He calculated quickly, working out where he was. The bus must have been heading south, and the houses were starting to thin out, so the town centre had to be behind and to the north of him. Good. The Massa research station was somewhere around here, in the countryside south of the town. He had to find out what had happened to Cat. He began to walk again, wondering how far away the place was.

After another few minutes, he stopped. The things he was seeing in his mind were so clear that his feet were starting to wander like those of a sleepwalker. His chest was hurting as if he had breathed in a dangerous gas. He leaned against some railings, gripping the cold iron of one of them in a hand that seemed suddenly weak.

Slanting glass let the sun come beating through, but the place was not hot. It smelled of flowers, but there were no blossoms, only the vast rubber plants that stretched their big leaves up to the glass. White-painted pipes brought in flower-scented fresh air, cooled to a comfortable temperature.

Luma drifted past the vast armchairs made of grey leather and the pedestal ashtrays, past the big desk, the swivelling office chair, the bank of computers. And then he made himself look at what was going on in the middle of the huge room.

Cat was lying on a narrow table. They had moved a modern sculpture off it in order to make room for her, and it now stood on the floor. It looked like a bull that was half machine, and a rather large hat made of white straw had been casually hung on its head. Cat wore a pale blue overall buttoned across her normal clothes, and her dark hair streamed across the polished wood of the table. Her eyes were open, and her face looked completely calm.

The two men examining Cat were in white coats,

like doctors or scientists, but the third, the oldest and thinnest of them, wore a dark suit. He stood back a little, watching the others. He was smoking a cigarette, and Luma could see how the fumes spiralled up into the air system and were removed through vents in the glass roof.

"She's certainly been in contact with the guardians, sir," one of the men said. "Nothing else could account for these burns except long-acting phosphorus vapour. Exactly what we're incorporating into the dogs."

The man in the suit nodded. He approached Cat and stood with his elbow cupped in one hand, cigarette cocked at an angle in the air. He looked down at her and said, "Tell me what happened to your legs, my dear."

Cat did not answer. Her eyes were beginning to close, Luma saw as he drew closer. Then he knew Mara was in the room as well. She stood at the head of the table, with her hands on either side of her daughter's face, thumbs gently stroking across her cheekbones.

"What do you want us to do, sir?" the other scientist asked.

The man in a suit stubbed out his cigarette and delicately removed a scrap of tobacco from the tip of his tongue. "Euthanize," he said without interest. "Do it now." He walked away and sat down at one of the computers that lined a whole wall, clicking on a new program.

The men looked at each other, then the first one who had spoken shrugged. "Orders," he said.

The other rubbed his face unhappily. Then he bent over Cat and stroked her hair. "Listen, sweetheart," he said, "we're just going to give you a little injection. Your legs won't be sore any more. You'll go off to sleep."

Cat heard him. She rolled her head a little to one side, and her face still wore its peaceful smile. "Yes," she whispered. The word was no more than a breath.

The first man was holding up an inverted bottle, drawing yellowish liquid from it into a hypodermic syringe. He turned Cat's right hand palm up and gripped her arm firmly, squeezing with his thumb. Then he slipped the needle into a vein on the inside of her elbow. Slowly and gently, he pressed the plunger home.

Luma, with one hand still clutching the iron railing, found that he was weeping.

Chokker stared at Stan with fierce excitement, but Sue was in tears and Abby had her hand over her mouth, struggling not to cry. Neil was staring down, frowning.

Fraser said, "But Cat's not really dead, is she? It's just that she's changed into something different. To be with her mum."

"That's the general idea," Stan agreed. "Sorry if it's a tough one. We're going to see her again, though; she's still in the story."

Sue blew her nose and said, "It's just so sad."

"Well, of course it's *sad*," said Stan. He sounded slightly irritated. "You can't kill a character off and not feel sad. Remember what I said about Dickens. But she'll be marvellously useful to the book this way. What's more, we've got a murder now, and that's great. It gives the whole thing a shape. Luma's upset, naturally enough, but he'll still be in touch with Cat. And, of course, he's not going to leave it at that. A crime has been committed, and he has to be the detective."

"Why didn't he stop them doing it?" Chokker asked.

"Because he's only there in a dream," Stan explained. "He doesn't have any physical presence. He can't touch anything or speak to anyone, only watch and listen."

Chokker frowned. "How's he going to get them, then?"

"I'm working on it," said Stan. "Thing is, there are two sorts of people involved in this crime: real ones who live in the actual world, like Pat and Terry and the Massa staff; and dream ones, like all the people who are dead. Cat belongs to them now. Luma can get into that world sometimes, but he's basically in the real one. So it's quite complicated." He looked at Abby, who was still struggling. "You OK about this?"

Abby swallowed hard. After a few moments she managed to say, "When people – when they've died, are they really all right?"

Stan looked at her carefully. "I don't know," he admitted. "That's the honest truth. Nobody knows. We all choose what to believe."

Abby nodded. "But—"

"Me, I think being dead is fine," Stan went on. "It's the people left behind who have a bad time, because they've lost someone they loved, and that hurts. Being dead doesn't hurt. It's the same state babies are in before they're born or even thought of, and we don't worry about that. It just kind of – *is*. Like air or something. The stuff we all come from."

After a much longer pause, Abby nodded again. "Yes," she said. "Yes, I suppose so."

The thought had a strange lightness about it. She felt almost like Cat, calm and weirdly happy. She could have curled up and gone to sleep.

Eleven

On Saturday morning a lot of people crowded into the summerhouse. Abby, Sue, Fraser and Neil were there, and so was Chokker, but Kirsty Baker arrived as well, and Ian Kerr and Kevin Dobb and two or three of their friends. They'd brought drawings and poems, and they were bursting to find out what had happened in the book after the bit Stan had read at school. They looked stunned when they heard about Cat.

"Wow," said Ian. "They really killed her?"

"Will the police come?" asked Kirsty.

"They don't know she's there," Sue pointed out. "Nobody knows, only Luma."

"The men who killed her know," said Fraser.

"And the Administrator," said Abby.

"Is he the guy in a suit?" asked Kevin.

Neil nodded and said, "He's really scary, isn't he?"

"Horrible," Stan agreed. He sounded pleased about that. "We need a name for him, I think."

"Can't he just be the Administrator?" asked Ian.

"Yes, maybe. Perhaps it's better for him to have no name. Just the man behind the scenes. The ordinary workers probably never see him."

"He could be the Eye," Sue suggested.

Stan nodded. "We might go a bit further than that," he said. "What if he's a sort of mechanized person?"

"Like a robot?" Sue looked doubtful. "They're kind of old-fashioned, aren't they?"

"I don't mean something that clanks around, saying things in a mechanical voice," said Stan. "We're well past all that. The whole point of this GM thing is to design living things in whatever form we choose. People have already started demanding designer babies, to fit in with their particular needs. More and more things are getting to be possible. Our book is set in the future, and by then we could well be seeing all menial tasks done by people who are half-cloned to machines."

"Ugh, yuck," said Kirsty.

Fraser was looking excited. "Could be the Administrator's a hologram. Like those things on bank cards that change according to which way you look at them."

"Now there's a thought," said Stan.

"He can be whatever shape he likes," Fraser went on. "Nobody ever sees what he really is."

Sue said, "He could lie on a table with wires

stuck to him, going into a machine. Only nobody sees, because it's behind a curtain, or in a different room or something."

"Like Frankenstein," said Stan. "But who's going to work the machine?"

"Technicians," said Kevin.

"Can't be," Sue said. "Nobody's got to know."

Fraser had more ideas. "He can work his own machine. That way, he can turn himself into whatever he wants."

"You mean, look like someone else?" asked Ian.

"Yes, why not?"

"That's really useful," said Stan. "Nobody will know what the Administrator really looks like. They'll see a lab technician or an office worker or someone from the laundry – whatever he's chosen to be. So he's got a built-in alibi for whatever he does." He beamed at them. "Aren't you brilliant! You've just solved all the problems."

"Oh, good," said Sue.

Abby's mother looked round from the sink as Abby came into the kitchen. "There you are," she said. "I never know where to find you these days. What are you up to?" She was scrubbing carrots under a running tap, and putting them in a saucepan.

"It's just the book," said Abby.

"Yes." Her mother frowned. "I don't know that I'm very happy about this book."

Abby didn't answer. She hadn't said anything about what they were writing, but one of the other mothers had probably been talking about it.

The silence grew longer. "From what I hear," her mother said, "it isn't very suitable."

"Why?" Abby tried to sound innocent, but the word came out with a tell-tale squeakiness. She knew why. It was because there were dead people in it.

Her mother put her knife down on the draining board. She dipped her hand in the saucepan and turned the carrots in their water, then her fingers came to rest on its edge. "I think you know why," she said, not looking at her.

They were on the edge of what couldn't be mentioned, and Abby felt her heart thumping hard. *Be brave,* Mara had said. *Do the thing you fear.* She took a breath, then let it out because she wasn't ready and took another. *Now, say it now.* "Because – because there are people in it who've died."

For a long moment her mother stared out of the window, with her back to Abby. Then she said, "Well, I don't think you should get involved." She reached for the towel and began to dry her hands.

Words were running about in Abby's mind, but she couldn't catch them. "It's not like that," she said, because she had to say something. "It's not awful or anything. The girl in the story who died – well, she's all right." Tears were welling up. "Mum

– she's all right. She is." Her voice was difficult to manage. "Honestly. She is." She tried to smile, but it didn't work. Her lips were trembling, and then the tears overflowed.

Her mother turned to her. "Oh, Abby." The words came on an outrush of breath, then she put her arms around Abby and gathered her close.

"Mum, don't cry." But they were weeping together, for Sylvie and for the years of trying to forget her, and the crying was like a river that had burst in freedom out of some dark, underground place.

Stan switched his computer on and sat there for a few minutes, thinking. Then he began to write.

It was strangely light here, Cat found. Nothing to do with daylight or moonlight or electric light; it wasn't about seeing. Everything *felt* light. No weight of the body to carry around, no restriction. She could be wherever she wanted. She only had to think herself into the new place, and she was there.

Nobody scolded her for wasting time. There wasn't any time here, so you couldn't waste it. Nothing was late or early. You didn't miss anything if you went somewhere else for a while. The thing you had left waited for you as if it was on *pause*, and continued when you came back.

It was a bit like the daydreams she used to have in the old life, when she could be sitting in her school classroom and at the same time be somewhere quite different in her own mind. She didn't have to choose between one place and another: she could be in them all.

She understood now how Luma had been able to dream his way in and out of the Massa building. She herself could dive into houses and schools and offices whenever she chose to. She went back to her old school once or twice, and was touched to find how worried people were, and how deeply they feared she was lost from their world.

Cat drifted around the outside of the Massa building for quite a time before she made up her mind to go inside. From above, the low, oblong blocks of its packing factory looked like white bricks plonked down among the fields of bright yellow rape. She circled the tall tower that housed its offices and laboratories, looking through its windows, and then went down to the animal pens. There she stared with compassion at the dogs and mice, the cats and rats and monkeys and patient cattle that waited their turn to be taken from barn to laboratory.

She flinched away from the tall chimney that gave off a smoke full of particles that were the remains of living things. No, she could not face Massa today.

She went off instead to visit Pat and Terry, who were driving their lorry along a lane. They were even more worried than the school people, she found. Neither of them was speaking, but they were both thinking of what had happened the previous day.

They'd come back from Massa with some useful steel bars and a sack of cement and were having a couple of beers with Davey, who was going on about the authorities. They'd hauled him and young Lew up that afternoon, and Lew had made a bolt for it. He hadn't been seen since, and Davey was worried he might have been caught. "They'll take him away," he said. "Put him in some home."

Then the boy himself came into the caravan, white-faced and silent. He went out again when he saw them, and Davey didn't say a word, just got up and followed him. When Pat and Terry met him in the pub afterwards, he was looking troubled. Luma had told him some weird tale about a girl smuggling herself into Massa in the back of their truck, and being killed there. The same thought was tormenting the two men.

That lassie couldn't have been in the back, could she? Did we take her into that place, and leave her there? God save us, we didn't know.

You didn't know, Cat agreed.

Pat was too agitated to listen. *And what about that puppy? I should never have told Mum I'd keep one for her.*

Terry's mind was running along the same lines.

Bad idea, saving that pup. The blasted thing's getting hotter every day. We'll have to get rid of it somehow.

Then the pair of them were worrying about Cat again.

What if the boy's right? He's a funny one, that. Got the seeing eye, same as Davey's old ma had. Did we take that lassie to her death? We never meant to. Lord knows we never meant to.

It wasn't your fault, Cat told them, more firmly this time. *You mustn't worry. It's lovely, the way I am now. I'm with my mother now, and I never knew her before. Honestly, it's all right.*

After a few moments both men gave a shrug.

"Ah, well," Pat said to Terry. "What's done is done. Could you fancy a swift pint at all?"

"I could," replied Terry. And they spent the next hour playing darts.

Cat smiled. These were kind men at heart – but they were not the ones who mattered. The darkness and fear that she had to confront had nothing to do with them. It came from someone else, at the heart of Massa. Someone who was hardly a human being at all.

You have to face him, my darling, Mara told her. *He can do nothing to hurt you now, and you need to understand. Go and look.*

Yes, Cat said. And she knew there was no point in delaying.

Stan took his hands off the keyboard and joined them behind his neck, leaning back in his chair as he thought. The Administrator would have to kill the scientists, because they knew what had happened to Cat. How was he to do it? He went on thinking. After a few minutes, the typed lines on the monitor changed to the snaking patterns of its screen saver. Stan stared at the shifting colours. This was the computer's resting state, when nothing active was going on. The Administrator could be the same.

"Got it," he said, nudging the mouse. The lines of printing returned to the screen, and he began to type.

Cat dropped through the glass roof into the huge room where her old life had ended. The man in a dark suit was not there, but as she watched, the door opened and a very fat young man in a brown lab coat came in. As he walked across the soft carpet, his appearance changed. He was not fat at all, but lean and cold. The lab coat melted away, and he was wearing a dark suit. A shock of recognition ran through Cat. This was the man who had looked up as she walked dizzily into the bright room in the last minutes of her previous life. This was the Administrator.

The man sat down at one of the computers and

began to work. As Cat watched, his appearance altered again. The thin shoulders became plumper and rounder, the hair thinner, the face more pudgy, the suit a little rumpled. He was no longer a sharp, ruthless executive. He could have been any office worker, doing a bit of overtime.

Cat watched him, astonished. This man could look like any human being he chose. Before her very eyes he was shifting again. His face lost its heavy-chinned solidity and became thin and sharp, and his hair changed from balding wispiness to a curly crop that was carroty red. His body wasn't dumpy any more; it was athletic and strong.

The new guise only lasted a few moments. The Administrator had started to change once more, from young to middle-aged, from athletic to paunchy. Cat realized that he was in a constant state of slow movement. Sometimes he would stay for several minutes in one form, while he studied something on the screen, but then the changing would start up again. She guessed he could hold an appearance for as long as he liked if he so chose, but now he was altering rapidly. The dark suit gave way to a chalk-striped grey one, grey to navy, navy to brown, shiny shoes to trainers, jacket to sports gear. In another couple of moments he changed sex and sat before the computer as a secretary in a neat skirt, then as an older woman in black jacket and trousers, with short hair dyed pale blonde. She in turn gave way to a slim boy with cropped hair and a single earring.

Cat moved nearer to the man's shifting form, even though every instinct told her to keep away from this unnatural thing. After all, she reasoned, he could not harm her now. She needed to find out the working of this strange mechanism. Had the Administrator known she was there, he could have brushed her off like a fly, but he did not know.

She travelled across the lapel of a blue suit that was becoming black-striped even as she explored it, and past its top pocket that held nothing but a folded handkerchief. She moved over a tie that was shifting from striped red and blue to a bright yellow with horses' heads, and across a dark silk shirt that changed to white cotton, aware all the time that the body inside the clothes was giving off a vibration like a silent hum. It made her uncomfortable, but she travelled on, across the skin of his neck that became wrinkled and then firm, over his chin and his ever-changing face. She reached his head under the constantly altering hair – and met a blast of electrical energy from the brain inside it that made the air quiver.

Cat recoiled. She retreated for a few moments, surveying the man from further away. Looking very carefully, she saw that under the skin of his wrists and on many places in his neck and face were microscopic swellings where something had been implanted. From each of these spots came a small vibration that echoed the main one sent out from his brain.

Cat approached him again, even closer this time, so that the pores and wrinkles and hairs of his skin were as large as the features of a landscape. And then she knew the truth. This stuff over which her gaze travelled was not skin at all. It was a form of plastic, perfect in every detail. It could slacken to show the blue veins of old age or be taut and firm with youth, and its colour varied from paleness to a freckly red, from suntan to the pasty flabbiness of the desk-bound indoor worker. Underneath it was the unvarying pulse of a mechanical pump and the steady rise and fall of air-powered lungs. The plasticized muscles that had perhaps once responded to the impulses of a normal, living man were now moved by mechanical stimulation, controlled by the vibrating apparatus housed in the Administrator's skull.

Cat backed away. Exploring above the man's head, she found a quivering pathway of invisible, perhaps electrical, connection. It led, she discovered, to the wall at the end of the room. She followed it, and found the wall to be thin, a sliding partition that could be opened. It was closed now, but she went through it.

A bank of grey machinery confronted her in the dimly lit space. Needles flickered on dials and the green numbers in display slots were in constant movement. An empty couch lay before them, and as Cat watched, the wall slid aside and the Administrator came in.

He sat down on the couch, swung his feet up and lay back. Then he pressed a button on the side of the couch. A mechanical arm unfolded from the machinery and reached across with uncanny certainty to place a grey, metallic hand above his chest. His clothes melted away to a simple white gown, open to the waist, and the hand located this opening and paused. An electrical plug on a long flex was fed down between its plastic-tipped fingers, which gripped it and felt for the heart. Finding it, they inserted the plug. The needles on the dials flicked over to *high*, and the body on the couch ceased its constant changing. It lay as peacefully as a baby being fed.

At the same moment, a radiance bloomed from the outer room. Cat stared in fresh astonishment. A being sat in a solid, grey leather armchair, but he consisted only of light, presenting an image of the Administrator that shifted according to where the viewer stood.

A hologram, Cat thought. She understood then that this was the man's resting state. While his physical body was being recharged, he existed only as a virtual creature, made of light.

A presence at Cat's side startled her, and she

turned to see who it was. She found a man who had only just come into the world of dream and spirit that she now inhabited. She knew how he felt, shocked and uncertain, but she didn't understand the waves of wretchedness that surrounded him.

Then it was clear.

This was the white-coated man who had bent over her in the last moments of her old life. *Listen, sweetheart,* he'd said gently. He'd told her what they were going to do, but not that it would kill her. He'd wanted to make sure she wasn't frightened.

I am so sorry, he was saying now. *So sorry, so sorry.* His whole being was blurred with guilt and regret.

Don't be, said Cat. *I'm all right. Truly.*

Another presence was arriving beside him, and he too was as helpless and vulnerable as a child newly born. He was in a worse state, shuddering with pain, and Cat knew why. His was the grip that had encircled her arm, squeezing the vein as he pressed in the plunger of the syringe with his other hand. When he had withdrawn the needle, he had released the pressure, letting the lethal stuff run through her bloodstream to her brain and her heart. This man had killed her.

When he knew Cat was standing beside him, the man shrank away in horror, and the thought in his tormented mind was clear.

I will never deserve forgiveness. I cannot forgive myself.

Cat did not know what to say to him. It was terrible to watch his pain, but she had no way to soothe it.

Mara was at Cat's other side, in a sudden blossoming of warmth and comfort. *Grieve for him if you must, my darling,* she said. *It may help him – but you can't change what he has done. Some people make such a burden of badness for themselves that they carry it for ever. He may be one of them.*

What happens to them? Cat asked in fear.

Mara looked at the man, who was curling away with his arms over his head as if he still thought he could hide. *They are in what living people call hell.*

Cat felt a wave of compassion for her murderer. *But what was he to do?* she asked. *If he'd refused, the Administrator would have killed him.*

Mara did not bother to look at the shimmering hologram in the leather chair. The truth was plain.

He did kill him. He has just killed both of them. As will be discovered.

A shrill noise of bleepers and alarm bells rang out, and the Massa building was suddenly alive with the sound of running feet.

Stan's wife opened the door of the summerhouse and looked in. "Tea's ready," she said in the Polish she and Stan spoke together.

212

"Mm," said Stan vaguely. "This is just getting interesting. Thanks, though." But he turned back to the screen.

Stasi came in to look at what he was doing. She was surrounded, as usual, by a flotilla of dogs, and a very small puppy weighed down the front pocket of her anorak, sleeping in there like a baby kangaroo. "Do you mind my wellies?" she asked, looking at her boots. "They're a bit muddy."

"Since when have I minded?" Stan turned in his chair to stroke the puppy's head with one finger. "How's she doing?"

"Coming on well now, poor little thing." Stasi was reading the words on the screen. She laughed. "And this is a children's book?" she asked.

"Yes, it's a children's book," Stan said firmly. "Anyone who thinks kids can't get their heads round a bit of murder and a discussion of hell is regarding them as something less than properly human. And if nothing else, I've learned not to do that."

His wife laughed again. "Would I argue?" she said. "Now, come along, or things will be burning. And don't forget to save that," she added, nodding at the screen. "I know what you're like."

"You do, my love," Stan agreed. "You do."

🌿 Twelve

The next day was a Sunday, and a lot of them crowded into the summerhouse. At the end of the reading, Fraser asked, "How did the Administrator kill the scientists?"

"He changed the label on a bottle of chemical," said Stan, "during the lunch break when nobody was there. He knew the men would be using it when they came back. By itself, the chemical was fine, but as soon as they combined it with the other stuff they were working on, it gave off a lethal gas."

Kevin Dobb frowned. "The Eye would have seen him doing it," he said.

"He could have switched it off, couldn't he?" said Sue. "I mean, he controls everything."

Neil didn't agree. "There must be technicians who watch it as well. They'd know if anything happened to it. There'd be alarms and things."

"It can't be off," Chokker said. "It's got to be on, that's the whole point. The Administrator wants people to see him, because he'll be looking like someone else. And the person he looks like will get the blame."

"The lab assistant," Fraser agreed.

Stan nodded and said, "That's why I made the lab guy fat, so he's easy to recognize on the screen. The police will be sure they've got their man. Even though they haven't."

"That's awful!" said Kirsty. "But the Administrator *is* awful, isn't he?"

"He does need a name," said Fraser. "You get sick of saying *the Administrator* each time."

"I think you're right," said Stan. "So what shall we call him?"

People looked at each other, thinking.

"It wants to be short," said Kevin.

"And hard," Stan added. "I mean, he's very cold. A man of no feeling at all."

Everyone piled in with suggestions.

"Stone."

"Iron."

"Ice."

"Winter," said Abby.

Stan repeated it. "Winter. That's good. The time when nothing grows. Cold earth. A cold mind. Are we happy with that?"

There were nods all round.

Fraser had still been thinking about the plot. "After the gas and everything, who'll find the men?" he asked.

"I thought they'd be working in a small lab on their own, because their stuff is particularly secret," Stan said. "So nobody actually sees them collapse. But sensors pick up the presence of the gas and trigger the alarms."

"It'll be on television," said Sue. "Everyone's going to know."

Stan nodded. "Yes, we'll need a bit of public excitement. Demonstrators outside the gates, and all that."

Chokker was getting impatient. "Someone's got to kill the man. Winter or whatever he's called."

"What if he can't be killed?" said Abby. "If he's just a machine?"

Stan said, "He's mostly mechanized, but I think he has to be human, deep inside. To me that's the scary thing about him. He started as a child like any other, and grew up into a man, then got so taken up by the idea of power that he turned himself into something else."

"You just want someone really strong, who can do anything," Chokker said. *The Master could see him off, no problem. And Luma would help.*

"Well, yes," said Stan, "but that's a bit of a cop-out. If there's someone super-powerful knocking around, then Cat and Luma never need to do anything. Just call in Superguy, and he'll take care of it."

Chokker scowled. The Master wasn't some stupid cartoon character.

"And if they do that," Stan was going on, "they're thinking the same way that Winter does. He wants to be Superguy himself."

"Yeah, but he's bad," Chokker argued. "You can have someone powerful who's good."

Fraser said, "He might start off good, then get to be bad. You can't be sure."

Lots of people nodded.

They were all wrong, Chokker thought. They didn't understand, any of them. He got to his feet, intending to go out and leave them to it, but at that moment, the door of the summerhouse was opened from outside and Stasi came in, carrying a tray with a big jug of orange juice and a plate of biscuits. A couple of dogs followed her, and a small puppy was tucked into her pocket.

"You are all I think needing refreshment," she said in English.

"You haven't met my wife, have you?" Stan said to everyone. "Stasi."

The parrot started climbing around in her cage, shouting things in two languages, and everyone laughed. Chokker didn't. This book was getting into a mess, he thought. It was going all wrong.

The others were all cooing over Stasi's puppy.

"Runt of the litter," Stan explained. "We took the mother on because her owners moved abroad, and she had these pups. Five big ones and a little one. She didn't want the little one, pushed it out.

217

They do sometimes, especially if they've been upset. So we've been hand-rearing it."

Sue was stroking the puppy's pale head with one finger. "What sort is it?"

"Golden retriever," said Stasi.

"Sweet. Just look, Abby, isn't he lovely!"

"She," said Stan. "It's a bitch."

"Hold her while I pour out drinks," Stasi said, and handed the pup to Abby. "Don't drop her."

In her anxiety to keep the little creature safe, Abby was hardly aware that she was holding a dog. The puppy felt very warm and solid, and her coat was soft. She made a small noise like a cork turning in a bottle, and pushed her nose against Abby's fingers.

"She's hungry," said Stasi. "I feed her in a minute."

Abby smiled. She lifted the puppy to her shoulder, and it nuzzled in against her neck. "She's very nice," she said.

Sunday afternoon was a drag. Chokker wanted to argue with Stan about his stupid book, and get him to see he was wrong. How could you win a fight without someone really strong on your side? Luma didn't have a hope of winning against Winter at the moment. He'd got nobody to help except a couple of ghosts and maybe the vet woman. The whole thing was ridiculous.

Chokker and Dorothy were on washing-up duty after lunch. There was a rota system.

"How's the book going?" Dorothy asked.

"All right."

"What's it about?"

Reluctantly he started to explain. "There's this place where they're making GM stuff, only it's all gone wrong. This girl called Cat gets killed. She's all right, because she lives in a sort of spirit world, only she and a boy have got to stop what's happening."

"It sounds fascinating," said Dorothy. "And I do think this GM thing is terribly dangerous. Nobody knows what could happen. I'd love to read a bit of it. Is that possible, do you think?"

"Dunno," said Chokker. "It's at Stan's." Then he had an idea. "I could ask him, if you like." It would be an excuse to go back to the summerhouse. Better than hanging around here.

"That would be lovely," said Dorothy.

"I'm busy right now," Stan said when he opened the door.

"I know. I just wondered if I could borrow a bit of the book. Someone wants to see it."

"Who, exactly?" Stan sounded suspicious.

"Dorothy. Mrs Finbow. She's like my mum." Only she wasn't. His mum would never have organized a rota for washing up. She never washed up at all, as far as he could remember. There used to be dirty stuff everywhere.

"Tell you what," Stan said. "There's a bit more that I didn't read out this morning. We got kind of sidetracked, what with refreshments and the puppy. I'll lend you that. Your Dorothy person can read it, then you can show it to the others. Only let me have it back, right?"

"Sure," said Chokker.

Stan put the pages in his hand. "There you go," he said. "Now I've got to get on. I've hit a really good streak. Sorry to be antisocial."

"It's all right," said Chokker. "Thanks."

He went away down the path. He'd meant to tell Stan he was all wrong about Luma and the Master, but it hadn't happened, somehow.

He took the pages down to the beach and sat with his back against the sea wall, reading them. It wasn't easy, but there was nobody looking over his shoulder or nagging, so he puzzled it out slowly. It was a good feeling, knowing he was the first person who'd seen them.

Luma sat on the caravan step in the afternoon sun with Cat close beside him in his thoughts. The puppy hidden in the lorry pen was snarling. It did that a lot. Luma let his mind drift away from it, following Cat into that other place.

In the Massa building, policemen were measuring and photographing and asking endless questions. But the questions were about the two scientists, not about Cat. They still didn't know she was dead.

They can't know, Cat pointed out. *Nobody has told them.*

I want them to know, Luma said.

Cat looked at him with concern. *You mustn't worry about me,* she said. *I'm all right; I like it in this world.*

Luma shook his head. *That man killed you. He mustn't get away with it.*

His name's Winter, said Cat.

Is it? How do you know?

I just do. And he won't get away with it. When the police find out I went to Massa, everything will change. *She sounded certain.*

Luma wondered if he could find the courage to go to the police himself, but he knew he couldn't. Authorities were to be left strictly alone, especially since he'd run out on the interview with the woman called Mrs Pimm.

You could tell my uncle and aunt, Cat suggested, reading his thoughts. *They'll do the rest.*

Of course. Why hadn't he thought of that? Luma was back on the caravan step, getting to his feet. *I'll go right now,* he said.

Yes, said Cat. Her smile filled his mind like sunshine. He knew she would be with him.

Cat's aunt opened the door a small crack, as far as the safety chain would permit. "Yes?" she said.

"It's about Cat," Luma began.

"Ah. You know where she is?"

"Well – not exactly." Cat was standing at his side, but he could hardly tell her that.

"Then what *do* you know?"

"Just ... where she went."

The uncle appeared in the hall behind his wife and said, "You'd better ask the boy in."

Luma, with Cat beside him, followed them into a front room that smelled unused. The curtains were drawn to keep out the sun, and the aunt twitched them back a little to let in a thin finger of light. "She's a very naughty girl," she said. "Giving us all this worry."

"Where is she, anyway?" demanded the uncle.

"She went to a place called Massa. It's a research institute."

"The place where those two scientists were found dead?" He looked startled. "Why on earth did she go there?"

"I was going to go with her, only I couldn't. We wanted to find out what was happening to the dogs." Luma went through the story of Mrs Jordan's dog.

"That's nonsense; it was nettle-rash," snapped the aunt.

Cat laughed. *That's not what the vet said.*

Luma repeated her words.

"Who is this vet?" the uncle demanded. "It all sounds extremely unprofessional to me. And whose lorry was it?"

Luma supplied the details, and the uncle wrote them down. Then he looked up suspiciously. "What's *your* name, anyway? How do I know this is true?"

"You don't," said Luma, hating the pair of them. Even now, they didn't really care about Cat.

"There's no need to be impertinent," said the aunt. "Have you told this story to the police?"

Tell her you're going to, said Cat.

Her advice surprised him. Surely she knew he—

Doesn't matter if you're not. Cat's voice was firm. *Just tell her.*

OK.

"Not yet," he said firmly. "But I will."

The uncle looked offended. "We'll go ourselves. They're aware that she's run off; we notified them. We've done everything we can."

"More than she deserves," said the aunt. "Cathleen's our niece, but she's been very thoughtless. So headstrong and selfish."

Let's go, said Cat. *You've done all you can.*

Luma ducked past the uncle and out of the room. They'd put the chain back on the front door, and he had a brief struggle to release it.

He felt a grab at his shoulder and tore himself away. Then he was out into the fresh air and running.

Yes, Chokker thought when he got to the end. *That's OK.* It would have been great if Luma had flattened the uncle, but perhaps he couldn't do that yet. Save it for Winter.

"Goodness," Dorothy said when she read the pages that evening. "It's very complicated."

"Not really," said Chokker. "You'd understand it better if you'd read the beginning."

"I expect I would." She looked at the pages again. "Luma seems a very sensible boy," she said. "He's having a difficult time, though, isn't he?"

"Sort of." Was Luma sensible? It seemed an odd word to use.

The little ones were in their pyjamas, watching *Mary Poppins.* It was almost over. Chokker stared at the screen as well, so that he didn't have to talk any more about Luma.

After a few minutes Dorothy said, "Can I show this to Gerald?"

He couldn't really say no. "All right. Only I've got to have it for school tomorrow."

"Of course. Thanks."

Mary Poppins was flying around with her umbrella. Dorothy got up and went out to the kitchen with the pages. It was Gerald's turn to wash up.

Everyone read the pages the next day. Mrs Long read them too, though Chokker wasn't sure if Stan would like that. He took them back to the summerhouse after school but there was a notice on the door that said BUSY, so he didn't go in.

For a couple of days nothing happened, then Abby came rushing in and said the busy notice had been crossed out, so they went up to Stan's for the next bit. Kevin and Kirsty came too.

The police didn't hang about. That evening Terry and Pat came to the caravan, looking shaken.

"They went over the truck like they were hunting for fleas on a cat," said Pat. "Blowing bits of dust about, looking for fingerprints. They took great lumps of mud away to be analysed."

"Then they had us down at the cop shop," Terry said. "For questioning. Lord save us, what a lot of questions. Where had the sugar beet come from? Did we see it loaded? Had the lorry been left unattended? Did we know Michael Farrell at the gate? Was he a friend of ours? We'd been seen playing darts together. I think that was a lucky guess about the darts, mind, but I'd nodded me head before I thought of it. Then they had Michael in to join us. Questions all over again."

"And what are they up to now?" asked Davey.

"We didn't ask," said Pat. "I was afraid they'd heard about the dog. I'll have to tell Mum she can't have it. Blasted thing's going to cause a heap of trouble."

Terry nodded gloomily. "It's getting hot as Hades and the straw all round it looks like toast. Costs a fortune too. It wolfs up dog meat like it's a starving tiger."

"And fries it first," added Pat.

"I want it out of here," ordered Davey. "All very well for you two, but what do I say if the fuzz turn up?"

"We'll move it, Davey, don't you worry," Pat promised. "We'll get rid of it somehow. Look on the bright side," he added. "The cops never noticed the truck's run out of tax. Could have been worse." He opened another can of Guinness. "Cheers."

Luma sat on his bunk and said nothing. Neither did Cat, but they both knew the pup with the Massa infection meant trouble.

The breakfast television news said a laboratory assistant was helping the police with the deaths of the two scientists at Massa. It showed a fat young

man being bundled into a police car. He looked as
if he was crying. Then it switched to a shot of the
goods delivery gate.

"A girl missing from her home in the village of
Skeltorpen is now thought to have entered the
Massa building a few days ago," the announcer said.
"Forensic tests have proved that the girl, Cathleen
Ingleby, climbed into a lorry laden with sugar beet,
delivered last Tuesday afternoon to the Massa
building. Investigations are continuing."

Davey whistled quietly. "Looks bad for Pat and
Terry," he said.

Luma exchanged a glance with Cat, who said,
It's started.

Suddenly Davey looked up sharply at the sound
of an approaching vehicle. Luma turned to kneel
on the seat so he could peer out of the caravan
window, and saw a police car with a lemon-yellow
stripe along its sides pulling into the muddy
lay-by.

"Uh-oh," Davey said. "Here comes trouble."

Don't run away, Cat warned as Luma's muscles
tensed. *They're not looking for you.* He made himself
sit down, but his palms were sticky with sweat. The
years spent with Davey had taught him that the
police were the enemy, though he had not always
understood why.

The two officers who came in, a man and a
woman, seemed very bulky. They wore yellow

jackets over their uniforms, and their broad belts were hung about with lumpy stuff – handcuffs, a baton in a leather case, a radio. Somehow they made the caravan seem much more crowded than Pat and Terry had done last night.

The police realized quite quickly that Davey didn't know anything, and they concentrated on Luma. When did he last see Cathleen Ingleby? Had she told him where she was going?

At Cat's silent prompting, he told them the truth. She might have gone to Massa. Why? Because there was something funny going on. He told them about Cat being burnt by Mrs Jordan's dog, about their visit to the vet, about what the nurse had said. He wondered whether to come clean about the dog in the lorry container, but Cat said quickly, *Don't*.

"Why didn't you come to us?" the policewoman asked. "You knew where your friend was, so why didn't you tell someone?"

"I wasn't sure," said Luma. "We were going to go together, but I couldn't. I didn't think she'd go without me – not at first."

"But you do now?"

"Yes."

"Why?"

"I just – do."

He could not tell them he had seen what had happened to Cat in the glass-roofed room high up in the Massa tower. He had no proof of that in their terms, and it would only make them disbelieve whatever else he said.

The police took him through the story again and again, and they wrote it all down, including the Jordans' address and everything Luma could remember about the visit to the vet.

"Do you like dogs?" the policewoman asked him suddenly.

Luma wondered what she was getting at. "They're all right," he said.

"You've never been bitten by one?"

"No."

"Never been attacked? You don't dream about them?"

Then he saw what she meant, and felt angry. "I didn't make it up, if that's what you think," he said. "It wasn't a dream; it really happened. You can ask the vet."

"We've checked all the local vets," the policeman put in. "Not one of them knows anything about this visit of yours. And they've never heard of a vet called Angie."

"But she was a – what's it called? – a stand-in," Luma said.

"Locum. What's her other name? Angie what?"

Luma closed his eyes and frowned, struggling to remember. *McIver,* Cat said in his ear, and he repeated it aloud.

That seemed to impress them. After a few more questions, they closed their notebooks and left.

"Whew," said Davey as the car pulled away. "That's all right, then. Good thing you never went to that Massa place, Lew. I don't know what happened to your friend, but it sounds like bad news to me."

"Yes," said Luma.

As he had often done, he wished he could talk to Davey about the other part of his life. But he'd never mentioned it to any living person. Sometimes he thought Davey knew – but Davey liked a drink and a gossip. If he didn't know, to tell him might be the same as telling everyone.

Chokker was disappointed. He'd hoped Stan would get Luma into the Massa building and start some action. "It's like there's nothing happening," he complained.

Sue turned on him. "Yes, there is. The police are asking questions."

"And everyone knows Cat went to Massa," said Kirsty.

"What do you suggest?" Stan asked Chokker. "It's all open to changes."

"Luma's got to get in there and fight," Chokker said. "He knows someone who can help him. They kill Winter, and then this friend of Luma's takes over

Massa and runs it properly." The Master would know how to do that. He knew everything.

"I don't want anyone to run Massa," said Abby. "I want it to close down."

"Me too," said Sue. Fraser and several of the others nodded.

They're so boring, Chokker thought. "That's no good," he argued. "They'll just start up again somewhere else. There's got to be a fight."

"Why has there?" Abby demanded.

"Because that's the way it is. There's always bad people. So you need fighters. They know how to do it, all the moves and weapons and stuff. Someone teaches them." Now that he'd started, he rushed on. "People have got to have someone stronger than they are, to tell them what to do."

"But what if that person gets to be like Winter?" Abby asked.

Chokker was too angry to stop. "Winter's all right," he said. "He just went too far, that's all."

There was an outbreak of disagreement.

Fraser frowned and said, "You think it's all right to kill people?"

"Yeah, why not?" said Chokker recklessly. *Disable your enemy if you can, but if you have to kill him, do it mercifully and fast.* A hot feeling was starting to build up in his mind. "Some people deserve to be killed," he said. *People who shout and hurt. People who go off and leave you. People with thick, hairy*

231

wrists and expanding metal watch straps.

"*Who* deserves to be killed?" Abby demanded. "Who do you mean, exactly?"

"Doesn't matter," said Chokker. *Don't start.* He should never have mentioned this; nightmares were private things.

"It *does* matter," Abby said. "If you won't say, then you don't know."

"Oh, shut up." He flung himself back in Stan's dilapidated armchair, and folded his arms across his chest.

"What about Winter?" Stan asked Abby. "Does he deserve to be killed?"

She frowned. "He's a machine; he's different."

"But if he's human?"

"He might have a good bit hidden away somewhere."

Chokker snorted. "Just shows you don't know anything, that's all."

"You said that before," Abby said. Her face was flushed.

"Yeah, right. I said you didn't know bad things could happen, and you said you did. And you couldn't come up with anything, could you?"

Abby stared at him, and he saw her mouth tighten. For a moment, he thought she was going to cry, but she didn't.

"All right," she said suddenly. "I'll tell you." She took a deep breath. "I used to have a big sister. Her name was Sylvie. It was in Greenock, where we lived before we came here. We were out one day, Sylvie and me and Mum. It was raining. A man came towards us with a big dog, and it went for Sylvie. She was really scared of dogs. She ran away from it, off the pavement into the road." Abby swallowed hard. Everyone was very quiet. Her voice was quavering as she began again. "Mum couldn't grab her quick enough. There was a car coming. It – it couldn't stop."

"Oh, Abby!" Sue looked appalled. "I didn't know. Oh, poor Abby." She got up and hugged her.

Kirsty was in tears.

"It's all right," Abby managed to say. "It's better now. But things happen; everyone has bad things happen."

In the fuss, Chokker got up from his armchair and went to the door. Stan said, "Hang on," but Chokker took no notice. He felt as if Abby had hit him, and he had no way to hit back. At least, none that he was willing to use. He went out, and shut the door behind him.

Thirteen

I'm finished with them, Chokker thought as he sat in his room. Abby had made him look a real prat, coming out with that stuff about her sister. Worse than a prat – they'd think he was really mean because he'd made her say it. None of them would speak to him now.

I don't care. The whole book thing had been stupid, anyway. He shouldn't have got sucked into it. He'd been stupid himself, thinking it was OK, starting to enjoy it. Letting them have Luma. That was a big mistake.

I must get him back. That was the only thing to do now. *If they want a boy in their story, they can call him something else.* He'd go and see Stan one more time, and tell him.

The video was running, but Chokker hardly watched it. That other place with its quiet courtyards and its view of the smoking mountain didn't seem real any more. That was Stan's fault as well. *Going on about being in charge of your own thoughts.*

Saying things are only real because you choose to believe them. Stan would never believe in the Master. *Superguy,* he'd called him, like he was Batman or something.

Chokker stared at the video, trying hard to get into it as he used to, but it was no good. The man in the dark cloak wasn't the Master; it was just an actor, speaking words that had been typed by a scriptwriter. He'd known that all along, really, but it hadn't mattered before.

I was right, Chokker thought bitterly. *Stan was the enemy, right from the start.* He hadn't meant to be. He didn't even know he was. He'd beaten the Master simply by not believing in him.

The deep voice on the video repeated the familiar words. *Trust me. I can help you defend yourself against those who wish you harm.*

Chokker lay back on his bed and put his arm across his eyes. *You can't trust anyone,* he thought.

After a few minutes, a crumb of comfort came. Luma wasn't an actor. He was a part of Chokker's own self; they couldn't get at him. Luma still had a way into that tranquil place where sunshine filtered through the screens. Once again, he sat cross-legged on the smooth wooden floor, a barefoot boy in black trousers and a belted tunic, listening to the words that were so real to him.

Then fight for him, my son.

Chokker hit the remote and stopped the video.

He'd already said he'd get Luma back, and he was sick of thinking about it. He got to his feet and put some music on the CD player, turning the volume up very high. The thumping rhythm pulsed in the small room, so loud that it was like being inside a drum someone was beating. The noise poured in through his ears and filled his head, drowning every thought in it. He shut his eyes. *That's better.*

He knew it wouldn't last long. One of the Finbows would be up in a minute. Not shouting – they never shouted. Just a head round the door and a worried face. *Charlie, the little ones are asleep – could you turn it down a bit? Please?* Even now, he seemed to hear their footsteps on the stairs.

He went to the summerhouse the next day after school.

"Come in!" shouted Stan and the parrot.

The others weren't there. That was good.

Stan turned from his computer. "Hi," he said. "How are things?"

"OK." *Got to find the words; got to tell him I want Luma back.*

Stan looked back at the words on the screen and said, "I've been having terrible struggles with this book. The fight's got to be in the spirit world, but I'm trying to work out what Winter's going to do."

Chokker didn't want to talk about the spirit world. He wished Stan wasn't so relaxed and casual;

it made things more difficult.

"Could be he's devised dream-sensitive software," Stan went on, pulling at his lip thoughtfully. "Cat would know, I suppose."

Got to tell him. Chokker cleared his throat.

At that moment, the door opened and Stasi came in, followed by several dogs. She smiled at Chokker then said to Stan in English, "Publisher woman on the phone."

"Oh, good." Stan got up. "I'll come and talk to her."

"Why don't you have a mobile?" Chokker asked irritably. He didn't want Stan to go off to the bungalow right now.

"Hate them," said Stan. "Back in a moment." He followed his wife out.

"BYE-BYE," said Agatha.

The screen saver on Stan's computer was snaking around slowly, changing from one colour to another. Chokker watched it for a bit, then turned away. He wished Stan would hurry up – waiting made it hard to stay angry.

"GIVE US A PEANUT," shouted the parrot.

Chokker went over to the cage and looked at her. She looked back at him with her head on one side, and raised the feathers on her neck a bit, as if she was about to scream at him. Then she lowered them and scratched under her chin with a grey-clawed foot.

There was a bag of peanuts on the shelf under the cage. Chokker picked one out and offered it to her, and the bird took it gently in her curved black beak. She nibbled at it, then dropped it on the floor of the cage.

"What d'you want, then?" asked Chokker. He put out his finger and touched the top of her head between the cage bars, scratching gently into the soft base of the feathers. The parrot arched her neck like a cat, as if she enjoyed it. He tickled her some more, and she stretched her head sideways and shut her wrinkled grey eyelids. It was funny how the bottom one came up instead of the top one coming down. Birds were different from humans. Chokker moved his finger round the side of Agatha's head to tickle under her chin. Cats liked that. He'd tried to get Gerald and Dorothy to have a cat, but Dorothy said she was allergic.

The parrot bit his finger, hard. The curved points of her beak sliced through the flesh on either side of the nail, and Chokker gasped with the pain of it. Agatha made a chattering noise and started climbing round her cage, looking at him out of one eye and screeching with what sounded like laughter.

Blood was pouring from the wound. Chokker nursed his finger in his other hand and looked about for something to wrap it in. He couldn't find anything – Stan didn't seem to use tissues – so he went to the waste-paper basket and fished out a handful of typed pages. Tearing them to a better size was a messy affair with his dripping finger, but he managed it after a fashion. The bits of paper weren't much good as bandages, and he was still fiddling about with them when Stan came in.

"Heavens, what have you done?" he asked.

"I was stroking the parrot."

"And she bit you? Horrible old baggage. She did that to me once; I think it's her idea of being affectionate. Come down to the house; Stasi's got first-aid stuff there."

It wasn't until afterwards, with his finger wrapped in a white bandage and a mugful of hot chocolate inside him, that Chokker remembered about Luma. The chocolate had been very good – Stasi had made it with a topping of whipped cream. Walking home in the cold wind that blew across the sea, he cursed himself for losing hold of what he'd meant to say. It had been very cosy in the bungalow, warm and untidy, with dogs all over the place and the puppies curled up in a heap in their basket. The little one looked a bit bigger now. Stasi had given her to him to hold for a bit. The business about Luma had somehow slipped away. He'd have to try again.

Chokker hung about in the village after school the next day, thinking about Stan. He couldn't go and see him now; the others were up there in the summerhouse. He hoped they wouldn't be long.

Rain started to blow in the wind. He might as well go up the path and get a bit of shelter in the bushes – wait there till the other kids had gone. Chokker walked along the road and past the bungalow. They were still in there. Moving closer to the glowing windows, he could hear Stan's voice, reading.

Wetness dripped from the rhododendron leaves. A cold trickle fell down the side of his neck and found its way under his T-shirt, and he rubbed at it impatiently. *Who cares what they think?* He opened the door and slipped in very quietly, sitting down on the floor with his back to the wall. Nobody looked at him except Abby, and she quickly looked away again. Stan didn't stop reading.

When humans aren't allowed to dream, Mara said, *they become ill.*

That's right, another woman put in. A countless crowd was listening quietly, standing among the trees and the shafts of sunshine.

A boy laughed. *I used to sleep all morning at weekends, to catch up on my dreaming,* he said. *It drove my parents spare.*

Other young voices agreed. *We all did that.*

But what about Massa? Cat asked. *What shall we do?*

The answer came in a wave of certainty.

We must defend the dreamers.

Stan turned over a page, but nobody moved. "Next bit," he said, and went on reading.

Luma was dreaming. He stood on the soft carpet in the Administrator's office. The sliding wall that hid the room at the end did not stop him from seeing the inert body of the man who lay on a narrow couch. An electrical lead coming from between the buttons of the white garment he wore was connected to the bank of machinery alongside it, while in front of the closed wall, the shifting hologram of Winter occupied its grey armchair.

A buzzer sounded, and from outside the door of the big office, Luma heard a mechanized voice say, PLEASE WAIT.

Either the man or the machinery heard it too. A telescopic arm extended and removed the plug from his chest, and the flickering green lights turned to red. After a few moments Winter stood up, brushed with a rapid hand at the dark suit he was now wearing, adjusted his tie and went out to his desk. The hologram had vanished.

There was a sharp click as the automatic locks on the door were released, and Magnus Chip came in.

"Ah, Magnus," said Winter. "Good of you to look in."

"You're welcome," Magnus said. It wasn't good at all, as they both knew. A summons from the Administrator was a serious affair.

"We have a problem," the dark-suited man went on. "Mental escape is getting worse. The new software was supposed to take care of that, but the place is leaking like a sieve."

"Mental escape. I guess that's a tough one," said Magnus. This huge office with its dazzling sweep of slanting windows always made him uneasy, and so did the impeccably groomed man who sat behind the enormous desk. He didn't like the modern sculpture on the coffee table either. What the hell was it supposed to be?

I am privileged to be here, he reminded himself. Very few other Massa employees had access to the old man, and he suspected that those who did were fobbed off with a deputy, for none of them seemed to know the true Cornelius Winter. Some said he was a big, florid man who wore brightly patterned jerseys, and others reported him as elderly and shrivelled, with a hearing aid. Not one of them had seen this efficient, dark-suited man with his iron-grey, neatly cut hair. *I am the only one who knows the truth,* Magnus thought, and felt a little braver.

"The isotope's working OK, sir," he said. "I did like you said, put it through the food line in the canteen. I've run a constant check. It's in the meat and the soup and the puddings and the chips, every day." He tried a smile. "They've had their chips, you might say."

The Administrator did not return his smile. "They hear the control voice in their heads, that is true," he said. "They are obedient to all commands. But there are blanks, Magnus. Moments of mental absence, which the software cannot interpret. We can detect the presence of incoming virtual invaders. There is one with us at this very moment." He glanced towards the place where Luma stood, and Luma automatically ducked, even though a part of his mind told him this was a dream.

"We should be able to account for every moment of a worker's waking life," Winter went on, "but these blanks mean the person is dreaming of something else. At such times, our contact with him is severed, and we have no means of controlling him. Or her. The women tend to be more determined dreamers, which is why I do not promote them to managerial posts."

Magnus nodded, knowing this to be true. "Yes, sir," he said.

Luma went on watching the two men, one of

them sweating uncomfortably, the other cool and precise. Winter spoke again.

"I want this problem solved, Magnus. And I want it solved now."

"Sure," said Magnus, then put it more formally, since the old man was in one of his nastier moods. "I mean, yes, sir, I'll see to it."

"I sincerely hope so." The piercing, pale blue eyes skewered him. "I may point out, Magnus, that your own record is less than perfect. I am not pleased, for instance, that you think of me as the *old man*."

Luma heard Magnus Chip's silent, panic-stricken words. *He knows what I'm thinking. He can't – the tracer isn't in me. I haven't eaten the canteen food since the isotope's been in it; I bring my own sandwiches. What in hell's going on?*

"You forget the water," Winter said. "Very pleasant, cool water, pale blue dispensers of it in every office, with plastic cups. Treated at source, Magnus." He smiled. "Did you imagine you were the only person handling the isotope? I always back up my actions."

"Yes, sir," said Magnus, dry-mouthed at the very thought of it. "Of course." Some mad part of his mind was wondering why the Administrator's eyes were blue. Surely he remembered them as a light, foxy brown? He met them again, and the eyes were not blue at all: they were greenish grey, the colour of shadowed ice.

"You may go," said Winter. "And," he added pleasantly, "do be careful, won't you?"

Magnus made an inarticulate sound, then turned and stumbled back across the carpet. He almost fell through the door as it opened in front of him.

Luma in his dream watched as the man in the dark suit got up from his desk. He looked older now, cardiganed and stoop-shouldered. The wall slid aside for him as he shuffled towards it. He lay down on the couch and touched a button. The telescopic arm extended and felt for his heart, and when it had found what it sought, the plug slid down between its metal fingers. Green lights flashed on, and needles leaped across gauges. In the glass-roofed room, a shifting, glinting hologram was back in the grey leather armchair.

"What's Luma going to do now?" asked Neil.

"Tricky one." Stan sat back in his chair, frowning thoughtfully. "To be honest, I'm beginning to wonder if we need Luma at all."

"But we've got to have Luma!" said Abby. "He's with Cat the first time they go into Massa – he told her how to dream her way out of there. And he goes with her to the vet. And we'll need him for the fight."

"Besides, he's nice," said Mandy.

"Yes," agreed Sue.

Stan wasn't convinced. "It might be better just to have Cat," he said. "Simpler for the readers."

Chokker felt as if things had turned a somersault. He'd come in here to get Luma back, and now Stan was saying he didn't want him anyway. Chokker felt strangely insulted.

"But Luma's the hero," said Neil.

"I know. But so far he hasn't done anything essential, has he?" Stan was looking bothered. "The trouble is, I can't see through to the end yet. This fight is looming ahead, but I don't know how they're going to get into it."

Everyone started talking at once.

"The vet could help."

"And the engineer man – what's his name?"

"The one at the meeting."

"Eddie Molotov," said Stan. "Yes, we need to use him again."

Abby had been thinking about something else. "Does Cat have a father?" she asked. "There was something about him at the beginning, wasn't there? Aunt Madge said Cat would end up like her father."

Stan took his glasses off and rubbed his eyes. "You're absolutely right," he said.

"So where is he?" asked Fraser. "Did he die?"

"He can't have done," Abby said. "Or he'd be in the spirit world, and Cat would have found him."

"So he's got to be still alive," said Mandy. "Why didn't he keep in touch, though?"

"He could have gone abroad," said Kirsty.

Fraser frowned and said, "That's no excuse. There's email and stuff. Mobile phones."

"Laptops weren't as common ten years ago," Stan said. "Flat batteries, no signal – if the guy had gone off somewhere really remote, it might have been tricky even to send a letter. I've been in places like that."

Questions started again. "Is he a writer then?"

"Or an explorer?"

"My Uncle Dave's a press photographer," said Kirsty. "He goes all over the place."

Stan looked at her with interest. "That's good," he said. "Perfect, in fact. He could have written to Mara, but if she'd moved on somewhere she might not have got his letters, so the contact would be lost. He'd never know she'd died – never even know he had a daughter."

"Then he comes back to Britain," Abby said.

"And tries to get in touch with Mara?" asked Sue.

"I don't know." Stan was pushing his fingers through his hair. "He might think it was all in the past."

"But he's got to find Cat," said Fraser.

Sue was waving her hand excitedly, like she did in class when she had something to say. "I know,

I know! When she goes to Massa and doesn't come back, the papers start writing about it, and her dad gets sent to take pictures of her house, so he meets her uncle and aunt and they tell him Cat's his daughter."

Stan thumped himself on the forehead. "Of course." He thought fast. "They won't know who he is, though. And he won't know them; he'll just think it's some kid gone missing. But I can work round that, find a reason." He beamed. "Aren't you brilliant!"

Sue blushed.

"He'll have to meet Luma," said Fraser. "Then he can help him get into Massa."

Chokker forgot that nobody would want to talk to him. "And he can kill Winter," he said. *If Luma's going to stay in*. Did he really want him to?

"Well, OK," said Stan, "that could work." He was looking as excited as Sue. "So we'll be at the end of the book, at least in its first stage."

"What d'you mean, *first* stage?" asked Neil.

Stan shrugged. "Then I go back to the beginning and rewrite the whole thing, properly."

"What a lot of work," said Kirsty.

"Yes, but work can be fun if it's interesting," Stan said. "Like playing chess. You have to think hard, but you're doing it because you want to."

"I'm in the chess club at school," said Fraser.

"You'll know what I mean, then." Stan looked at

his watch. "It's time you lot went home. You've been a big help about Cat's dad," he added. "If you'd like to do some pictures of him, that would be great. And anything else you can think of."

"OK," said Neil.

Everyone started towards the door.

Stan looked at Chokker, who was the last to get up. "How's your finger?" he asked.

"All right." He stayed where he was, waiting for the others to be gone.

Sue was the last. She turned to wave, then shut the door behind her.

Stan looked at him, frowning. "This business about Luma," he said. "He's a great character, but to be honest, I don't quite understand him. I don't know what he's about. That's why I thought of dropping him."

Chokker didn't answer. He felt very odd, as if he'd gone to pick up something heavy and then found there was no weight to it at all.

"I can't get his background right," Stan went on. "I'm not happy about his parents dying in a caravan fire – it's too close to Cat's mum dying in a car crash. Parents are a nuisance in books because they stop their kids doing anything dangerous, but we can't go killing them off all over; it gets monotonous."

"Could be they just – went away."

"Would they do that? It sounds a bit unlikely."

That's all you know. "They might. If they were kind of no good."

"Criminals, d'you mean?"

Chokker thought about it. *Could have been.* "His mum was nice, but she had to do what his new dad wanted." *That was her excuse, anyway.*

"What about one of these home alone things?" Stan was getting interested. "There was a case in the papers about a kid who got sent home from the airport because his passport wasn't right. His parents gave him the key to the flat and put him in a taxi, then shoved off to Majorca for a fortnight. Can you believe that?"

Yes, he could believe it. *Only there wasn't any airport. They just went. Probably scared I'd die, all bashed up like that. Then they'd get put in prison.*

"What about Davey, though?" Stan went on. "How does he get to look after Luma?"

Chokker shrugged. *Rugs, car, hospital. Police. The home.* He pulled his mind away, trying to think about Davey, and found a sudden memory of being lifted up to pat a horse that was looking over a stable door. *Good smell of straw and horse; everything safe, warm.* "He had these horses," he said.

"Someone Luma knew since he was quite small, then."

"Yeah. But afterwards, he was with the Master. Learning how to fight." Chokker scowled. Stan didn't believe in the Master.

Stan thought about it. "This Master guy might adopt him, perhaps. Maybe he runs some kind of wacky community where kids end up when everything's gone wrong. Can you do the fight thing?" he added suddenly. "Kicks and all that?"

"Sort of. You have to know the patterns."

"That would be terrific for the book." Stan sounded really keen. "Can you write some of it down for me?"

Write it down? The thought filled Chokker with panic. "It's best to see it." Perhaps he might lend him the video.

"Could you show me a bit?" Stan asked. "Just for a couple of minutes. It's getting late – time you went home."

Chokker had never shown it to anyone, but he nodded. "I'll do the start." He stood up and closed his eyes, letting his breath settle. The voice spoke in his mind. *Head and spine in a straight line, shoulders relaxed, arms loose by the sides, knees straight but not locked. Breathe through the nose, tongue in the roof of the mouth. Take a minute to steady yourself.*

Chokker went into the familiar sequence. *Ready stance. On guard, hands in defence position. Crouch, parry, turn, throw. Step, kick, step again, punch, turn, elbow jab, left-foot kick, step, turn, second throw. Back to ready stance.*

"Wow," said Stan. "That's impressive. Is it Japanese?"

251

"Yes."

"Could you kill someone? Or is it purely self-defence?"

"The Master says you should disable your enemy if you can. But if it's your life or his, you may have to kill him." Chokker had never quite understood the next bit, but he repeated it all the same. "And if you do, you must beg his pardon, so you release his soul."

"The Tibetans do the same when they slaughter a yak," Stan said. "They ask the animal's forgiveness. That way, its soul is set free to become another yak, and the man is not burdened by the sin of killing. I like that idea."

Chokker wasn't sure if he liked it. He didn't want to forgive anyone; he just wanted to be strong.

There was a pause, then Stan asked, "What do you think about Luma? He's your character, really, not mine. You invented him. Shall we drop him, or keep him in? It's your choice."

Chokker knew what he was going to say, and it surprised him. He delayed his answer for a few moments, finding a sharp pleasure in being free to decide. Then: "Keep him in," he said.

🌿Fourteen

For a good few days after that, there was a notice on the summerhouse door that said: BUSY, SORRY. Then on the following Friday, Abby came into school waving a very bad drawing of a parrot, with "OK" coming out of its beak. "It's Stan's," she said. "It was there this morning."

Chokker was the first to get to the summerhouse after school, but the others weren't far behind.

"What have you written?" asked Sue. "Is it the fight yet?"

"Almost. I had to fill in some other bits first." Stan picked up the new sheets of printing. "This runs on from where Luma has seen Winter putting the frighteners on Magnus Chip. See what you think." Everyone settled down to listen.

Cat wandered through the offices and laboratories of Massa, past the desks and animal cages and stainless-steel benches. She saw how people did not raise their heads from their work, afraid even to glance at the person beside them – and saw too how Winter moved among them in one guise or another, as technician or manager or canteen worker, watching and noting, recognized by nobody.

Outside, the crowd at the gate had got larger. Some people had started camping there all night, in tents pitched on the grass between the ornamental rose beds. Tea was being brewed, and banners said in large, hand-done letters: LEAVE NATURE ALONE, and NO GM. Others asked stark questions: MURDER? WHERE IS CATHLEEN?

Drifting among them unseen, Cat could have told them where she was. What had been her body was part of the sky now, released in a waft of gentle smoke from the tall chimney that stood at one end of the Massa building. Nobody would ever know. Even if the people at the gate managed to get into the place and searched it from roof to basement, they would find no trace of her.

Cat was not greatly concerned. A question of her own occupied her attention, and it grew more urgent with every moment. She was sure that, quite soon, she was going to find her father.

He does not know you, Mara had warned. *He has never known. He went away before you were born.*

It wasn't much of an explanation, Cat thought. Perhaps Mara hadn't known the whole truth of it in life, and she was waiting for things to become clear. In a world where time was everlasting, there was no hurry.

When Cat mentioned it, her mother agreed. *When he comes here, it will all be understood,* she said, and sounded untroubled.

Moving restlessly from one group to the next, Cat could not share Mara's tranquillity. She prickled with excitement. The discovery was waiting to be made – and it was coming closer. Her lost father was here somewhere, among these hundreds of people. She was sure of it.

The feeling grew stronger as she moved towards the edge of the crowd.

And then she saw him.

Jim McQueen was standing by a car, looking through a digital camera at the scene around him. He wore a waterproof jacket with a lot of pockets, and his eyes were narrowed in a thoughtful frown. *Need a better angle,* he was thinking. *Something worth looking at. Human interest.* He shifted to get a shot of a woman fixing a flower to the closed gates of Massa, then moved closer to her. He took his notebook from a top pocket.

"*Daily Courier,*" he announced. "Could I have a word or two? What do you think about the missing girl? Any idea what's happened to her?"

"I reckon she's dead," the woman said. "She went in there, didn't she? We all know that. So what have they done with her? How come they say no one saw her? And what about those scientists?" she went on. "You can't tell me it was the bloke they arrested. He was in a terrible state, poor lad, I saw him on telly. Crying his eyes out, saying he never did it. He wasn't there. It was his lunch break; he was up in the canteen."

"The security cameras picked him up," Jim pointed out.

The woman wasn't convinced. "They picked *someone* up, but those video pictures are dead smudgy. Could have been anyone about that size."

Jim nodded. She was right, but he pressed her a bit further. "Why didn't his mates speak up for him? If he'd been in the canteen like he said, they must have seen him. But they all said they couldn't remember."

"Yes, and why couldn't they?" the woman demanded. "There must be some reason why they're keeping their mouths shut. Are they scared or what? There's no way that poor bloke's a murderer. Murderers don't cry. I saw that man on telly who'd killed his wife and kids, and he just looked horrible."

Murderers don't cry, Jim McQueen repeated to himself. *Good headline.* He wrote it down. "Thanks," he said. "Can I have your name?"

"Ann Watt. Am I going to be in the papers?"

"Could be. You never know." *Depends what other stuff they've got. They might use the photo, though.*

256

He made his way back to his car, started it up and bumped slowly over the grass, heading for the road. Next stop the aunt and uncle.

Yes, Cat said from where she leaned close to him, *go and see them. Please.* And Jim smiled with the sudden conviction that he was doing the right thing.

Cat inspected him carefully as he drove. His face was lean and hard, but his grey eyes were steady and his hands on the steering wheel looked capable.

You are my father, she thought, newly amazed at the discovery. *You made me, you and my mother.* And she felt a great warmth for him, despite the mystery of where he had been through all the years of her life.

Jim pulled up outside a suburban house and checked the number above the front door. Yes, this was the one. He took a photograph of it, then slipped the small camera into his pocket. He got out of the car and rang the bell.

The woman who peered through the chained slit of the door looked hostile. Jim decided not to risk a smile. "*Daily Courier.*" He showed his press pass and said sympathetically, "I'm sure you've had a lot to put up with in the last few days."

"So?"

She sounded forbidding, but he ploughed on. "I thought you might like a chance to put your own point of view. No interruptions, no slanted questions.

And anything we use will be paid for." *If all else fails, try bribery.*

"Oh," said Madge. "Well, that makes a change. You'd better come in." She closed the door to release the chain, then opened it wider.

"Thank you," said Jim.

Cat went in beside him as her aunt took the visitor into the front room.

"I take it you are Mrs Ingleby."

"Yes. My husband is out."

Jim gazed at her small eyes and the thin mouth with its over-bright lipstick. "You're very photogenic," he said, straight-faced.

"Oh." Madge touched her tightly permed hair and almost smiled. "You think so?"

"It's – remarkable," said Jim.

Cat giggled. It was nice to know her father had a sense of humour.

He was looking through his camera now. "May I take a couple of photos? As I said, we pay quite well for their use."

"Well, yes. Not that it's the money or anything."

"Of course not. Thank you."

Jim McQueen walked around the woman, looking for a decent angle. *She's got as much expression as a block of concrete,* he thought. He said aloud, "The missing girl is your daughter, right?" It didn't matter if he'd got it wrong – anything to get her talking, loosen her up a bit.

"Cathleen is my niece," Madge corrected. "The child of my adopted sister."

"Adopted?" Jim made a mental note. This was something new.

Adopted. Cat said it as well. She was astonished. So her mother wasn't actually Madge's sister. She'd come from a different family altogether. That meant Madge and Arthur were not Cat's true aunt and uncle. She had never belonged in this stuffy, sun-excluding house. She'd been free all along, and she'd never known it. The relief was tremendous, but so was the sense of time wasted.

"I was an only child," Madge was saying. "My parents seemed to think I needed company, so they imported this baby when I was six years old. I can't say I ever really liked her. Mara was such a *dramatic* child. I left school as soon as I could, and got a job with the gas board. That's where I met Arthur."

Mara, Jim thought as he circled round the woman, looking at her through the lens. *No, it can't be.* The name was uncommon, though, and an old memory stirred in his mind. *Mara of the dark hair and the sweet smile.* His first love. Lost and gone.

"This Mara," he said. "Did she work for the gas board as well?"

Madge snorted with contempt. "Not her. She persuaded my parents to send her to art school, of all the useless things."

259

Art school. Yes. A mad suspicion was growing in Jim's mind.

Madge was still talking. "She'd just about finished there when she got pregnant by some feckless man."

"And the baby was Cathleen?" Jim made himself sound calm. The name was a coincidence, that was all.

"Yes. She and the child lived a gypsy kind of life, moving from one place to another. And three years later she was killed in a car crash." Madge sighed. "It was Arthur's idea to take on Cathleen. We had no children of our own; I've always been delicate."

She looked about as delicate as a hippopotamus, Jim thought. He concentrated on the camera. Click, click. *Nice one with the stuffed trout in its glass case. Two old trouts together.* Part of his mind thought it was quite funny, but he was panicking as well. *Dear Lord, don't say lovely Mara is dead. No, it can't be the same girl. Mustn't be.*

"Arthur would have preferred a son, of course," Madge went on. "A boy might have been easier to discipline." She sighed again. "It all proved extremely tiresome. But I suppose a child of Mara's was bound to be tiresome. And now this."

I've got to know. I'm happy with May – she is my wise and beautiful wife – but I must find out what happened. Jim tried hard to sound casual as he asked the vital question. "What was Mara's surname?

Did she take your parents' name when they adopted her?"

Madge nodded. "Mitson," she said. "We were Madge and Mara Mitson. But I used to explain to people that she wasn't really my sister."

Mara Mitson. Jim's hands froze on the camera.

"And she called the child by its father's surname," Madge went on with immense disapproval. "Some man we hadn't even met. We gave Cathleen our own name of Ingleby, as you know. But when she came to us she was Cathleen McQueen."

After a stunned moment while his thoughts splintered, Jim managed to say, "Yes. Yes, I see."

A dark-haired, slender mother and her girl-child smiled at him. They were still there in his mind as he turned away to look out of the lace-curtained windows, beyond which was nothing but a privet hedge and the houses across the road. His throat was aching with tears.

"Oh, poor Jim," said Sue. "How awful for him."

Kevin was looking confused. "So is Jim Cat's dad?" he asked.

"Yes." Stan pushed his fingers through his hair. "Sorry if there's rather a lot to explain. I might put some of it in earlier. Have Mara tell Cat about it or something. I'll think about it."

"You haven't said what Jim was doing all that time," said Fraser. "Why he didn't know Cat had been born."

"I didn't want to clutter it up with explanations right there," said Stan. "I've given a clue, having Madge say Mara moved around a lot. The rest can go in later. She wrote to give him her first new address, but he was out in some jungle with a war going on, and never got the letter."

"OK," said Fraser.

"Jim's very nice, isn't he?" said Kirsty.

"A good sort, yes," Stan agreed. He glanced at Chokker. "If Luma is staying in the story, he needs someone with a bit of sense on his side."

"So what happens?" Chokker asked. "Have you done any more?"

"Next scene's the caravan." Stan picked up his pages again. "A bit drastic, but I had to loosen things up so Luma can start doing different stuff."

Chokker was all impatience. "Go on, then," he urged.

"Right."

Jim McQueen drove up the rutted track towards the caravan. His mind was still reeling from what Madge Ingleby had told him, and the car seemed strangely full of the presence of his lost daughter. *She can't have died in that place,* he thought. *She's around somewhere – she must be. She escaped. I've got to find her.*

The smell of smoke cut into his thoughts. For a moment he wondered if something was wrong with his car's engine, then he saw the spark-filled greyness that billowed over the hedge ahead of him. Fire was raging in the junkyard that surrounded Davey Gowan's caravan. Jim drove past then swerved the car into a lay-by, grabbed the fire extinguisher from its clip behind the driving seat and ran back.

A boy was directing a hose at the inferno, but the thin jet of water hissed into steam and made little difference. Jim ripped the top off the extinguisher to start it, and moved in beside the boy.

"Go and phone," he shouted. "I'll stick with this."

"Already have," said the boy. His face was streaked with black and his eyes were red-rimmed from the smoke.

A siren sounded from down the track, and a fire engine screamed to a halt behind Jim's car, men jumping off it as it was still moving. They ran their hoses out fast, but the flames had already reached the caravan, and it was burning like a torch. In a few minutes of frantic activity it was saturated with water and steam mingled with the acrid smoke.

"Mind," said a fireman, rolling out another hose past Jim.

"Sorry." He stepped out of the way, tossing the

empty extinguisher towards the gate. He felt in his pocket for his camera and took shot after shot of the firemen and the grimy boy who stood looking at the smoking wreckage with the useless garden hose in his hands.

"What's your name?" Jim asked him when he'd done enough.

"Luma Gowan. Well, Lewis, really. Cat's friend."

"Cat. You mean – Cathleen? The girl who went to Massa?" Jim had to confirm it, though there was a weird sense of inevitability about what was happening. It was like riding a surfboard on big Australian breakers. Once on that wave, you were held by it, carried along. All you had to do was trust it. And keep your balance.

"Yes." Luma was staring at him with interest, as if he already knew who he was.

Jim stared back. This boy, Lewis or Luma, would know all sorts of things about Cat. He'd know what sort of things she liked, what she chose to wear, what she said, what she looked like. All Jim knew of his lost daughter was the photo that had appeared on TV, an out-of-focus shot taken some years ago, showing her in a primary school group. Madge and her husband had evidently never bothered to get a decent photo of their adopted daughter. The school shot had given Jim a vague impression of dark hair – like Mara's, now he came to think of it – and blue eyes. His own eyes were blue. He tried desperately to recall more details. She'd had a snub nose and determined mouth, hadn't she, just like the face that looked at him every morning from the mirror. Or was he kidding himself because he so much wanted her to look like him? He returned his attention to the boy, who stood silently watching him.

"Tough for you," he said, "your friend going missing." He could not accept yet that it might be something worse. "And now this." He waved at the devastation that surrounded them.

Half the caravan was still standing, but it was charred and smoking.

"Davey doesn't know yet," Luma said. "He's away at a horse fair."

"Is Davey your dad?"

"Sort of."

"And what now? This is your home, right?"

"Was."

"That's what I mean. Have you anywhere to go?"

The boy shook his head. He rubbed the back of a dirty wrist across his forehead. A police car was coming up the track, with its blue light flashing.

The police had no qualms about asking questions.

"How did this start? Any idea?"

"Were you here?"

"What did you see?"

Luma's face tightened. "Could have been the electrics," he said. "The wiring was a bit grotty."

265

He would not tell them about finding the crazy animal playing in the fire that raged like a furnace in the lorry container. Staring away from the policemen, he saw again how the dog picked up a burning bar from the hurdles that had penned it and went rushing through the stacked and untidy stuff in Davey's scrapyard. Flames leaped up behind it, catching at an overturned roll of roofing felt and licking up from the open door of the shed when it burst into there. Luma had tried his best to stop it, but the dog was like a fast-moving incendiary bomb, setting stuff alight wherever it went. Bottles of turps and paint stripper fell and smashed, and a drum of diesel toppled and started to leak. There had been a whoosh like a soft explosion, and the fire burst into larger life. In another few seconds it was everywhere.

He pulled his mind back. The questions were going on, about exactly what was stored in the shed and why it was there and what Davey did with it. "I don't know," he said, suddenly weary of the whole thing. "You'll have to ask him."

A fireman came out of the gutted remains of the caravan and walked across to them.

"I'm afraid your dog's had it, son," he told Luma. "Sorry about that."

Luma nodded. He felt very relieved. He'd been worried that the fire-raising beast might emerge again at any moment, in front of the police.

"He's not burnt," the fireman went on. "Not a mark on him. Odd, that. Could have been the shock of the cold water."

Luma nodded. He knew Cat was beside him. *I must bury the dog, before anyone finds out,* he said to her, but she smiled.

You won't have to, she told him. *But do it anyway.*

He didn't understand what she meant, but there was no time to ask. The policemen were going on with their questions. Where were Luma's parents? How long had he been with Davey? Did he have relatives he could stay with? Was a social worker involved? Who would look after him?

"If I can help at all," Jim said, "I'd be very willing. My wife is at home; we've rented a flat in the village, over the baker's. It's not far away."

"That's a very kind offer, sir," said the senior policeman. "Perhaps you could look after the boy for an hour or two, while we contact Mr Gowan. I'll check with social services."

He turned away to speak into his radio.

Luma murmured quietly to Jim, "I have to bury the dog."

"Won't it do later?"

"No."

You must help him, Cat urged her father. *Go and look at the dog. Please, it's important.*

Jim didn't get the words, but he had a strong feeling that Luma's request was urgent. "OK," he said. If it was going to make the kid feel better, that was fine by him.

There was something strange about this dog, he thought as he looked at the saturated body on the caravan floor. Its wet fur was hard and matted, and it was steaming although it had been lying in a lake of cold water. He touched the animal and found it was very hot. He glanced at Luma and raised his eyebrows.

"Tell you later," the boy said quietly.

Jim nodded. "OK if I take some pictures?"

Yes, Cat urged. *You are going to need them.*

Luma knew she was right. "That would be good," he said.

Jim circled round, focusing each shot carefully. He wanted one of the boy holding the dog, to show the size of it. He asked, "Could you pick him up?" It might be something the kid wouldn't want to do, but Luma didn't seem to mind.

He stooped, then drew his hand back because of the heat. "I'll need something to hold him with," he said.

A water-sodden towel was hanging by the caravan's sink, and they cushioned the dog on that. The steam from it rose around the boy's face as he stood holding it. Jim took more photos, then slipped the small camera back in his pocket. "OK," he said. "Let's find a spade."

A policeman intercepted them as they came out

of the caravan. He looked at the dog. "What are you doing with that?" he asked.

"We're going to bury him," said Luma.

The man shook his head. "Oh, no, you're not, son. Not till the incident report's complete."

The heat from the wet bundle was getting through to Luma's arms. He knew he couldn't hold it much longer.

The policeman knew it too. "Put it down," he ordered. "Before you get burnt."

Luma laid the wrapped dog on the grass, and stepped back from it.

"Was it yours?" the policeman asked.

"No."

"Mr Gowan's?"

"No."

"Whose was it, then?"

"I don't know." Luma didn't want to get Pat and Terry into trouble. "There's a lot of people come here, buying and selling stuff." He knew he sounded a bit half-witted, but it didn't matter.

Don't worry, Cat told him. *This is all right.*

The policeman turned to Jim. "Do you have a car here, sir?"

"Yes." Jim nodded at where it was parked. There were several more police cars there now.

"An officer will follow you, if that's all right. You can leave the dog to us."

"What will you do with it?" Jim asked.

"There's a procedure," said the man. "Now, if you don't mind…"

"OK."

Something very weird was going on, Jim thought as he and Luma followed the policeman into the lane. He touched the camera safely hidden in his pocket. Somehow he was glad the police had not seen him taking photos of the dog.

Jim's wife was Chinese, and her name was May. She wore jeans and a black sweater, and smiled when she saw Luma. "Hi," she said. "Jim phoned me, said you'd be coming. Are you hungry? I've done fried chicken."

"Great," said Luma.

He sat by the window with a glass of orange juice while Jim and May had a private conversation in the kitchen. He knew what it would be about. Even before Jim had turned up at the fire, Cat had been full of excitement about the finding of her lost father. Jim hadn't mentioned it to Luma. Coming here in the car, with a police car behind them, the conversation had been all about the dogs and Massa. And May knew nothing about that either. He'd have a lot to tell her.

Outside, the sea lay beyond the roofs of the shops, calm and tranquil today. Seen from up here, the horizon looked higher than it did when you were on the road. Everything was the same, yet it was different. Things felt strange, as if every tiny event was weirdly important, though Luma didn't know in what way.

They ate at the table by the window. May served the chicken with noodles and a spicy yellowish sauce, and it was very good. Jim repeated to his wife what Luma had told him in the car about the dog whose scorching breath had burnt Cat's legs, and about the vet and what she had told them about Massa. May listened carefully, frowning with concentration. Her eyes were full of concern.

Luma felt worried. *What's going to happen?* he asked Cat, who was still beside him.

Lots of things, she said. She still sounded excited.

He wasn't sure what she meant. *But will it be all right?*

Oh, yes.

They'd only just finished eating when the police came back, together with Davey and, to Luma's dismay, Mrs Pimm. She put a bulging file down on the table, retrieved her chained glasses from where they hung on her chest and stared at him through them.

"We meet again," she said.

It wasn't a question, so Luma didn't answer.

To his relief, she concentrated on Jim, firing questions at him. How long he had been back from abroad? Five months. Was he here permanently?

Yes, probably. Did he have a regular job? Freelance, but doing a lot for the *Daily Courier*. Married? Yes. Children? No. Police record? No.

She wrote all the replies down. Then she turned to Davey.

"And what are your plans, Mr Gowan?"

Davey shrugged. "I can doss down at Pat and Terry's. Dare say they've room for the boy and all."

Mrs Pimm wasn't having that. "I'll make arrangements for Lewis to go to a residential home," she said, "while we check the other possibilities."

"No!" Luma was on his feet. "You can't make me; I won't! I'll run away!"

Mrs Pimm glanced at one of the policemen, who moved quietly to the door and stood with his back against it.

Cat rushed to her father. *Don't let them,* she said. *Luma's got to be with us. There are things to do.*

Jim was already protesting. "Don't force the boy to do something against his will. He doesn't have to go to a home. He can stay here."

"Of course he can," May agreed. She glanced at Luma. "Would that be OK?"

"It would be great," said Luma. And everyone looked at Mrs Pimm.

She clicked the top of her retractable pen a couple of times and frowned. Then she said, "Well, just for tonight. You'll understand that we have to be careful."

"Of course," Jim and May agreed. They both spoke together, which sounded funny, but nobody smiled.

Luma wondered if Davey would mind him going off with other people. "Is that all right?" he asked him.

Davey's shrewd eyes met his with understanding. "You do what you want, Lew," he said. "You're big enough."

It sounded careless, but Luma knew it wasn't. In his odd way, Davey would always be there if he needed him.

"Thank you," he said.

That evening Cat said, *Please, Luma, tell my dad what happened. I'd do it myself if I could, but I'm not in his world any more. Tell him about Massa. Make him see I'm all right. Please.*

He could not refuse her, but he wondered if she knew what a hard thing she was asking. He'd never talked to anyone about the other world of his dreams, not even Davey, who kind of understood it.

Dreams are private, Luma said.

I know, agreed Cat. *I'm sorry. But I need you.*

Yes.

Part of his mind envied her. The events of her life had gone terribly wrong and she would never have any new experiences in the real world, but at least she knew she was loved. Each in their own state, her parents cared deeply about her. Luma himself had only a wisp of sweet early memory to grasp at, something about his mother carrying him through some place that he liked. Holding him up to pat a horse. He didn't want to think about any of the things that had happened later. And he had no idea what he would say to the two people who were his mother and father, should he meet them at some point in this world or the next. He could not think about them calmly. They were best left behind.

The evening dragged slowly on. He watched the TV unseeingly while Jim and May talked quietly to each other. Cat waited in silence. A programme ended, and Jim looked at Luma. "You all right?" he asked.

Luma nodded. As if it was someone else's voice, he heard himself say, "I've got to tell you about Cat."

Jim touched the remote, and the screen blanked. "Go on," he said.

"It's going to sound stupid."

"Never mind."

He couldn't start.

Jim prompted him gently. "Tell me about Massa. Do you know what actually happened there?"

"Yes."

He went through the story, starting with the burns on Cat's legs, then the visit to the vet and the plan to get into Massa. Then he said what happened to Cat when she went there alone, and Jim's face darkened with grief and anger. May took her husband's hand in her own slim one, and Jim gripped it tightly as he stared at Luma. "You're sure?" he said at the end. "That's – the way it was?"

Luma nodded. "I'm really sorry." He wished he was grown up, so he'd know what to say. "But Cat's all right," he added. "She's here. And Mara too."

This was true. Mara's presence was strong in the room. She was very calm, Luma thought. There was a lot to explain and to catch up with, but she had all the time in the world. And one day Jim would have it as well.

Jim was frowning. Luma could see he was finding the thing hard to believe. Then he said, "I love the thought that they're all right. I want to believe that, because it would be such a comfort. But – can you tell me how you're so sure?"

This was the question Luma had dreaded. He plunged in again, hoping his words made sense. "It's kind of dreaming, only not really. It might be because I nearly died when I was small. I think Davey kind of knows about it – his mother was like that. She could see things."

May nodded as though this made perfect sense. "There is spirit life as well as physical life," she said.

There was a long moment of not uncomfortable silence while the three of them thought about it. Then Jim looked at Luma and took a deep breath. "I can't thank you enough for all this," he said. "But we've things to do, haven't we?"

"Yes," said Luma.

Jim reached for a notebook. "Who do we have to see? Your vet girl, to start with. And the Jordans. What about people at Massa?"

Luma shrugged. He had a confused impression of men at a meeting, but there was nothing clear.

Eddie Molotov, Cat said.

Luma repeated the name experimentally, and Jim wrote it down. "Molotov. Spelled with a *v*?"

"I don't know," said Luma.

Jim looked at the name, frowning. "Could be tricky, finding him. But never mind, it's something to go on. What else is there?"

Cat was full of suggestions.

There were people in Massa who saw me. Someone in a corridor. A man in a laboratory, and the men in gas masks at the dog pens. And there's a woman who knows a hat and overall went missing, with a swipe card in the pocket. I've been watching her. She thinks she ought to tell the police, but she's scared.

Luma passed it all on, and Jim listened carefully. "We can't identify the Massa people," he said. "Maybe they're your department – yours and Cat's. You can dream your way into the place, and I can't. Do be careful, though," he added. "I don't know how this world of yours works, but it sounds scary stuff to me. They've obviously got some very powerful software. It may even have an input into the human brain. Don't take risks. Don't try to be too brave."

"Course not."

But Luma was not as light-hearted as he sounded. Someone had to be brave. And it probably had to be him.

Fifteen

Everyone started talking at once.

"Is Luma going to stay with Jim?"

"What are they going to do about Massa?"

"Will they get in there?"

"Hang on," Stan protested. "This is your book as well as mine; I don't have to come up with all the ideas. What about you lot?"

"But it's difficult," said Kirsty.

Stan shrugged. "It's difficult for me too. I've been working like a horse in the last few weeks, and what have you been doing? Sitting back and enjoying the story."

"We've done all these pictures of Jim," Mandy reminded him.

Sue added, "And at school we've been writing poems about nature."

"Very nice," said Stan. "But I'm talking about work for our book."

"So am I," said Sue. "Mrs Long read the bits we took to school. You gave Abby some, then Chokker.

She thought they were great. She said it makes you think about what people are doing to the natural world. That's why we did the poems."

"Oh, I see," said Stan.

"And we've been doing it in art," said Ian.

"Mrs Long wants us to have an event," put in Abby. Secretly she found the idea rather alarming.

"A what?"

"Like readings and some music and stuff," Fraser explained. "I said I'd play my saxophone. And you can explain about the book."

Kirsty joined in. "All our mums and dads will come. Lots of them were asking about it at the parents' evening last week. They want to know what we're doing."

"Heavens," exclaimed Stan. "Well, I suppose we could." Then he added, "There's good news about the book, by the way. My publisher says she definitely wants to do it. I sent her the first chapter and a sketchy sort of plan, and she's really keen."

"You mean it's going to be in the shops and everything?" Kirsty asked.

"That's right."

"Oh, brilliant!" She clapped her hands. "Wait till I tell my mum – she'll be thrilled!"

"Will we all get lots of money?" asked Kevin.

"I doubt it," said Stan. "They'll give me what's called an advance, so I've something to live on while I'm writing it, but the book itself has to earn that amount before I get any more. If it turns into a bestseller, you'll be in for a share," he added. "But don't hold your breath."

"When does it have to be finished?" asked Abby.

"Next summer. And it's November now."

"That's *ages*," said Mandy.

"It's not ages at all," Stan said. "There's a huge amount to do." He glanced at his watch. "Can't talk about it now; you've been here long enough already. And I'm all tied up tomorrow – my daughter's coming, with her new boyfriend. We've never met him, so I guess I need to be there. Tell you what – I'll print out all the stuff we've written so far, the whole lot of it. You can have it in the morning. Read it through this weekend if you've time: it'll help refresh your minds. Then think about the ending. I will too, because I still don't know what's going to happen."

"Can we show it to Mrs Long?" asked Mandy.

Stan hesitated. "Well, all right, since she's seen some of it. Nobody else, though, or it'll turn into a committee. I can't bear committees – they wreck everything."

"Why do they?" asked Fraser.

"They're full of people who talk. Quite often they don't know what they're talking about, so things that were simple get in a mess. If you want to change anything in the pages we've done, feel free," Stan went on. "Use a pencil, so we can rub it out if we need to change it again. Ballpoint's hopeless."

Mandy said, "Do we have to write the end bit?"

"No, just bung down some ideas. Remember, nobody knows how Winter works. He's going to be our big problem."

"Luma knows," said Chokker.

"That's right," Stan agreed. "He's the only living person who does, though Eddie Molotov might have his suspicions. Now Luma's staying in the book, we have to make him central to the whole thing. I guess I've been thinking about it in my sleep. Stasi says I sat up in bed the other night and said, *Not the circus*. She thought I'd gone bats."

"Was that about Luma?" asked Abby.

"Yes. Two caravan fires in one book isn't on," Stan explained. "Now Davey's van has gone up in flames, we can't use the same thing in Luma's background. We still need the stuff about him nearly dying when he was small, to explain why he's got one foot in the other world. But the circus stuff is out, I think."

"The bit you read out said his parents were alive, but not around," said Fraser.

"Yes. Chokker suggested they might have gone away." Stan didn't look at Chokker.

"It sounded like his dad beat him up," said Kevin.

Stan shrugged. "Nothing's fixed. Whatever we settle on, it'll be something you're all happy with.

Now, go home and get your tea, for goodness' sake. I'll do those pages for you when I've had mine."

"I won't be here to read it," said Sue, making a face. "We're going to my gran's."

"Doesn't matter," said Stan, shooing them out. "Any time will do. Go on, out. You can come for the stuff about ten tomorrow morning. If anyone turns up here before that, I'll bite their heads off."

They laughed, and went.

"Can I use the computer?" Chokker asked that evening.

Gerald was watching television. "What for?"

"I need to write something."

"Oh. Yes, sure, that's fine."

"Thanks."

Chokker went into the other room and switched the machine on. He thought for some minutes, then started to type slowly.

Luma got a new dad. His mum was all write but she let the new dad do what he wanted. he hit Luma and he got broken bones. They didn't want any one to no. So they went of. Luma was alone he cried but the people up stares were out it was a long time then he herd banging and the door got broken down. the police came.

Luma was in hospital he nearly dyed. he went to the place where Mara was then he got better so he came back his mum didn't come back they didn't ever find her or the new dad.

he new Davie. when he was small his mum said lets go see the horses they went lots of times before the new dad came. Davie was grate. he let Luma ride on the horses he held him so he didn't fall. In hospital Luma was shouting Davie Davie. they didn't no Davie but the police went and got him and then Luma was better.

they took him to a home but he wanted to be with Davie so he ran away.

the police came. Davie went to caught and the judges herd watt Davie said. They decided Luma cud stay in his caravan he worked with the horses he didn't like school he went away to be with the Master in japan.

he new about fighting he got very good. In the end he was a master to.

The end.

C. Bailey.

Chokker scrolled back and read what he had written. It was pretty good, he thought. Picking the right words out of the spell-check box when the red line came up took a bit of time, but it was worth it. Stan would understand a bit more about Luma now. He clicked on *print*.

Stan never normally worked in the evening, but after he and Stasi had eaten their meal, he took a cup of coffee up to the summerhouse and printed out the promised chapters. He read them through, thinking about his conversation with the children. He began to put some notes down about the next bit, then got interested.

The next day, Jim and Luma went to see the vet. Cat was with them. As Luma expected, Angie McIver wasn't there. Mr Morris was walking stiffly and seemed in a bad temper.

"I am not responsible for anything a locum may say in my absence," he snapped when Jim asked his opinion about Massa and the dogs.

Further questions were useless.

"I have nothing to say, least of all to a member of the press. Now, if you don't mind, I'm very busy."

The nurse, Isabel, came out with them to call the next animal owner in.

You remember me, Cat said to her, and the woman paused.

"Is there any news of your friend?" she asked Luma.

He shook his head. "We wanted to see Angie."

Isabel glanced over her shoulder at the closed door of the surgery. "Phone the veterinary college," she said quietly. "Number's in the book. They'll give you her address. But please don't mention me."

"OK," said Jim. "And thanks a lot."

Mrs Jordan asked them in for a cup of tea.

"My husband's outside with his pigeons," she said, putting a plate of biscuits on the table. "Blooming things. I miss the dog. She was company."

"And the puppies," Jim said.

Mrs Jordan shook her head. "I never meant her to have puppies, but she got out. Milk?"

"Yes, please."

"Help yourselves to sugar."

"So you don't know who their father was?" Jim asked.

"No idea. I don't think it matters. Beauty picked up something from that pigeon food, I reckon. Or from the men who delivered it." She sat back and sighed. "Look, I'm sorry about your caravan, son," she said. "It wasn't Pat's fault. I was that upset about the dog, he offered to keep a pup for me. I shouldn't have let him do it. I might have known." She shook her head. "That blasted place."

"Massa, you mean?" asked Jim.

"Where else? My husband won't hear a word against it, but if I had my way, they'd close it down. When I think of that poor girl – and those scientists dying as well. There's something really bad going on there."

Luma nodded. Cat said in his ear, *Ask her about Eddie Molotov.* Jim seemed to pick up the idea without any prompting. He flipped open his notebook. "You haven't heard of a Mr Molotov, by any chance? Eddie Molotov? Works at Massa?"

"Oh, I know him," said Mrs Jordan. "He lives out near my daughter. She used to babysit for them. Hasn't done it lately, though."

"Why not?" asked Jim.

"She says he's changed. He was always such a lively man, a great one for a joke. But the way he walks about now, never smiling, he looks more like a machine."

Of course he does, Cat said, and Luma nodded again.

Mrs Jordan glanced at him and asked, "Do you know him, then?"

"No," he said quickly. He could not tell this woman what he had seen in his dream.

Jim said, "Perhaps we could talk to Mr Molotov."

"He doesn't talk to anyone," said Mrs Jordan. "Gets out of his car and goes into the house like he was programmed, my daughter says. If she sees him and says hello, he says hello back, but he doesn't even look at her. And that's not like him. Not like him at all."

Luma thought of the isotope in the Massa canteen food and in its water dispensers.

"Do you have his address?" asked Jim.

"Hawthorn Gardens," said Mrs Jordan. "I think it's number fourteen. That's in Primwell. But I don't think he'll see you."

I'll talk to him, Cat promised. *He can't keep me out.* Luma was careful not to nod this time.

"More tea?" asked Mrs Jordan. But she saw they were getting to their feet. "Well, it's been nice talking to you."

She came out to see them off. Luma looked back as they drove away, and she was still standing at the gate. She looked very lonely.

The veterinary college promised to ask Angie McIver to phone Jim, and she called him that evening.

He explained who he was and asked if she remembered a boy and a girl who came to see her about Mrs Jordan's dog.

"Heavens, yes," she said. "Those dreadful burns. Is she better now?"

"You don't understand," said Jim. "She's the girl who went missing. The Massa girl. I'm – I'm her father."

"Oh, no! I didn't know her name, so I – oh, how awful. I'm so sorry."

"I want to get an interview with Massa," Jim went on. "Ostensibly to do an article about their work. I don't know if they'll talk, but in case they do, will you come with me? Some expert knowledge might be extremely useful."

Angie did not hesitate. "Yes," she said. "Gladly."

"There may be some risks," Jim warned her. "They're a very tough bunch."

"I know that." Her voice was steady. "But playing with mutations could change animal life completely. If it gets out of hand – and it's not far off that now, I suspect – then vets will be helpless. They won't have the power to make a stand, and they'll be sucked into the Massa system because that'll be the only way to make any money. I'm only new in the profession, but I can't stand by and watch. I've got to do something."

"Good for you," said Jim, smiling into his phone. "I'll be back in touch."

Now for Massa, he thought.

It was surprisingly easy to get an interview.

"Mr Chip will see you tomorrow," a secretary told him. "Three o'clock."

"Thank you. I would like to bring a vet with me," Jim said, "in case there are points I don't understand – is that all right? And a lad who knew the missing girl."

He was put on hold while the woman enquired further, then she came back and said, "Yes, Mr McQueen. Three o'clock." She sounded very mechanical.

It was weird, Luma thought, walking into this place in real life. It was exactly as it had been in his dreams, except that it had a smell about it. Coffee, and air-conditioned air that carried a faint reek of perfume. They were escorted up in the lift, and he expected to find himself in the big room with the glass roof. Instead they got out at the floor below it, and waited on a leather sofa outside Magnus Chip's office.

Winter's in there with him, Cat said quietly to Luma. *Telling him what he has to say. Chip doesn't know who he is, because Winter looks like a smart woman. Chip's nodding. He's thinking, Yes, I know, I've done it often enough. Don't need this woman to tell me. Winter knows what he's thinking, and he's not pleased.*

A few minutes later the door opened and a silver-haired woman in a navy suit came out with an armful of files. There was no need for Cat to say anything – a shiver ran over Luma's skin at the sight of her.

"This is Magnus Chip," the woman said, indicating the man who followed her. "Our director of planning. He will answer any questions." Then she got into the lift and its doors closed. It went, Luma noticed, upwards.

"Good to see you." Magnus shook hands with Jim and Angie, then turned to Luma. "And who's this young man?"

"Lewis Gowan," said Jim. "A friend of the girl who disappeared."

"Right." Luma's hand was shaken as well.

"Come in, come in." Magnus ushered them into his office, indicating comfortable armchairs. "Coffee?"

"No, thank you." They had agreed not to eat or drink anything they were offered at Massa. Just in case.

"Well, then – how can I help you?"

Jim produced a small tape recorder. "OK if I use this?"

"Sure, sure. Fire away."

"What's your feeling about the missing girl? Do you accept that she came here?"

"Not a chance," Magnus said. "You can see for yourself that there are security cameras all over this place. You really think some strange girl could walk in here without being spotted at once? I know the police have got fingerprints or some damn thing from that lorry," he went on, "but they can't prove it. Who's to say she didn't get in there some other time? Could have been playing a game or something – you know what kids are like."

"She didn't," Luma said. "I know she didn't."

Magnus ignored him. "I'm telling you, she was never here. Totally impossible."

Angie took over. "What about these dogs?" she asked. "I saw the girl a few days before she came here – if she did – and she had severe burns on her legs. She insisted they'd been caused by the breath of a dog owned by a Mrs Jordan."

Magnus waved a dismissive hand. "Yeah, yeah, there's been a lot of crazy talk about this. Fact is, we're working on a vaccine that'll deal with an imported disease that's killing a lot of dogs."

"What disease?" asked Angie.

"We haven't identified it yet. That's why it's a tough problem."

Angie wasn't satisfied. "If there's something new around, why isn't the veterinary college aware of it? Why have there been no reports in the professional journals? Do the ministry people know?"

"Of course they know," said Magnus. "We work very closely with those guys. How long have you been in practice?"

"I qualified last summer."

"So you're the new kid on the block." He smiled condescendingly. "The point is, honey, we don't want to cause public alarm."

"But there *is* alarm," said Angie. "You have about three hundred people in front of this building, and they are alarmed. And don't call me honey," she added.

Magnus ignored this. "All registered veterinarians in this area are cooperating. We're getting this thing licked."

"In *this* area." Jim picked up his words. "You mean the outbreak is a local one? It centres around Massa?"

"Massa has nothing to do with it." Magnus was becoming irritated. "As a leading research establishment, we're anxious to help, that's all. As soon as we know the nature of this thing and develop a safe vaccine, we'll put it on the market, and that'll be that. Meanwhile, we just have to eradicate it by more traditional methods."

"Like killing everything you can find," said Angie.

"Whatever."

"Animals with this disease apparently develop very high temperatures," Jim put in. "Do you know the reason for this?"

"Animals get sick, they get a fever," said Magnus. "What's odd about that?"

"We're talking more than fever, aren't we?" said Jim. He felt in his inside pocket for the envelope containing the photos he had taken in the caravan. "I think there's some mutation going on. This dog's fur was stiff and spiky, not normal at all. And it was hot enough to burn you, even though it was dead and soaked in cold water."

For a moment Magnus's smile slipped. He leaned forward, hand extended for the photos. He studied them carefully, then looked up. "Where did you get these?"

"I took them yesterday," said Jim. "In the caravan where Luma here was living. It had just burnt down."

"And what was this dog doing there?"

"Some misguided people had kept it."

Magnus lost his temper. "How in hell are we to keep tracks of this thing if folks don't do as they're told? Any animal that gets this thing should be sent to us, right away. Whose was this dog?"

"I can't tell you," said Jim.

"Oh, no? Well, where is it now?"

"The police took it," said Luma.

Magnus rounded on him angrily. "That's garbage. The police have been told what to do. We've not been notified of a new case."

"Perhaps the police are investigating it themselves," Angie said smoothly.

"And what's that supposed to mean?" Magnus glared at her. He stood up and put the photos on his desk. "These are staying here until I can get them checked out."

"Too late," said Jim. "I posted them on my website yesterday."

Magnus's eyes bulged. He took a deep breath – and at that moment, the door opened and the silver-haired woman came in. "Excuse me." She walked across and put her finger on the button of the tape recorder. "I'm sorry to interrupt, but you are wanted upstairs, Mr Chip. I understand it's urgent."

"I'll be right there," said Magnus. "Sorry, folks – interview concluded."

Jim retrieved his tape recorder and the photos, and the woman stood back to allow them access to the lift. She still clutched her armful of files.

On the smooth descent to the ground floor, nobody spoke. The small monitor screen mounted above them in the lift's corner watched them with an unblinking eye.

Cat said silently to Luma, *There's a woman at the tea trolley downstairs. Talk to her. She runs the laundry department. She knows I took a hat and overall from there.*

Luma touched Jim's hand, and got a quick glance of enquiry. As the lift slowed, Luma let his eyes slide sideways to the unknown event that was waiting to happen outside.

Jim understood. "Whatever," he said, echoing Magnus Chip's senseless word. And the doors opened.

The tea trolley was there, as Cat had said. A girl was dispensing drinks in plastic beakers, and a stout woman with red hair had just picked one up and was sipping from it. The name badge on her overall said: LORETTA TEBBITT.

Go on, go on, Cat was urging Luma. *Speak to her.*

He wished he could explain to Jim and Angie, but with the monitor screens everywhere, he didn't dare.

He tried to look natural. "Oh, hi," he said to the red-haired woman. "I've a friend who says she knows you."

"Go on?" said the woman. "Who's that, then?"

"You wouldn't know her name. She came here a week or two ago." He was talking fast in case he was stopped. "She got in through the laundry room; she took one of the overalls and a white hat. It was a bit big for her."

Loretta Tebbitt gasped. The tea she was holding jerked in her hand and spilled. "What happened?" she whispered. "The things never came back. I put in a missing report, but it wasn't—"

Alarms screamed out. Bells started ringing all over the building. Doors were flung open and uniformed guards arrived at a run. They hustled Luma, Angie and Jim into the vestibule, where more guards pinned them against the wall.

"Excuse me," Angie said with amazing coolness, "but we are bona fide visitors to this place. We have our badges, issued at the entry desk."

The guards stared at them, stony-faced, and did not answer. Then they parted to let an elderly, slightly stooped man make his way between them.

He took a remote control from the top pocket of his grey suit and touched a button, silencing the alarms. In the sudden quietness he said, "I must inform you that we do not allow the unauthorized questioning of our staff."

"But we didn't ask any questions," said Angie. "It was just that Luma thought he knew this lady."

She lives near Terry and Pat, said Cat in Luma's ear.

He used the information at once. "She lives near where I do. I just kind of said hello."

"You said rather more than that," the elderly man

remarked. His eyes looked paler than when Luma had first seen him, a faint, icy blue. "If I am not mistaken, you mentioned a girl. You made certain allegations."

"I just … said she came here."

The man's eyes were almost white now. "And borrowed certain items from the laundry room?"

"Yes."

"How can you possibly know that?"

"I…" Luma swallowed hard. "I dreamed it."

There was a long silence. The man's eyes shifted to the colour of dry stone, and the muscles around his mouth produced a short-lived smile. "Did you, indeed," he said. "How very interesting." He turned to the guards. "Dismiss."

The men left.

"May I know your name?" Jim asked the man.

"Cornelius Winter. I am on the administration staff." And then, to Luma's astonishment, he led them to the front entrance, relieved them of their visitor badges and tapped in the exit code. He did not offer to shake hands, but as the doors opened he gave a slight bow. "We at Massa are reasonable people," he said. "Goodbye, Miss McIver. Mr McQueen."

As Luma passed him, Winter's icy, green-grey eyes rested on him thoughtfully. "Goodbye, Lewis Gowan," he said. "Until we meet again."

Nobody spoke until they were safely in the car and heading back towards Jim's flat.

Angie broke the silence. Very quietly, she asked Luma, "How did you know about the woman?"

Luma put his hand to his head. Now he had to go through the story all over again.

Jim saved him. "Believe it or not, he has second sight."

Angie thought about it for a moment. Then she said, "Well, whatever it was, it certainly worked." She and Jim exchanged a glance, then Jim returned his attention to the road, and they drove on in silence.

🌿 Sixteen

Stan leaned back in his chair and stretched his arms above his head. *I don't work at night,* he thought. *This is madness; I'll be wrecked tomorrow.*

But tomorrow Anna was coming, so it would not be a work day. And since his head was unusually clear about the book, he might as well do a bit more. The kids would like some new stuff to read.

There was silence in the car for a few moments, then Angie said, "Loretta Tebbitt. At least we know her name."

"Handy of them to label their staff," Jim agreed. "I think we should go straight to the police with this."

"Too right," said Angie. "We've got a bit of real evidence at last."

But we haven't, Luma thought. *It all depends on Cat.*

Jim glanced over his shoulder at Luma in the back seat. "The only thing is," he said, "we may have to come clean about – you know. The way you communicate with Cat."

"Yes," said Luma.

"You don't mind?"

Luma did mind, of course, quite a lot. All his life this had been a secret. Even Davey, who kind of understood, had never expected him to talk about it. But if he backed out now, Jim would think he'd been kidding about the whole thing. Or else that he was off his head. "No, it's all right," he said.

The policeman was Sergeant Muir, the same man who had taken charge of the dog after the caravan fire. He asked all the obvious questions, and soon came to the important one.

"How did you know this woman?"

"She lives near Pat and Terry," said Luma. "Cat knew her."

"So you were already acquainted with Loretta Tebbitt."

"I don't think she knew who I was." He didn't want to tell a direct lie, but neither could he admit that he'd never met her.

The small office was very hot. Sergeant Muir sat back in his chair behind the desk, tapping his pen on his thumbnail as he stared at Luma.

"You hadn't spoken to her previously."

"No."

"And you didn't see your friend, Cat, after she went to the Massa building?"

"No."

"Then how did you know about the missing hat and overall?"

It'll be all right, Cat said. *Just tell him.*

Luma cleared his throat. "Cat and I – talk to each other," he said.

The policeman looked at Jim and raised his eyebrows.

"I know," said Jim helplessly. "It's crazy. I can't ask you to believe it. I didn't believe it myself at first. But it works. Loretta Tebbitt was shaken rigid. She agreed at once that the things were missing. She said she'd put in a missing report, and it had been ignored."

"I'm a witness to that," Angie put in.

Sergeant Muir nodded. "We in the police are not as narrow-minded as people think," he said. "We have been known to take the advice of dowsers, crystal-gazers, clairvoyants – anyone who claims to have knowledge. Most of the time it's useless, but if they turn up a fact that can be proved, fair enough. If you learn nothing else in this job, you find out that human beings are pretty weird animals."

"So will you talk to this woman?" asked Angie.

"Oh, yes," said the policeman. "We certainly will."

There was no word from Cat while they dropped Angie off and drove back to Jim's flat. Luma had the feeling she was up to something else.

He was right. She was waiting for him in Jim's front room, full of excitement.

Winter's found something new! He's going to replace Magnus.

With someone else, you mean?

No, with himself.

Luma didn't get it. *You mean he's going to do Magnus's job?*

Worse than that. The two scientists have been telling me. They can see it all now.

See what?

Cat sighed, trying to be patient. *Winter can change his appearance, right?*

I know that, said Luma.

But he's had this breakthrough. Up to now he's stuck to inventing people who don't exist. That silver-haired woman who came in and stopped the interview, then the man who showed you out of the building. They're not real; they're just Winter. He made them up.

That's what I thought, said Luma.

He's never known how to copy real people. Not properly.

He did the fat lab assistant, though.

Yes, he did, Cat agreed. *But nobody saw him except the cameras, so it didn't matter if it wasn't perfect. He was the right size and shape, good enough to be recognized on the monitor screens. The lab assistant's friends would have known it wasn't the real him – that's why he picked a time when they were away in the canteen.*

But now… Luma felt himself turn cold at the thought.

Yes, said Cat. *He's found out how to do it. Come and see.*

They were in Winter's glass-roofed room. Beyond the sliding wall, Magnus Chip lay on the couch. His head was encased in a transparent helmet, from which a multitude of cables ran to the bank of machinery.

All his brain pulses are being loaded into the computer system, Cat explained. *Magnus Chip's personal hard drive. The thing that makes him who he is.* Her voice in Luma's ear was quiet, even though both of them knew they could not be heard. *When it's complete, Winter will have it on disk, ready to transfer into his own mind.*

And then? asked Luma.

He'll be an exact replica of Magnus. A clone. Everyone will think it's Magnus himself.

Luma closed his eyes for a moment in horror. Then he thought of something. *What's going to happen to the real Magnus while Winter is using his body and mind?*

He'll tick over as a hologram, said Cat. *Like Winter does. It's the same as putting a video on hold. It just waits for when it's needed again. When Magnus gets himself back at the end of the day, he'll remember all the things he's been doing, just as if he'd really done them. But his memory is downloaded to him as Winter chooses. Magnus will only remember the things that are fed to him.*

Winter could go on taking person after person, said Luma, *until there are no real ones left. Everyone at Massa, from the bosses to the cleaners – they'd all be Winter's clones.*

That's the plan, Cat agreed.

How horrible. Winter is going to steal people. Their bodies and minds – all of them.

Yes, he is.

They were back in Jim's sitting room, looking out of the window. Beyond the roofs opposite, a full moon made a silver path over the dark sea.

You'll have to be careful, Cat warned. *Winter knows now that you've been dreaming your way into Massa. He'll steal you if he can.*

Luma felt a rush of fury. *He won't,* he said. *I'd rather die.*

Cat was silent, but there was no disguising her unspoken words. *You may have to.*

When Eddie Molotov came home that evening, Cat was watching him. She was with him as he turned his car in off the street and as he let himself in through his front door and hung his jacket up. His wife wasn't in from her work yet, and his children were still with the neighbour who looked after them until six. He poured himself a drink and sipped it, then sat down and leaned his head back. His thoughts were circling madly, and the frantic nature of them was perfectly clear to Cat.

Can't go on like this. Careful, careful, mustn't be caught thinking that sort of thing. Can't go on being careful, though; I can't bear it. I'm going crazy. No choice. I've got to go on.

A stronger pulse cut in.

I AM PRIVILEGED TO WORK AT MASSA. I OWE THE FIRM MY TOTAL LOYALTY. ITS DECISIONS ARE THE RIGHT ONES, ALWAYS.

Eddie's closed eyes flickered. *Believe it,* he told himself in despair. *Believe it, why don't you? Just accept it. So much easier.*

Cat moved closer to him. *What is your dream?* she whispered. *If you could do whatever you wanted, what would it be?*

No words came, but she saw what Eddie was seeing. Children played in the sunshine and he lounged on the grass, laughing with some friends. They were joking and being wonderfully silly.

The sunshine and the grass ran wordlessly through Eddie's thoughts, and brought a wave of sleepiness. He reached to put his drink down on the table by the chair, and gave a little sigh. His body slackened.

DO NOT DREAM. THAT IS AN ORDER. YOU WILL NOT DREAM.

He jerked as if an electric shock had run through his body. He made a sound like a sob, and slow tears oozed from under his eyelids. *I'm so tired,* he said.

Listen, Cat told him. *It's going to change. Very soon now, all this at Massa will end. You'll be free. There are thousands of us. We'll help you.*

He put a hand across his forehead. *I'm not thinking this,* he said, flinching from the loud voice that was going to shout in his mind. *It didn't come from me.*

Strangely, the voice was silent.

It can't hear me, Cat explained. *It knows when you are slipping into a dream, and it tries to stop you, but it can't see what you are dreaming. It only pretends it can.*

Only pretends. Hope and relief flooded through Eddie Molotov, and Cat warned him quickly, *Don't think in words. Just let the dream come to you. It's all right – you can trust it.*

Eddie's face relaxed. His hands slackened, and his breathing became slower and deeper.

DO NOT DREAM! the voice screamed in his ear, and he jumped a little, but that was all. His head fell sideways, and in the next moment, he was more deeply asleep than he had been for weeks.

Cat watched him. She let her own picture of the coming battle drift out, ready for him to pick up when he chose, but for now she would not disturb him.

Chokker was at the summerhouse before any of the others the next morning, waiting by the walnut tree for Stan to come up from the bungalow.

"Oh, good grief!" Stan said as Chokker stepped quietly out. "Don't do that, boy; you'll give me a heart attack."

"Sorry." He followed Stan into the summerhouse, pulling the tight-folded sheet of paper from his pocket. "I wrote this about Luma." He watched him read it.

Stan didn't seem to know what to say. He looked at Chokker, then back at the paper.

"Is it all right?" Chokker asked. "I put it through the spell-check."

"It's more than all right," said Stan. "It's terrific. Believe me, there are grown-up novelists who couldn't tell that story." He looked at Chokker again. "Are you sure it's OK to use this? It's not too ... personal or anything?"

"It's about Luma," said Chokker.

"Sure." Stan looked at the note again. "Well, thank you very much. Luma's really clear now. Brilliant." He turned to his desk and picked up a supermarket bag that looked quite heavy. "Here's the printout. There's quite a chunk of new stuff as well; I had a go at it last night. Can I leave it to you to show the others? I'm going to be stuck with Anna and her young man today."

"OK," said Chokker.

He stood outside the summerhouse and watched Stan go away down the path. With the bag of papers in his hand, he felt very much in charge of the whole thing.

The others were excited to hear about the new bit.

"Where shall we go?" asked Kirsty. "I'm dying to read it."

Abby had been thinking about this. She said, "My house is just up the path."

"That would be great," said Fraser.

Chokker scowled as he trailed after the rest of them. He was still carrying Stan's pages, but Abby was in charge. She used to be so quiet, but she was different now.

"Goodness!" exclaimed Abby's mother. "Yes, of course, come along in." She seemed pleased to see so many of them arriving, Abby thought. It had never been a house that people flocked in and out of, not until now. "Take them through to the sitting room," her mother went on. "Or would you rather be in the kitchen? There's the big table—"

"The kitchen's fine," said Abby.

"Is this about the book?" her mother asked.

"There was a letter from the school this morning – Mrs Long wants a meeting with all the parents."

"That'll be about the event," said Mandy.

Chokker put the bag on the table. "Stan did some new stuff."

"Let's read that first," said Kirsty. "Fraser, you do it."

"OK." He shuffled through the pages. "Here's the start of it."

"Go on, then," said Neil.

It took quite a time. Abby's mother stopped wiping the stove. She leaned against the sink with her arms folded, listening. When Abby's father came in halfway through, she put a finger on her lips, and he sat down with his earthy hands resting on his jeans.

"Did you children write that?" he asked when Fraser got to the end.

"Stan did the actual writing," said Abby, "but it's mostly our ideas."

"I can see why the school's interested," her father remarked.

"It's very exciting, isn't it?" said Abby's mother. "What's going to happen about this boy? The one called Luma?"

"There's going to be a fight between him and Winter," said Chokker. "And Luma's going to win."

"He's not going to die, then?" Abby's mother sounded anxious.

"No," said Chokker firmly. "He's not going to die." He waited for someone to disagree, but nobody did.

"There's all the early stuff to read as well," Kirsty said.

"We can do that later," said Neil.

Somehow the morning was turning into a sort of party. Abby's mother gave them juice and biscuits, then her father let them get in the trailer behind the tractor and took them down to the greenhouses. He showed them all the stuff growing in there, including the big vine that filled a house of its own, and they ended up mucking around in the adventure playground.

"Aren't you lucky," Kirsty said to Abby. "All this space." She'd never been to the house before.

"Do you have a dog?" Mandy asked.

Abby shook her head.

"You ought to have that puppy." Mandy was inclined to be bossy. "The one you were cuddling the other day."

Abby's father looked at her with an unspoken question.

"It's Stan's," Abby explained. "It was very small when it was born. His wife's been hand-feeding it with a bottle." She knew her face was red, as if she'd been caught doing something disgraceful. "We can't have a dog here," she told Mandy. "It would dig things up and make a mess."

To her astonishment her father said, "Not if it was trained."

"There you go then," said Mandy.

The Finbows had a letter about the event as well.

"Such a good idea," Dorothy said, retrieving a paintbrush that one of the little ones had thrown on the floor.

"Excellent," Gerald agreed. "And it's good to see you getting stuck into something, Charlie."

Chokker looked at him suspiciously. He thought he'd deleted his page about Luma from the computer, but perhaps he hadn't. Maybe Gerald had read it. To his surprise, he found that he didn't really mind.

They didn't see anything of Stan until Wednesday, when Abby found a single word stuck on the summerhouse door. MORE, it said. So they all crowded in there after school.

"You know the worst part of a book?" said Stan. "It's the end. You can't do it until all the rest leads into it. You wouldn't believe how many endings I've tried to write, and they've all gone in the bin. I think you'll have to help."

"Course we will," said Sue. "Winter's going to do something awful to Luma, isn't he?"

Chokker nodded in agreement. They'd spent most of Sunday rereading the book from the beginning, at Sue's in the morning and at Abby's after lunch, and he could see the whole thing in his head now. It just needed the big fight at the end.

Stan was leafing through his notes. "Jim's photos of the dog are in the papers next morning," he said. "There are more protesters than ever outside Massa, and a lot of them want to storm the place. The dreadful Madge and Arthur have been on television, saying how desperate they are to get Cat back. Jim's been to see the lab assistant in prison, who swears he was in the canteen when the scientists died. He says his mates won't back him up because they are all brainwashed. He was like that himself, he says. He thinks it was something to do with the food at Massa, or maybe the air-conditioning. His mind is starting to clear now he's away from the place."

"What about Eddie Molotov?" asked Fraser.

"I'll read you the bit about him. As you'll see, Cat's visit has left him feeling rather different."

It was strange, Eddie thought the next morning, how wonderful it all seemed now. Ever since yesterday's sudden, deep sleep in his armchair, he felt lighter and happier. The stern voice still shouted in his mind, but it was more distant, as though it came through a wall from a room next door. It didn't concern him as it used to.

He noticed other things instead – small things that he'd written off as unimportant. Getting into his car this morning, he was aware of the brightness of the sky and the patterns of cloud that drifted above his head. He saw the yellow, square-edged petals of dandelions growing in cracks between the paving slabs.

He watched himself with interest as his body went through the routine of starting the car, backing out into the road, moving off. He could feel the pressure of the seat belt across his shoulder and noted how efficiently he looked ahead, changed gear, kept a reasonable space between his own car and the one in front – but all the time, his real self was drifting free. He had stopped thinking in words; he simply gazed in wonder at the changing picture that surrounded him. He did not try to decide if one thing was more important than another – just to exist was enough, like a cloud or a buttercup.

The crowds outside Massa were being kept back by police, who joined arms and leaned back against the shouting people, clearing a way for Eddie's car. A man with a camera in his hand was close enough to ask a question through the car's half-open window. "What do you think about Cat, sir?" A lean-faced boy with hair the colour of straw was at his side, and his frowning eyes met Eddie's with a strange intensity.

Eddie made no answer. He had no wish to be unfriendly, but the question meant nothing. His brain had stopped its busy patterns of thought. He paused at the checkpoint, noting with distant interest how his hand showed his pass to the uniformed man inside, and how he caused the car to move smoothly forward when the red and white striped bar lifted. He parked the car, and heard birds singing as he walked across the tarmac and into the building.

"Hi, Eddie," Magnus Chip said as they met in the corridor.

Eddie smiled at him. "Hello," he heard himself say.

Chip paused and looked at him again. "You all right?"

"Wonderful," answered Eddie, still smiling. His mind noted that Magnus had never asked that kind of question before, but it didn't wonder why. Above the roof of this building, there was the sky.

"Why the happy face?" enquired Magnus. "You won the lottery?"

"No," said Eddie. "There's no need." Things were perfect as they were. Perhaps he wouldn't stay here this morning, he thought. It might be nicer outside. He'd like to have another look at the dandelion. He turned to walk on.

Magnus Chip caught Eddie's arm. "Hey, you seem a bit crazy. You been taking drugs or something?"

Eddie felt himself smiling. "Just sleep," he said.

"It was very enjoyable."

Magnus glanced with unusual shrewdness at the Eye monitor that stared down from the wall. It had begun to flash: DREAM ALERT, DREAM ALERT. He looked back at the man in front of him, who still seemed ridiculously happy. "You've been talking to someone," he said, narrow-eyed. "Come on, Molotov – who was it?"

Eddie's smile was not disturbed. "I didn't talk to anyone," he said. "She talked to me."

Cat, who had been with Eddie since he left the house, saw the cold presence that was using the mind and body of Magnus Chip, and knew what Winter planned to do. As soon as the apparatus could be made ready, he would send for Eddie Molotov. And up there, in the room with the glass roof, Eddie would become the second of Winter's clones.

Magnus released Eddie's arm. "OK," he said kindly. "See you later, Eddie. Have a nice day."

Stan looked up. "That's where I've stopped."

"But you *can't* let him clone Eddie Molotov!" cried Sue.

"Absolutely not," Stan agreed. "This is where we have to muster all the troops, both in Cat's world and Luma's. We're going to write the big fight."

"What d'you mean, *we* are?" asked Fraser.

"I can't do it without you," said Stan. "I've tried it all ways round, and never been sure if it works. So it's you and me together. Right now."

✿ Seventeen

Stan picked up a pencil and an untidy handful of notes. "These are the things to tackle," he began. "First, Luma's got to get into the Massa building. Second, he has to warn Molotov. Or someone has. Third, there's the final set-to with Winter."

"That's all right, then," said Fraser, as though he could see no problems.

"What do you mean, *all right*?" Stan demanded. "It's full of awkward questions. How's Luma going to get into this place, to start with? We're not talking dream stuff here; this is for real. And we've got Jim in the picture now, so it's even harder. He's going to take great care of the boy, especially as he knows what happened to his daughter."

"And there's Mrs Pimm," said Sue. "If she thinks Jim's no good at looking after him, she'll put Luma in a home."

"Exactly," Stan agreed.

"Jim will have to go in as well," said Abby. "To Massa, I mean."

Stan nodded. "That's what I've been thinking. But then he'll be watching Luma all the time in case he does anything dangerous. We'll have to get rid of him once he's in there, so Luma can get to grips with Winter. This fight is a private affair. Or is it?" he mused. "Could it happen in the middle of a general battle?"

Chokker had always imagined them fighting alone, but maybe people could be watching. "Yeah," he said. "Could do." But it didn't seem quite right.

"We could have a riot, couldn't we?" Stan went on. "The protesters outside could storm the place."

"That's how Jim and Luma get in!" said Fraser. "If they're in the crowd, they just go barging in with everyone else. They can't help it."

"Great." Stan made a note. "That's fine; they just get swept along. So they're in the building. What's happening there?"

Everyone had ideas.

"Guards."

"Stun guns."

"Tear gas."

"All the doors get automatically locked," said Sue.

Fraser shook his head. "There's a swipe-card system. That's how Cat got in, with the card she found in the overall pocket."

"So trusted personnel can still get in and out," Stan agreed. "OK. We've got all this security going on, but the crowd's broken in. People are coughing and choking in the gas, getting thumped over the head by the guards: it's general bedlam. What about Molotov?"

"Could be Winter's already got him," said Neil.

There were shouts of disagreement.

"We said he wouldn't."

"Luma's got to rescue him."

Stan held up a hand for some hush. "Let's think this through. Molotov's in a happy mood today. Cat's made him see the Eye isn't as powerful as he'd thought, so he's feeling much better. In fact, he's so drunk with happiness, he might do something quite peculiar."

"He was thinking of going outside," Sue said, "because he wanted to look at dandelions and things. If he's out there when the riot starts, he might join in."

"Oh, that's good," said Stan. "Cat knows him, so she'll put him in contact with Luma."

Fraser took up the idea. "Molotov can take him in. He'll have a card."

"But what about Jim?" Fraser objected. "He's not going to let Luma go off into the building without him."

Neil said, "He could get gassed."

"Right, that gets rid of him." Stan made another note. "Then there's Winter. Is he still pretending to be Magnus Chip, or what?"

Kirsty shook her head. "He's gone back upstairs, ready to clone Eddie Molotov."

"So does he know the place has been invaded?" Stan asked.

Everyone agreed that he did. The Eye screen would show it, they said, and the alarms would have gone off. It was probably Winter who'd ordered the guards out, and the stun guns and tear gas.

"OK," said Stan. "We're nearly there. We just have to get Luma up to the room with the glass roof, to tackle Winter. Or else we get Winter out of there, and have the fight somewhere else."

"Luma's got to be in there," said Chokker. An idea was growing in his mind. "He's going to attack the machinery."

"Of course!" said Stan. "Why didn't I think of that? It could be the way Luma finally kills him – if he's going to kill him," he added.

"You mean, perhaps he won't?" asked Abby.

"He's got to," said Chokker. He'd hung on all through this business so that Luma could win the fight with Winter, and nobody was going to take it away.

Stan looked at them carefully. "This is the big question, isn't it?" he said. "We have a difficulty about death. We're saying in this book that dying doesn't actually end anything. It just shifts you from the world that people live in now to another one."

"Where Cat is," said Sue. "And Mara."

"And the two scientists," said Kirsty.

"Plus millions of others," Stan agreed. "Whether that's right or not, we're working to those ground rules. We can't make it different for Winter. If Luma kills him, he's not getting rid of him completely; he's just moving him to the other world."

Chokker didn't like the idea. "But then Luma hasn't won," he said.

"Yes, he has," said Abby.

Stan was still thinking. "Maybe Winter should stay alive, so he gets punished in the real world. He'll be arrested and imprisoned. Cat and Mara can afford to wait. Winter will come to their world one day, same as everyone else."

"No," Chokker said. "That's *boring.*"

"Dead boring," agreed Kevin, who hadn't said anything.

"Forget it, in that case," said Stan. "If the readers get bored, they'll chuck the book away and go back to watching the television. Winter has to die, OK."

Chokker was thinking frantically, All this stuff about the other world was just getting in the way. Luma had to win, he just had to. And then he realized something.

"Luma's in both worlds!" he said. "Winter can't get away from him. If he dies, Luma can follow him."

"Of course!" Stan thumped his forehead. "I'd

been thinking of his two states as separate, but when it comes to the fight with Winter, they can come together. If Luma gets knocked out, the readers will think he's done for, but he's not – he's just shifted into Cat's world. The fight will go on there, but it's a fight of souls."

"They can't kill each other," said Fraser. "Because a soul is what's left when a person's already died. So if Winter and Luma are fighting, how do they know who's won?"

"The best one wins," said Chokker, as if it was obvious. *Submit, submit.* "The other one has to give in."

"The best," Stan repeated. He nodded a couple of times. "Yes, that's it. This battle is to prove who is the best."

Chokker shrugged. "Of course."

Everyone had started to talk, arguing about how to prove you were the best, and about what would happen after Luma had won.

"There could be an explosion," Neil said. "Massa could blow up."

"They could make a new factory but it would all be different," Sue suggested.

"With Eddie Molotov in charge," said Neil.

Stan put his hands to his head. "If you give me any more ideas, I might blow up myself. Or collapse, or something. Thank you all very much, but that's enough."

"GOODBYE," said the parrot firmly, and everyone laughed.

"You said we were going to write the ending," said Neil, sounding disappointed. "And we haven't."

"Oh, yes, you have," said Stan. "It just needs words put to it, that's all. So off you go and write some. I'll write some too."

"When do we come back?" asked Sue.

Stan shook his head. "I don't know. I'll hang out a flag or something. Now – scram."

And they scrammed.

A couple of afternoons later, Stan found some papers under the stone on the summerhouse doorstep, and took them in to read what they said. Abby had written:

There was a blinding flash as the equipment blew up. Everything went black. When Luma came to, Winter was still there, but it was different. There were trees all around, and people were watching, but they weren't real people. Winter hit Luma again, but it didn't hurt. Nothing hurt any more. They struggled and pushed each other and Luma was stronger. He said, "You were bad to do all those things."

Winter didn't want to admit he was bad, but Luma was holding him, and at last he said,

"Yes, I was bad. I am sorry."
Luma had won. All the people cheered.

Fraser had written a lot of sensible stuff about the police coming, and Luma winning the fight with Winter by wrecking the machinery. Neil had written at the bottom: *I helped with this.*

Sue had written:

All the animals were glad when Luma won. People came and reskoued them, and looked after them propely. The black dogs upstares had to be put down, but it dident hurt.

Chokker's was word-processed:

Luma took a stick from a guard who was dead. He went up with Moletof. When he got in to Winters plaice Winter said I've been waiting for you. The fight started. Winter went all different shapes he was very strong Luma cud not get hold of him. He thawed I have to stop the machine so he smashed it with the stick. Their were flashes and explosions the plaice was all smoke. Luma cud not see Moletof then he fund him on the floor. He was all small and he had no skin, it was disgusting. So Luma killed him because he thawed it was the best thing to do.

Stan read them all, several times. Then he spread them on the desk near the computer, along with all his other notes, and began to write again.

For a week, nothing happened. Then one morning a large sock with a hole in its heel was hanging from a stick pushed into the top of the summerhouse door. The sock looked as if a dog had chewed it. Abby supposed it was the nearest Stan could get to a flag, and told the others. Some of them couldn't come, but she and Sue, Fraser, Neil and Chokker were there after school.

Stan looked at them and smiled. "The original five," he said. "Thanks for the stuff you left on the doorstep. It was a real help."

Everyone was impatient.

"What did you decide?" asked Sue. "What have you put?"

"You'll see," said Stan. He started to read.

As Eddie's car went forward under the raised pole, Jim tucked his notebook and camera away. He had enough for a good update piece on the state of things outside Massa. "Right," he said to Luma, "let's get out of here."

But it was too late. The crowd was surging in behind Molotov's car, and the pressure of suddenly moving people drove Jim and Luma towards the gate. A policeman who tried to check the stream of invaders was thrown aside, and Luma staggered and almost fell as a man barged into him. He clutched at someone's jacket and managed to stay on his feet, then found himself being swept on, like a bit of twig in a fast river. Countless people were ducking under the red and white striped bar and running across the tarmac to the grand entrance into the Massa building. Steel-helmeted guards rushed at them, hitting out with heavy sticks. Some of the protesters fell, and people tripped over those on the ground, but they kept going, and more were pouring in behind them.

Jim grabbed Luma's hand. He tried to pull him aside, out of the crowd, but in that instant, the figure of a guard was suddenly in front of them, black against the sky, stick lashing down. The blow brought Jim to his knees, then he pitched forward and lay still. Luma bent over him, but a couple of women crashed into them both and sent him flying.

Go on, go on! Cat said urgently. *He'll be all right; don't worry*.

Luma struggled to his feet. There was a hand on his arm, helping him. He found himself staring at a man whose dark hair was threaded with whiteness and who seemed in no hurry to go anywhere. His face was thin and deeply lined, but he was smiling.

It's Eddie Molotov, said Cat. *He'll help you.*

The man was walking away from the crowd, as calmly as though the car park held no one but himself. Luma followed him round the side of the building, keeping close behind him. Eddie stopped suddenly, stooping to stare closely at a weed growing near a drainpipe, and Luma almost fell over him. The man put out a hand to steady him, and smiled again.

"I have to see Mr Winter," Luma said. "It's very important."

He wasn't sure if the man had heard. His eyes were unblinking, but it seemed as if he was trying not to think about the question. Luma started to repeat his request, but an absent-minded nod stopped him, and Eddie moved on again.

Bucket, Cat said in Luma's ear. *And mop.*

Bucket? He wondered if she'd gone mad.

No, honestly, she said. *You'll see.*

Eddie Molotov swiped his card through the slot beside a service door where dustbins stood, and pushed it open. Luma followed him. They were in a utility room where floor polishers and vacuum cleaners stood parked. Brown overalls hung on pegs.

It made sense now. *This is what you did,* Luma said to Cat. *Overall. The perfect disguise. Polisher.* He moved towards the machines.

Bucket, Cat insisted again.

He found himself beside a large bucket, mounted on trolley wheels, with a wet mop in a clip behind it.

Water.

OK. If you insist.

Luma took the bucket over to one of the big sinks and filled it. Eddie Molotov watched. He put his hand under the running water, smiling at the way it changed the pattern of the flow.

Luma turned the tap off. "Sorry," he said, realizing that the man had been enjoying it.

Eddie gave an easy shrug as the boy fitted the full bucket back into its trolley. *The water is still in the pipes,* he thought. *Water is everywhere. Such wonderful stuff.*

DO NOT DREAM, the voice screamed in his mind again, but he hardly heard it. As long as he dreamed, he was safe.

Eddie moved out into the corridor, and Luma followed him, pushing the trolley. People rushed past, but nobody stopped to look at the slow-moving, absent-minded engineer and the cleaning operative in a brown overall.

The crowd had broken into the building. People were running through the corridors, yelling to each other. Luma saw one of them grab a white-overalled Massa scientist by the lapels and shout at him, "Don't you see what you're doing?" The scientist didn't answer. He seemed confused.

There was a sound of splintering wood and breaking glass from the main entrance, and a sharp thudding of guns began. A waft of something bitter-smelling drifted through the air, and Luma's eyes began to stream.

Tear gas, Eddie thought, then snatched his mind away from the dangerous words. Soon he would be out of here. Once this boy was on his way to do whatever strange thing it was that seemed so compulsive and right, a long walk waited. Somewhere there was a hill that stood sweet and quiet against the sky, and he was going to find it.

In a few more steps they were at the double doors of a lift. Eddie swiped his card to open them, then pointed silently to the top button. Luma pushed his trolley in, and turned to thank the man who had helped him.

Eddie waved a finger. No thanks needed. He was coughing, and his eyes, like Luma's, were pouring, but he still smiled. Luma pressed the top button as he'd been silently told, and the doors slid across. *Such a nice man,* he thought. And Winter, unless he was stopped, would invade his being and destroy him, this very day.

When the lift stopped, Luma found himself in a short corridor with doors on either side. All of them were blank except for the one at the end, where an Eye screen stared down. Its illuminated notice said KEEP OUT, but as he looked, it changed to ENTER. Luma pushed his trolley towards it, and the door opened.

It let him into a waiting room with low glass-topped tables and leather armchairs. This too had only one of its several doors illuminated. It opened as he approached it, to reveal the glass-roofed room he had seen in his dreams. A curly-haired girl in a black dress was sitting behind the desk, and she looked up and smiled.

"Hello," she said. "Have you come to see Mr Winter?"

She was so pretty and so friendly that Luma felt stupid, pushing the cleaning trolley with its bucket of water and mop. "Yes, please," he said.

Careful, Cat whispered.

The girl came round the desk and approached him with her hand outstretched. "I'm Mary," she said.

The handshake told him.

It was as cool as a rubber glove, and the grip was hard and strong. In the next instant, Mary had whipped round to try a neck throw, and he had to move fast to counter it. Even as he grappled with her, she was changing. Her arms thickened; she was taller now, a man in a black sweatshirt, using weight and strength against him. Luma freed himself and kicked, landing a hard blow on the thigh, then crouched and elbow parried the return blow, coming in with a double-handed chop to the neck. It made contact, but it didn't stop him. The man was older now, narrow-eyed and crop-headed, a cunning fighter, aiming to trip and unbalance. All the time, he was trying to work Luma towards the end wall of the room, behind which the machinery was hidden.

He's not trying to kill me, Luma realized. *He wants me alive. It's not Eddie Molotov he's going to change. It's me.*

He switched to a defensive pattern and took a couple of steps back, but the man followed. He was black-skinned now, a long-armed boxer, very fast. A couple of hard punches to Luma's body made him gasp for breath. *If he knocks me out, I'll be on that table and never know it.*

He was backed against the trolley now, starting to feel desperate. He had only his own shape and size to pit against this changing monster, and it wasn't going to be enough.

Mop, Cat said.

Frantic though he was, Luma almost laughed. *Of course!* That was why the cleaning trolley was here. He reached behind him, snatched up the wet, heavy mop and rammed it with all his strength into the man's face. The boxer coughed and ducked, and Luma swung the mop in a circle, bringing it down in a savage blow to the side of the neck.

The man collapsed to his knees. He seemed to be shrinking. The skin on his neck had split open, revealing an intricate detail of pinkish-coloured plastic moving parts. He looked elderly now, and shrivelled. He was crawling.

"Don't hit me," he said pathetically.

For a moment Luma paused. Then he caught the gleam of spite in the wrinkled eye as the man started to get to his feet, and slashed at him again.

The man was instantly larger, heavy-shouldered and muscular. He grabbed the shaft of the mop and thrust it back at Luma so fast that Luma was thrown off balance. He clutched at the trolley for support – then ducked behind it and drove the whole contraption at his opponent.

It knocked the man sideways. Water slopped into the gaping hole in his neck, causing a flash and a hiss of steam, and he screamed. He was losing size, going into a confusion of changing shapes.

Luma drove the trolley hard at him again, pushing him back towards the hidden room. He was wrinkled and grey now, hardly human at all.

"All right," he said in a grating voice. "All right."

He reached behind him, and the sliding wall opened. He dodged quickly behind the couch and stood with his hands on it as Luma came after him, still pushing his trolley.

The voice came out of the grey face again. "What a good move, dear boy," it said.

The machinery hummed quietly, its cooling fans whirring and its green lights blinking. *Ready to start processing*, Luma thought as he stood there, breathing hard. He had walked into the centre of the danger – but this was the only way. *I'd rather die*.

There was one chance left.

Moving very slowly so as to give Winter no warning of his intention, Luma felt behind him for the bucket. His fingers closed around the metal handle and his muscles tensed to take the weight. Then, with all his strength, he lifted it, swung round – and hurled gallons of water all over the machinery.

The explosion blew him flat. The room was in darkness. Flames flickered, and the place filled with smoke. The automatic sprinklers began to rain water from the ceiling, causing further small flashes and bangs from the wrecked and steaming remains of the apparatus. Alarm sirens were screaming and bells were ringing.

Luma got to his feet. His head hurt, and it was hard to breathe. He groped his way round the couch in the darkness, and stumbled over something at his feet. Dim emergency lighting came on, and Luma found that the thing was Winter. He stooped over him, then gasped in revulsion at what he saw. It had shrunk to something the size of a five-year-old child, but it had no skin. The bones of its monkey-like skeleton were covered by a complex structure of plastic parts joined by tiny, silvery-coloured motors. They were still twitching.

The eyes, as round and white as ping-pong balls in the skinless face, were moving. They circled until they found Luma, then fixed him in the gaze of their black pupils. He stared back at them in horror.

The mouth opened and the thing gave a thin, high scream, like a terrified rabbit. *I should kill it,* Luma thought, not because he wanted to win any more, but because he was sickened by the agony it must be feeling. Crouched beside it, he did not see the slow movement of one skinless, plastic arm that came up behind him. Silently, it laid its metal fingers on the back of his head, sending a blast of powerful current into his brain.

Several people gasped, and Sue gave a shriek of alarm.

Stan looked up from his pages. "Well, I had to get him into the other world somehow."

"Is Luma dead?" asked Fraser.

Stan shook his head. "No, it's just another mighty leap."

"Have you written the next bit?" asked Chokker.

Stan looked at his tense face and smiled. "Yes," he said. "Here goes."

Eddie Molotov was still in the building when the alarms went off. As he stood in the sudden darkness, his mind clicked into clarity from the non-thinking state that had been his only safety. Ideas were expressing themselves in words again, and the words seemed to carry no threat of being overheard and used against him. Something had changed. In the new lightness, a plain and terrible thought stood clearly above all others. The boy had gone up to tackle Winter.

Dear heaven, what was I thinking of, to let him do that?

Somewhere not far from Eddie, a man was shouting, "Luma, where are you? Where are you?" He sounded frantic.

The emergency lighting came on. Eddie ran for the stairs and hurled himself up them.

Magnus Chip was just behind him. "Don't know what in hell the old man's up to now," he panted, "but I've had enough."

Firefighters pounded past them, taking the concrete steps two at a time. *They're younger than me,* Eddie thought. *Fitter.* But he wasn't far behind them as they burst into the room at the top of the building.

A wall at the far end that he'd always taken to be solid had vanished. Smoke was rolling out from the space behind it, and the fire crew were already in there.

"What on earth—" he heard one of them say.

They were bending over something on the floor. Eddie joined them, with Magnus behind him, breathing heavily.

He thought it was a laboratory animal at first. It was moving slightly, and a high-pitched scream was coming from it.

"Jeez," said Magnus. "What in hell is it?"

"Some kind of machine," said one of the firemen. "Robot or something. Don't touch it – could be live wires in there."

Eddie bent over it. An arm lifted slightly, but he put his foot on it. Eyes rolled in the thing's head to look at him. A horrible conviction ran through Eddie, but he pushed it away. *I'm an engineer; I don't go in for mad fancies. And if it's right – well, he's got what he asked for.*

The screaming was still going on. *Must stop this,* Eddie thought. *Need insulation, though.* He turned to the fireman. "Can I borrow your gloves?"

The man stripped off his heavy yellow gloves and handed them to him.

"Thanks."

Very cautiously, Eddie parted the plastic muscles of the chest. In the smoke behind him he heard another fireman say, "There's a boy here. He's alive, but only just."

Eddie found what he was looking for. Under the mechanical lungs and above what seemed to be a human heart, the chest cavity was full of batteries. *Standby system,* he thought. He found the main lead and disconnected it.

The screaming stopped and the arm that had

been trying to free itself from Eddie's foot lay still.

"Wow," said Magnus Chip. "That's better."

There seemed to be trees, and bright sky. And eyes. Thousands of eyes. Millions. All watching.

Winter, Luma thought in his confusion. *I have to fight Winter.*

Cat was beside him. *You've done it,* she said. *You—*

Her words were cut into by another, sharper voice. *But I did better. I won.*

Luma found a fattish boy beside him, his spotty chin defiantly raised.

A lot of people were standing round, and among them was Mara. *Why do you say that?* she asked the boy.

Because I did what I wanted to. I had the power. I showed them all.

You made us cruel, a man said.

You made us into murderers, said another. *And then you killed us.*

Luma recognized the two scientists from Massa. *I had to,* said the boy. *I needed to be strong.*

He didn't look strong, Luma thought. He looked flabby and soft, although he hadn't felt like that when they were fighting.

You wanted *to be strong,* Mara corrected. *There is no pretending here; everything is understood. You, William Winter, will understand the truth, even if it takes for ever.*

Cornelius, said the boy. *I am Cornelius Winter.*

Laughter rippled through the trees. *You chose that name because you didn't like being called Willy,* Cat said. *It made the other kids laugh at you.*

The boy looked sulky. *Doesn't matter. I was right, anyway. I've won.*

Perhaps he has, Luma thought in utter depression. He felt exhausted. *I can't fight any more,* he said.

A wave of reassurance came from the countless watchers. *You don't have to. He will know what is true. He is learning it now.*

William Winter was starting to seem more agitated. *It wasn't my fault,* he said. *I never had a chance. You can't expect someone to be good when they had a start like mine. I was fat. My parents were stingy; I didn't have the right sort of trainers. People laughed at me. My father said I was a waste of space.*

That was very nasty for you, said Mara. She turned to Luma. *And what was your start?*

Luma shook his head. *I can't fight like that,* he said. *It's not fair.*

But it is true. Again the plain statement came from the watchers, or perhaps from the sky and the trees with which they seemed mingled. The clear picture lay before them all. Luma as a small child was seen cowering alone, bruised and beaten, left in a locked room until he almost died.

Winter saw it too, and his hands were over his face. *But I won,* he whimpered. *Please. Didn't I?*

Nobody answered.

Another truth opened, a recent one this time. Luma was crouching over the still-living thing that had been Winter. *I should kill it,* he thought. And everyone saw that the silent words were spoken not in anger, but out of concern and pity. Out of compassion.

If there is a fight here, said Mara, *then who is the better person? Who has won?*

Luma.

Luma.

Luma.

The word rolled through the sky, and hands were extended in salute.

Chokker found that he was crying.

✿Eighteen

"New chapter here," said Stan.

Nobody looked at Chokker; they were too intent on the story. He rubbed his face on his sleeve. He was OK, really. In fact, he felt rather amazing.

Stan was reading again.

Narrow bed, like a caravan bunk. Everything shaking. Engine noise.

"Hi," said Jim.

He was sitting on the bunk opposite. His arm was wrapped in a white sling.

Luma started to struggle up, but someone put a hand on his shoulder. Man in green overalls. "Just keep still, son; you're all right. Not feeling sick at all?"

"No." *Ambulance,* he thought. His head hurt. "What did you do to your arm?" he asked Jim.

"Broken collarbone," said Jim. "And you were nearly electrocuted."

"Nearly," said Luma. Then he found that he did feel sick, so there wasn't any more conversation.

He was in hospital all the next day, with sore lungs because of smoke inhalation as well as shock and extensive bruising. He slept a lot, but people kept coming to see him. The police, twice, and Jim and May, and Angie, who said she'd told the Veterinary Association about the whole thing. It wasn't exactly news to them, she said. The police had already been asking questions, and there was going to be a full investigation. One or two vets might find themselves in big trouble, Angie added. She didn't mention any names, but she and Luma exchanged a glance, and they both knew who they meant.

Cat was constantly there, with news of how everything at Massa was changing. *We're in charge now,* she said cheerfully. *They don't know we're there, of course, but they want it all to be different. We're helping them understand that it can be. They want Eddie Molotov to run it, when he comes back.*

Luma had a clear vision of Eddie walking on some distant hill, and smiled. *What about Magnus Chip?* he asked.

He flew to America this morning, said Cat. *He thinks he's going to run a fairground ride.* And although it gave him a pain in his chest, Luma laughed.

Davey came the next day, smelling of stables and clutching his greasy old cap in his hands as though he thought he had to be respectful in this official, medical place.

"Got a new caravan," he said. "Pat and Terry found me one. Said they owed me that. I reckon they did, and all."

"In the same place?" asked Luma.

"Yeah, it's a good field. I got rid of the junk," he added.

"What, all of it?"

"There wasn't much left after the fire. I kept anything useful."

Luma grinned. "Like almost everything."

"Never know when it'll come in handy."

There was a short pause, then Davey went on. "It's a good van, Lew. Bigger than the other one. There's a separate room you could have. If you were thinking of coming back."

Luma had thought about it a lot. He liked Jim and May, and wanted to go on being friends with them, but being with Davey was easy and comfortable. Not comfortable in the way people meant when they talked about houses – caravan life was tougher than that. Things froze in the winter, and there wasn't much space. But it was home.

"Yes," he said. "Please."

"That's all right, then," said Davey.

He looked away, and Luma knew what he was thinking. The newspapers had picked up the story about him telling the police about the laundry

woman, Loretta Tebbitt. SECOND-SIGHT BOY
REVEALS TRUTH, their headlines said. Jim had
brought Luma the cuttings apologetically.
It wasn't his doing, he said.

The nurses were fascinated. They kept asking if
Luma could tell their fortunes. There were reporters
outside, they said, desperate to talk to him, but the
hospital wouldn't let them in.

Davey gave a little cough. "Lot of fuss," he said.
"All this stuff in the papers. My old mum could do
that, same as you. See things."

"Yes," said Luma. He had always known this,
though he wasn't sure how. Had Davey told him
about it years ago, or was it just part of the stuff
they both knew and never talked about? He felt his
face redden. Davey might have wished he had
mentioned it. But Davey was a tough old horse
dealer, drinking beer with his dodgy friends and
talking with them about things a kid wasn't
supposed to understand. As far as anyone else could
see, he didn't take much notice of the boy who
shared his caravan. That was all right. It had taught
Luma how to keep his mouth shut and think for
himself – and Davey was always kind. No fuss, but he
was somehow there when he was really needed. He
didn't ask Luma stupid questions about where he'd
been or what he was doing, and Luma didn't ask
Davey much either, just practical things like getting
more pony nuts or whether he could drive the

tractor. Things were all right the way they were, and that was enough.

"I knew the way things were," said Davey, picking up Luma's thoughts as he quite often did. Only this time he meant something different. "I hadn't had you long when you came in and said there was a little black horse outside. You held your hand up to show me the size of it, level with your chin. *He's white here*, you said. Put your finger on your forehead. Three years old, you were, or maybe four. We went out and looked, but there was nothing there, of course. You said it was hiding. One of my mares foaled that night. Black colt, she had, with a white blaze on his forehead, just like you said."

"I don't remember that," said Luma.

Davey shrugged. "You wouldn't. It's a long time ago. But I knew then. There's been other things too. I never said anything. Best not, I thought."

Luma nodded. That's what he'd thought as well. *Leave it alone.* He wasn't sure what *it* was, but he sensed that asking might start up things that were best left undisturbed. Safer to keep going from day to day, riding the horses, doing whatever jobs had to be done. School was no good. Once he'd learned to read and add up, the rest of what they were doing just bored him, and he sat there dreaming. The dreams took him into scary places. He'd resisted them at first, but he knew now that they'd mattered more than anything. Perhaps the school had done him more favours than it knew.

He looked at Davey again, and Davey looked back. An old trouble was stirring uncomfortably in Luma's mind, the long unasked question about the mother who had left him. She was not in Cat's world. He had roamed there often enough, hardly admitting to himself that he was looking for her, but he'd found no trace of her. The living world was harder to explore through dream, but whenever he cast his mind into those fields of possibility, he met only pain and regret. Many times he'd almost asked Davey what had happened to her, and now he thought of it again. *Should I?* Perhaps this was the moment. He wasn't sure, but he took a breath.

Cat arrived beside him as if in a hurry, full of concern. Her anxiety told him what she meant. *Let it be.* Some things were better left undisturbed, at least in this life. All truth would be known in the end. *You must wait.* Luma released his breath. Then he took another one, and asked a different question.

"When can I come home?"

"Tomorrow," said Davey. "Pat's bringing the truck. Do it in style, eh?"

Somehow Luma imagined a grand procession with horses and banners, not just Pat's truck, and he laughed. It didn't hurt so much today, he found. His chest felt pretty much OK. He was recovering.

There was a silence.

"Is that the end?" asked Fraser.

"Yes, it probably is," Stan said. "But I've got to go through the whole thing again, of course. There's a lot more to add to it, probably a lot to change. But at least we have a book. Thanks to you."

"I liked the bit about throwing the water over the machinery," said Neil.

"Good, isn't it?" Stan agreed. "You lot triggered that off when you said the machinery would blow up. And I liked Abby's idea about the people cheering; that was a big one. And Chokker's terrific contribution about what happened to Winter." He glanced at Chokker. "Your phrase about it being the best thing to do really stuck in my mind."

Chokker nodded. Somewhere inside his chest he felt so warm that he was almost shaky. He couldn't have said anything.

"You didn't say what happened to the animals," Sue said.

"I will do," Stan promised. "Your note's here on the desk, look – all that stuff is waiting to go in."

"That's all right, then." Then she asked the question that was in all their minds. "What do we do now?"

Stan ran his fingers through his hair. "Not a lot," he admitted. "I have to slog through the donkey work, move the thing on to a more finished state. But keep thinking. If anything strikes you that we ought to change or add, drop in; I'll always be happy to see you. We'll get together about printer's proofs and jacket designs later on. Oh, and there's this event coming up," he remembered. "Friday week, isn't it? We'd better sort out who's going to do what."

The village hall was crammed with people – far more than would have fitted into the room where Stan had done his talk at the school. All the parents had come, and grandparents and older or younger brothers and sisters, and there was a reporter from the local paper, and even a man from the council.

Mr Grant gave a talk about what he called "the project" and about Stan coming to the school; then it was Abby's turn, and she explained how it had all started. There was music from the school guitar group next, and a "walking exhibition" of pictures held up by a parade of children. People read out the bits they'd contributed to the book, and Stan told everyone how the plot had been put together. Fraser played his saxophone, and Mrs Long's class read some of the poems they had written about nature and GM.

Chokker sat beside Gerald. Dorothy hadn't come, because one of the little ones kept being sick, and she said it wasn't fair to ask a babysitter to cope with that. She'd been very disappointed about it, and Chokker was sorry too. Secretly he'd been looking forward to her hearing him read his bit. He'd said he wouldn't at first, but Stan had talked him into it.

Sue finished reading a poem she'd written about animals. Chokker was next. As the moment drew closer, his palms were sweating.

"And now we have Charles Bailey," Mr Grant said, "reading two pieces: one written when the book was in its early stages, the other more recent."

Chokker was on the platform, standing in front of the rows of people, all looking at him. *Remember, they don't know what you're going to tell them,* Stan had advised him. *And you do. So you're one up. Just hang on to that.*

Some of the kids had sounded nervous and wobbly, but Chokker was determined to do better than that. He took a deep breath – another bit of advice from Stan – and heard his own voice begin.

"You got it wrong about Luma." He knew the words by heart. "He isn't just a kid – he can fight. He is different and special. He can do things. It needs more stuff happening. There's too much dreaming. I don't think people go on living after they are dead. Cat has got to get proper fighters." Everyone clapped while he changed to the next bit of paper, then he read the last note he'd written, about the fight and the blowing up of the machinery, and Luma's pity for the thing that had been Winter.

"That was terrific," Gerald whispered as Chokker sat down. "Absolutely stunning."

He didn't have to sound quite so surprised, Chokker thought. Still, it was nice of him to say he liked it.

The last item was Stan reading the final part of the book, from the Massa break-in to the end. When he'd read the last words, he started to explain that it was only a first draft, but his voice was drowned because everyone was clapping. When they'd stopped, he went on. "Thank you very much, but I do hope it's the children you're applauding. Without them, none of this could have happened. And I want to make it clear that the names of everyone who helped will appear in the book as co-authors." The applause was even louder.

Everyone stayed for refreshments afterwards, and people were milling round the table where Stan sat, signing copies of his earlier books. He looked rumpled and astonished, but very pleased.

Abby's parents were talking to Stasi about the book. Then Abby's mother went on to something else. "I believe you have a puppy," she said. "The little one whose mother didn't want it."

Stasi smiled. "She is getting big now. Nearly time for finding a home for her."

"Well," Abby's father said, "we could help with

that. We've never had a dog, but – it's time we did."

Abby gasped. Her father looked at her. "All right?" he asked.

She thought of the heavy warmth of the puppy, her soft ears and the almost transparent claws on the pink pads of her feet, and nodded in amazement. "Oh, yes," she said. "Yes, please."

"A puppy is soon becoming a dog," warned Stasi. "It has to know how to behave. So you must know how to behave with your dog, yes? To teach her."

"Yes," Abby's father agreed. "I hope that's part of the deal. If we want to know something, can we come and ask you?"

A big smile spread across Stasi's face. "Of course," she said. "I will be very pleased. And so, I think, will the puppy."

Walking home with Gerald afterwards, Chokker felt unusually happy. It had gone well. He hadn't done anything stupid; everyone had said it had been OK.

"That was quite a night," remarked Gerald.

"Yes."

They went on for a bit, with the dark sea washing up against the sea wall on their left. Then Gerald said, "I'm sorry about what happened earlier on. Big mistake."

"It's all right," said Chokker.

"You have to be so careful. It seemed the right thing at the time, but..." Gerald shook his head. After a moment he said, "That stuff about Luma, in the bit Stan read out. When he says what happened to him as a kid. Did it come from you?"

"Yeah," said Chokker. "Sort of."

"I thought it must have done."

So he knows, Chokker thought. When he'd come to live with them, Dorothy had told him, *This is a fresh start.* They'd never said anything about what had happened before. He could see now that they must have known. They'd have been told before they took him on. But he'd never been sure.

They were almost home before Gerald spoke again, then he said, "You know how your mates call you Chokker. Do you think we could too?"

Chokker thought about it. Gerald and Dorothy drove him bats in lots of ways, but they cared. And they were the best he'd got, or was likely to get. "OK," he said. "Yes, all right."

"Great," said Gerald. "I've often thought of asking you. Dotty will be chuffed."

Dotty, Chokker thought. He smiled. It suited her.

He waited while Gerald opened the door. Light streamed out through the bare branches of the fuchsia bush, together with a waft of warm air. It had that family smell, Chokker thought – food and milk and children, clean washing, and just a trace of sick.

He looked back. The summerhouse was over there somewhere, tucked into its place on the hill. Nobody could see it now, because the lights were out and it was hidden in the darkness. Tomorrow it would be gleaming like a spaceship again, and Stan would be in there, getting on with their book.

Gerald looked back from the doorstep. "Come on in," he said. "It's cold out there."

It wasn't, really.

Never mind.

Chokker followed him into the house.